THE SLAUGHTER AND THE TERROR

WAR TORN BOOK SEVEN

ROBERT VAUGHAN

with

BRENT TOWNS

WOLFPACK
PUBLISHING
— EST 2012 —

The Slaughter and the Terror
Print Edition
© Copyright 2021 Robert Vaughan

Wolfpack Publishing
5130 S. Fort Apache Rd. 215-380
Las Vegas, NV 89148

wolfpackpublishing.com

Paperback ISBN 978-1-63977-032-8
eBook ISBN 978-1-63977-031-1

THE SLAUGHTER AND
THE TERROR

CHARACTERS

Anatoly Kozlov
Eva Kozlova
Katya Kozlova
Marya Kozlova
*Gerhard Meunch
Edmund Wagner
*Joseph Stalin
*Georgy Zhukov
Nicolai Sobol
Felix Glass
Hans Bauer
*General Heinz Guderian
Ivan Safonov
General Yevgeny Serov
SS-Untersturmfuhrer Karl Egger
Ilya Zorkin
*Senior Lieutenant Yevgeniya Prokhorova
*Andrei Yeryomenko
*General Friedrich Wilhelm Ernst Paulus

*Political Commissar Nikita Khrushchev
*Vasily Chuikov
*Vasily Zaitsev

*Denotes actual people

PROLOGUE

Berlin, Germany, April 1945

THE SMELL OF DECAY WAS EVERYWHERE LIKE THE DEAD. German soldiers, Russian soldiers, civilians, even a horse lay rotting amongst the rubble of the Berlin suburb. Eva Kozlova swept the debris-strewn street from the second floor with her Mosin-Nagant Sniper Rifle and the PU optical sight it had mounted on top. The crosshairs moved slowly left to right as she took in everything before her. Today was her birthday, her twenty-third, and she decided that it would be appropriate to start the day by killing another German.

Dark palls of smoke—too many to count—rose above the city, left to hang listlessly in the sky, without the aid of any wind to sweep it away. In one of the other Berlin suburbs the sound of artillery rocked the early morning. Somewhere else the rattle of an MG 42 could be heard and the pop-pop-pop of rifles.

A low grumble emanated from beside Eva, and she glanced down the young man who lay asleep on the hardwood floor. Anatoly was her brother and commander of Anatoly's Bastards, a small group of killers, formerly prisoners once considered by the Russian commanders, to be good only for the role of suicide missions. Eva had been with them since Stalingrad.

Stalingrad! The destroyed city on the Volga seemed like a lifetime ago. Yet she could still smell it. Hell, it smelled just like Berlin did now.

Movement flickered, drawing her attention back to the street. A soldier appeared fleetingly before disappearing behind a burned-out halftrack. Eva settled down again, drawing the rifle butt into her shoulder and looking through the sights with her right eye like she'd done so many times before. If she killed this one, it would be her 170th kill.

Patience was the key, plus she knew where he was going; the bombed-out building thirty yards to his right. The soldier was headed for the basement where the Germans had a small command post. However, those thirty yards he needed to cross with a sniper hunting him, might as well have been a mile.

It took a while for him to move. Perhaps it was the two German corpses lying out in the open that caused him to linger.

Eva could see his feet where a portion of the halftrack's front had been ripped away. He was sheltering behind the engine block, waiting.

Waiting.

Waiting.

Waiting for what?

Eva saw his boots start to move. She relaxed and let

out a long breath. Her finger started to take up the tension on the trigger and—

WHAM!

A bullet smacked into the wood desk she lay atop, positioned back from the shattered window, allowing her a good visual of the street but not completely exposing her. Splinters sprayed Eva's face, sharp splinters stinging as they bit into her flesh.

"*Der'mo!*" she hissed wildly and threw herself from the desk to the floor, hitting it hard, hurting her shoulder. "Shit! Shit! Shit!"

Beside her, Anatoly lurched awake. He grabbed his PPSh-41 submachine gun and crashed against the wall near the window opening. He blinked to clear his vision and was about to look out when Eva snapped, "Anatoly, stop!"

He froze and stared at his sister on the floor. "What are you doing down there?"

"Shitting German sniper," she growled. "I knew I should have moved yesterday. It was stupid."

Glancing up at her desk, he saw the gouge mark where the bullet had struck. Looking back at his sister, he shrugged; what was it? The tenth? Twentieth? Hundredth? He had lost count of how many times the Germans had almost killed his sister. He grunted. "Maybe you'll learn one day."

The sound of footsteps hurrying up the stairs reached out to them. Two men appeared. Captain Nicolai Sobol, Anatoly's second in command was closely followed by a young man they simply called Bear. Bear by name as his size was that of a bear.

"What is happening?" Sobol asked his commander.

"Eva is pissing with a German," Anatoly growled. "The first sleep I've had in days, and she stuffs it up."

She scowled at Bear once more and then walked over to the side of the window where her brother sat.

"What are you doing?" he asked her.

"I'm going to see if I can find that *ublyudok*." (*bastard*)

"Get away from the window," Anatoly growled at her. "The war is almost over. I'll not lose you now through stupidity."

Eva stared at him, deep into his brown eyes and thought for a moment she could see in them the love that they had once held for her and her sisters. Her sisters. Katya and Marya. She did not know where Katya was, and the last she had seen Marya was in Stalingrad. She had been driving a tank, of all things. By now they could both be dead.

"What are you looking at?" Anatoly snapped at her, annoyed by her prolonged appraisal of his soul.

The warmth once there was long gone, replaced by an iciness so unforgiving that she often imagined that the new Anatoly had killed the old one.

More footsteps on the stairs and another soldier appeared. This one, unfamiliar to the others. He was a new officer. Anatoly fixed him with a look of disdain. "What pissing rock did you crawl out from under?"

"Major Kozlov?" the young man asked nervously.

"Yes."

"You are to report to the colonel for orders."

Anatoly grunted.

Eva stepped close to the new officer. He was young, fresh. "What is your name?" she asked him.

"Taras, Lieutenant, Thirty-Seventh Rifle Brigade." His answers were short and clipped.

Eva leaned in close and took a deep breath causing him to flinch. She looked at her brother and smiled wickedly. "He smells nice and clean."

"So?"

"I want him."

Taras looked surprised. "What?"

Eva took him by the hand. "Come with me."

"What?"

Without granting him time to think, she dragged him towards an open doorway into another room. Anatoly called after her, "Be nice to him, Eva."

"Screw him," she called back over her shoulder.

"I think that's what she plans to do, Anatoly," Sobol said with a wolfish grin.

———

ANATOLY AND SOBOL waited at the doorway before running the short distance across the alley to the next twin floor apartment. Once inside, the first thing to hit them was the stench; the smell of putrefaction and death.

Anatoly looked at the heap on the floor and wrinkled his nose in disgust. By their attire he could tell it had been a German soldier, and judging by its condition, it had been there the four days since the Russian soldiers of the 37th Rifle Brigade had captured their current position. "Christ," he hissed. "Get that pissing thing out of here. Are you animals?"

One of the men present started to complain until Anatoly grabbed him by his uniform jacket and shoved him towards the rotting corpse. "Do it!"

"What is going on here?" an authoritative voice demanded.

Anatoly stared at Colonel Stepan Andreev. He was a bald man in his forties, with a scar on his left cheek, and wore only his uniform pants. His jacket and shirt were gone revealing an overinflated belly covered in a mat of black hair. Anatoly growled, "You let your men live in shit like this? Like animals?"

"Careful, Comrade Major Kozlov, you are speaking to a superior." The officer's voice was cool, almost cold.

"You think I give a shit?" Anatoly snarled. "I could be dead tomorrow. All of us could. But we don't have to live like damn animals."

Andreev stared at him thoughtfully. "Come with me, Comrade. Let us discuss why you are here."

Anatoly and Sobol followed him downstairs into a dimly lit basement. A radio operator sat at a table in the corner, headset on, furiously scribbling notes. In another corner was a bed, covers pulled back to reveal a naked woman lying there curled up into a ball. Andreev noticed Anatoly looking and said, "One of the local women looking for a handout. I made her work for it."

Anatoly felt an overwhelming urge of disgust surge through him, and with it a sudden willingness to shoot the officer before him. Sobol must have sensed it for he reached out discreetly and grabbed his commander's arm.

"Over here," Andreev said, motioning them forward to another table. On top of it was a map. The colonel stabbed a finger at it. "The Berlin Hotel. I have been ordered to take it. Now I'm giving you and your bastards that same order."

Anatoly's blood ran cold. He had a dozen men. At

last estimate, the Germans had maybe forty inside the hotel. Most of whom were hardened Wehrmacht troops. All would undoubtably be veterans of the Russian front and would fight like starving dogs after the last scrap of meat. He looked at the colonel and asked, "What support will I have?"

"None. It is a fool's errand, Anatoly. A waste of men. The hotel is of no strategic importance. The army can just go around it and push towards the Reichstag."

"Yet you are ordering me and my men to take it."

Andreev nodded as he sneered, "Yes. But you are all condemned men anyway, are you not? Thieves, deserters, murderers. Why waste my men when I can send you and your bastards?"

"What if we take it?"

The colonel shrugged. "Then you take it. But I doubt it. You will all most likely die in the attempt."

"Can we at least have some artillery?"

"I'll see what I can do. Dismissed."

———

The Berlin Hotel

Major Gerhard Meunch walked down the wide stairs of the hotel and stopped in the once grand foyer. He looked around him at the devastation caused by days of battle. The top floors were gone, destroyed by Russian artillery, killing ten of his men in the process. Now he was down to thirty-seven spread out over two floors. Above him he'd left his most trusted NCO, Feldwebel Felix Glass, in charge of the ten men on the first floor where two MG42s were placed, their field of fire along the street towards the Russian held buildings was unimpeded. The rest of his men were inhabiting the ground floor.

"Herr Major?"

Meunch turned around and saw a tired looking Gerfreiter standing there with a Sturmgewehr 44 in his hands. "What is it, Engel?"

"There is movement down near the Kaiserhof," Engel said wearily.

"Shit," Meunch swore and ran for the stairs. He took them two at a time until reaching the landing where he turned right. From this point on, the hotel was open to the elements. He found Glass near what had once been a window. Now it was a half square with exposed sandstone blocks around it. "What do we have, Unteroffizier?" he asked the sergeant.

"Down the street near where the old fountain used to be, sir," Glass said, pointing. "You can see them organizing for an assault."

Meunch lifted his field glasses and put them to his eyes. Along the street he could see the Ivans preparing. "How many did you see, Felix?"

"I'm not sure, sir. It wasn't very many."

"Do you think they are going to make one of their suicide assaults?" Meunch asked.

"It's possible, Major. They did enough of them on the Russian Front. There are more than enough troops, sir, why don't they just overrun us?"

The major continued observing the Russians before saying, "Wait, Felix. These are not normal Soviet soldiers. They are Shtrafbat. Have everyone ready."

"Sir."

Meunch looked around and saw a private near a broken wall, addressing him, "You, come here."

The man ran over to his commander. "Yes, Herr Major?"

"Go downstairs and tell Corporal Engel that the Russians are about to attack us. Tell him they are Shtrafbat."

"Sir."

The man disappeared and Meunch went back to watching the Russians. Glass appeared at his side. "The men are ready, sir."

"Good. Now, where is Johann?"

"Here sir," a young man in a dirt-stained uniform called out.

Meunch made his way over to him, looking him up and down. "Get me Unteroffizier Keitel."

Several moments later, Keitel was on the other end. Meunch took the radio operator's headset and hand-piece. "Keitel?"

"Major?"

"The Ivans are about to attack us. How many mortar rounds do you have left?"

"Fifteen I think, sir," came the reply.

"Have them ready."

"Yes, sir."

Moments later, the sky above their part of Berlin seemed to be torn apart before the first artillery round landed. It fell short and a giant explosion erupted in what had been the hotel's turnaround, now just a mass of craters and churned earth. Another shell landed, this one short like the first. Meunch hunkered down behind the sandstone wall of the second floor. He knew the next one would be on target and braced himself.

However, something else happened. Hell seemed to open and swallow the whole street as Russian Katyusha Rockets, or Stalin's Organs as they were known, rained down with terrifying effect.

Meunch hugged the hotel floor, his mouth open, so that the concussion from the blasts wouldn't blow his eardrums out. Debris fell upon him, one chunk big enough to make it feel like he'd been shot in the back. Meunch ground his teeth together.

Off to his right he heard a scream through the explosions, and then another. The floor beneath him seemed to leap and bounce and for a moment he wondered if it would collapse under him. Meunch could taste the dust in his mouth as it found its way in, turning his remaining saliva to mud.

Then as suddenly as it had started, the hellish bombardment stopped.

Now the Russians would come.

The major scrambled to his feet and looked around. More of the hotel had come down. He saw one of his men laying off to the side, his head smashed to a bloody pulp by a large sandstone block. Another lay moaning, his right leg bent at an odd angle.

"Unteroffizier Glass, report!"

"Coming right up, sir."

Hunched over, Meunch moved to the front of the hotel to take stock of the street before him. Once more the landscape had changed. More craters, more debris, more rotting bodies ripped apart.

He raised his glasses and could see the Russian troops. They were coming. This was it. Just another day in a dying Berlin.

———

ANATOLY HADN'T BEEN EXPECTING the rockets; however, he'd been more than pleased to see them falling on the German position. As soon as they stopped, he ordered his men and Eva to attack.

They used the scattered craters for cover, leaping from one to another. To their front two MG42s opened fire and raked them with a deadly fusillade. One of Anatoly's men cried out and fell forward, bullets holes stitched across his torso.

The rest of the defenders opened fire, sending Anatoly diving into a crater to his right. He landed hard, pain lancing through his back. A foul stench filled his nostrils, and he turned his head to see the eviscerated corpse of a German soldier, eyes open, flesh a mottled color, right there.

There was a thud behind him, and he turned to see Eva, the look in her eyes almost maniacal. Shuffling past him on her belly, she edged up to the rim of the crater and brought her Mosin-Nagant rifle up, taking aim through the optical sights.

Anatoly reached her just as she fired. One of the MG42s went quiet and he saw a smile come to her face. As she worked the bolt on the rifle she said, "One hundred and seventy, Anatoly."

He grunted and was about to press forward when the mortar rounds started to fall. One landed in front of their position sending dirt and sharp metal shards skyward. A second landed, this one to their left. Anatoly came to his feet and said, "Come on, Eva, move."

Seemingly untroubled with the events unfolding

around her, she fired a second time, calling after her brother, "One hundred and seventy-one."

Anatoly dove headlong into another crater ten yards ahead of the last one. Bullets whipped around him as he came up to the lip. He pulled the pin on a F-1 Fugasnaya grenade and threw it out. He counted in his head and heard the CRUMP! as it exploded. Coming to his knees, he opened fire with his PPSh-41, raking the German position.

Then he was up and running once more, bullets kicking up dirt at his heels as he moved.

When he next stopped, Anatoly found himself in a crater with Sobol. The captain had blood on his left sleeve, and it was dripping from his fingers. "Are you all right, Comrade?" Anatoly asked.

"I'm fine. I can still kill more of the German bastards," Sobol snarled. "At least the mortars have stopped."

Indeed, they had. It was the first that Anatoly had noticed it. He rose and immediately attracted attention from a shooter nearby. Looking at Sobol, he said, "Do you have any grenades?"

"One."

"Give it to me," Anatoly ordered, retrieving the last one from his own pocket. He waited several moments for the captain to hand his across before saying, "When they explode, we move."

"Don't miss."

Anatoly pulled the pin on the first grenade and threw it. He hurriedly followed it up with the second and the moment it exploded the two men went over the top.

Sobol's head snapped back as a bullet from a

German rifle punched into it. Anatoly pushed forward towards the opening in the hotel wall. "Follow me, Comrades! Follow me!"

Once inside he was confronted with a German soldier who was staggering around, an arm missing almost at the shoulder, helmet gone, his face a mask of blood. Anatoly fired a burst from his PPSh-41 and the soldier fell.

Behind him, those that remained of his men entered the hotel. They began spreading out and firing at the enemy.

Anatoly grabbed two men. "Come with me."

They hurried towards the stairs. Gunfire rattled throughout the ruins of the building as the fighting grew in intensity. Anatoly was halfway up the stairs when he heard a shout, "Anatoly! One-hundred and seventy-four!"

He saw Eva disappear through an open doorway before the room that she had entered exploded violently. Something flew through the opening and landed amongst the blood and debris on the floor. He blinked twice before realization hit him. It was an arm with the hand at the end still clutching a Mosin-Nagant sniper rifle.

Anatoly froze on the stairs, unable to move from what he'd just witnessed. Eva, his sister, darling Eva, gone. Hands grasped him roughly. "Comrade, move."

Brought back to the immediacy of the battle Anatoly kept climbing. He reached the top and sprayed a German soldier with his weapon. The man's chest was ripped apart by countless bullets. The magazine on the PPSh-41 ran dry, and Anatoly cursed. He detached the drum magazine and turned while replacing it with a fresh one.

Standing there with an MP40 was a German officer. A major with blood running down one side of his face, his uniform ripped in many places. The weapon was pointed at Anatoly who braced himself for the storm of bullets that was imminent.

The expression on the German officer's face was that of hatred which transformed into a snarl as he prepared to fire his weapon. The hotel chose that moment to implode, the floor beneath both men falling away, dropping them into the abyss.

CHAPTER ONE

June 1941

OPERATION BARBAROSSA STARTED WITH THE BOMBING OF Soviet-occupied cities in Poland. Then came the artillery barrage along the entire front, softening the defenses before 3,000,000,000 Wehrmacht, Finnish, and Romanian troops crossed the border in what would be the largest invasion of any country in the world.

Russian troops were either pushed back, surrounded, or completely overwhelmed by the German's lightning advance. In the juggernaut's path, waiting for the coming onslaught was the Russian 38th Rifle Division, furiously digging in under the watchful eye of their officers.

Shallow firing positions were dug across the grassy plain upon which the Germans would advance. Anti-tank positions were reinforced, and machine gun nests set up along the line. In the distance, columns of black smoke rose skyward as yet another village burned.

Lieutenant Anatoly Kozlov walked along the part of

the line where his section was digging in. In his arms he cradled a PPD-34 submachine gun. He could see the fear in their eyes as they worked tirelessly to be ready. Anatoly said, "Keep digging, Comrades. Glorious leader Stalin is depending on you to stop the Nazi horde here. There is to be no retreat. We must hold. Dying for the Motherland will bring pride to your family name."

It was a load of shit and Anatoly knew it. This was the third such position they had prepared before being ordered back to form new ones. Each time it was to stop from being encircled by the enemy's pincer movements where they would drive into the flanks of the defensive line and get in behind it, trapping those who were there, leading to total annihilation of those trapped in the pocket. The invasion had been going only a matter of days. Not weeks, or months, but days.

This time however, the division's 112th Rifle Regiment, was on the flank right in the path of the coming onslaught.

Ahead of them on the plain a figure appeared followed by another. Then before long they noticed others.

"Stand to, comrades," Anatoly called out and men dropped their shovels and took up their weapons. All along the line the rattle of loading could be heard and within moments each soldier was hunched over and aiming at the figures before them.

Anatoly raised his binoculars and breathed a sigh of relief. They were Russian soldiers coming towards them. Retreating in the face of the oncoming German thrust. A colonel stepped forward and halted beside Anatoly. "Cowards, Anatoly. Running in the face of the enemy. Well, they will run no more. They will join us here and die if necessary to protect the motherland."

"Yes, Comrade Colonel."

"Are your men ready to fight?"

"Yes, Comrade Colonel."

Colonel Mikhail Morozov turned his head to glare at his lieutenant. "Order your men to their feet, Anatoly. Have them present their weapons to the front. If these cowards will not stand then you will order your men to shoot."

Anatoly hesitated.

"Do you understand, Lieutenant?"

"Yes, Comrade Colonel," Anatoly said. Then, "On your feet. Get up. Stand—"

"Samolety!" (Aircraft!)

Anatoly looked to the sky and saw them coming. At first, they were dark specks against the blue background but as they grew closer, he could see that they were Junkers Ju 87s. Dive bombers.

"Take cover!" he yelled at his men who immediately dove back into their holes and slit trenches.

Meanwhile out on the plain the retreating Russian soldiers started to run.

Morozov drew his Tokarev semi-automatic pistol and waved it around. "Stop!" he barked. "Stop in the name of Stalin. Dig in, comrades. It is time to fight for our motherland."

They kept running like an unstoppable tide encroaching on the sands of a beach. Morozov lowered the weapon, aimed at the closest man, and fired. The scared soldier threw up his hands and fell forward to the ground.

"Stop! I order you to stop!" The colonel aimed again and shot another soldier.

The sight of this man shooting his own countrymen sickened Anatoly. The bastard was crazy. "Stop, Colonel. Can't you see they are afraid?"

"They are cowards, Anatoly. Order your men to fire. Shoot them down."

Anatoly held his tongue and looked up at the sky. The Ju 87s were rolling into their dives. Instead of giving the order to fire, he dove into a hole next to him and waited for the earth to shake.

The scream of the dive bombers filled the air and soon Anatoly couldn't hear anything except their ear-piercing sound. One pulled up and flew over his position. Its passing was followed by the shattering sound of a 550-pound bomb exploding.

Then came the colonel's voice, higher-pitched now, a shriek. *Shoot them! Shoot them! Shoot—*"

A second explosion from another bomb silenced the hysterical commander. A large splinter almost cut the man in half, shredding his guts in a hideous display. Blood sprayed across Anatoly's face, its warmth almost sickening.

He threw himself to the ground as another Stuka dropped its payload. Screams of pain cut through the sound of the explosion. Anatoly covered his head with his hands as a German plane roared overhead, strafing the Russian soldiers who had survived the onslaught.

Then, as suddenly as it had started, it was over.

Anatoly came to his feet, his PPD-34 clutched in his hand. "Sergeant! Sergeant Sobol! Where are you?"

"Here, sir."

The lieutenant turned to face his sergeant. "What are our casualties?"

"I'm still ascertaining that, sir. So far, I know of four dead."

"Get me the numbers as soon as you can. We can expect the Nazis to be here anytime soon. Make sure the men are prepared."

"What men, sir? Most of them ran away."

"Plug the gaps with what we have, Comrade."

"Yes, sir."

The wounded and the dead were taken out of the line. Anatoly walked along the line that the remainder of his company occupied. They looked scared and it was up to him to hold them together. A staff car appeared, the driver alighting and scurrying to open the rear passenger door. Struggling to haul his ass out of the seat, a fat general was puffing like an old steam train climbing a steep rise, his face red from the effort by the time he got to his feet.

He straightened up and looked left and right. "Who is in charge here?"

Anatoly stepped forward. "The colonel is dead, Comrade General. He was killed in the last air raid."

"Then who is commanding the battalion?"

"I'm not sure, sir."

The general suddenly looked puzzled. "Where are the rest of the men? Shouldn't you have more?"

"They ran away. One of the front divisions broke and when they came through, along with the bombing, some of them went too."

"Cowards."

"Yes, sir."

"Then I guess you will command the battalion. What is your name?"

Anatoly was stunned. "Lieutenant Anatoly Kozlov, sir."

"You are now Colonel Anatoly Kozlov. I will make sure that our great leader hears of your name and the sacrifice you have made here."

"Sacrifice, sir?"

"You are to fight until the last man, Colonel. Do not give an inch of this precious ground without giving your blood to hold it. I wish you luck."

While you run away, you fat swine. "We will do our best, sir."

Anatoly watched as the general climbed back into the staff car and was driven away. Sobol appeared at Anatoly's side. "What did he want, sir?"

"I've just been promoted to colonel, Sergeant."

"Congratulations, sir?"

A dry chuckle passed Anatoly's lips. "All the fat fool has given me is a death sentence, Nicolai. We have been ordered to hold until the last man."

"Does he not understand there is no hope of stopping the Germans?"

"I'm quite sure he does. Prepare the men."

———

THE FIRST INDICATION was the deep, low rumble of the tanks. Anatoly put his field glasses up to his eyes and could see them in the distance. As far as he could see, left and right, was wall-to-wall German armor and infantry. The sight sent a chill down his spine.

He looked behind him and, far in that direction, he

could see the small village of Korkino. They were too
exposed here. The Germans would run right over them.
The village would offer them more cover and give them
a better chance of mounting a good defense.

"Mother forgive me if I bring shame to our family,"
he muttered. "Sergeant Sobol!"

"Here, sir."

"We're pulling back to Korkino. Pass the word along
the battalion line."

"Yes, sir."

Soon the line echoed with the calls for the battalion
to pull back to Korkino. The Russians needed no
further encouragement as they left their trenches and
started running towards the village.

As soon as they were out in the open, the German
armor opened fire at long range. Great geysers of black
earth exploded skyward. To Anatoly's right, two of his
remaining three-hundred and fifty men disappeared,
smashed into oblivion.

Another soldier cried out in alarm. Anatoly looked
over his shoulder and saw what the man was pointing
at. In the sky, more Stukas had appeared.

"What have I done?" he muttered in despair. They
were all out in the open. Was his first order to be his
last?

The howl of the dive bombers was the signal for
them all to take to the ground. As one the Russian
soldiers fell to earth, hugging the damp earth for dear
life. The first bomb hit, and the vibrations rippled
through Anatoly's body. More came followed by the
harrowing screams of wounded and dying men. They
needed to get out of there.

Anatoly climbed to his feet and waved his arm in the air. *"On your feet! Get up! Move! Move!"*

The rest of the battalion followed his lead and started their desperate run across the open ground. Behind them the tanks kept up their fire. Anatoly focused on the village. Still a mile distant, he was already laboring under the exertion of running and carrying his heavy kit.

What had started out as a line was now a staggered mass of stumbling men being chased across the plain by the steadily gaining German armor.

Slowly, almost painfully, Korkino grew closer. "Sir, look," Sobol shouted from beside him.

Anatoly stopped and looked back to where his sergeant was pointing. Some of the battalion had ceased running and had dropped their weapons before sitting on the ground. "What will we do?" Sobol asked.

"Keep going, there's nothing we can do for them."

"Shit."

They turned and followed the rest of the battalion towards Korkino where they would make their final stand.

————

Korkino, June 1941

"What are you doing here, Colonel Kozlov?" the fat general demanded.

"The village is a better defensive position, sir. I gave orders to withdraw so we could meet the Nazis on better terms."

"What *were* your orders, Colonel?"

"To hold where we were, sir."

"Exactly and yet here you are. Tell me why I shouldn't shoot you where you stand?"

Anatoly pointed back behind him. "The reason is out there, sir. A whole armored division is coming our way. We are the only ones standing between you and them. Does it really matter where we die?"

There was fear in the fat man's eyes. He said, "I will see if I can get you more reinforcements. Although I doubt it; the army has fallen back to Minsk where they are forming to stand against the Nazis."

"Yes, sir, that would be good."

What the general really meant was that he was about to run away under the premise of finding reinforcements.

"This time, Colonel, hold this position."

"Yes, sir."

Explosions rocked the village as the German tanks opened their attack with another barrage. They had stopped short of the village, waiting for their infantry to catch up. Sobol found his commander. "Colonel, from the church spire I could see that they are starting to encircle the village."

Anatoly looked back at the general who was walking towards his vehicle. *Good luck getting away, General.*

"Have the company commanders report to me, immediately."

"Yes, sir."

It was only a matter of minutes before the company commanders joined him. They were all young, baby-faced, and most appeared too young to shave. "The Germans are encircling the village. My guess is once they've done that, they will attack in great numbers. Take up positions around the village square. It's the only place we can fortify properly. Otherwise, we'll be spread too thin. Occupy the houses where possible."

"Excuse me, sir."

Anatoly turned and stared at the new face. "Who are you?"

"Borodin, 231st Field Regiment. I have two 45mm anti-tank guns."

"Set them up on the two main approaches to the square. Make sure your position is strong." Anatoly sought out another officer. A young lieutenant. "Vasin, do we still have both Degtyaryovs?"

The Degtyaryov was a light machine gun. The officer nodded. "Yes, sir."

"Good. Set them up covering the approaches from the other directions. But make sure they can be turned to support the anti-tank guns if need be."

"Yes, sir."

"All right, deploy your men. Sergeant Sobol, back to the church spire with you. I want sharp eyes up there."

"Yes, sir."

———

OBERLIEUTENANT GERHARD MEUNCH was preparing the men of his company for the assault on Korkino. Their captain had been killed the day before, and being the senior officer, the duties of company commander fell to him. He turned to his sergeant, Unteroffizier Hans Bauer, and said, "When the tanks go forward, we will accompany them. Use them for cover."

"Yes, Herr Lieutenant," Bauer snapped. "I shall make

sure they keep up at all times. The Ivans won't know what has hit them."

Meunch shook his head. Bauer was a dyed in the wool Nazi. He was surprised that he joined the Wehrmacht and not the SS. "Let's just capture the town, shall we?"

"The Fuhrer will be proud of us this day, Herr Lieutenant."

"Carry on."

Meunch looked to the west and saw that the sun was going down fast. If the generals didn't order them forward soon, they would be fighting in the dark.

Suddenly a roar erupted along the front as the tanks came to life. Panzer IIIs and IVs started to roll forward, firing as they went. The lines of infantry fell in behind them. Meunch ordered his men forward. "Bauer, follow me."

With a tight grip on his MP40, the lieutenant fell in behind a roaring Panzer IV as it lurched forward over the uneven ground. He glanced behind himself and saw that the rest of his company was doing the same.

The Panzer rocked as its main gun belched fire, sending its high-explosive shell towards the village. Meunch turned o face his men. "Keep moving. We're almost there."

He peered around the side of the tank and saw the village burning. The strange part of the assault was that the Ivans weren't firing at them.

The tank stopped suddenly a hundred yards short of the village, its turret turning to the right. Meunch could hear the commander in the turret giving orders. The Panzer fired and a wooden building disintegrated under the assault of the high-explosive shell.

"Lieutenant! Lieutenant!"

Meunch looked up and saw the tank commander staring back at him. Meunch climbed onto the tank where he could talk to the man. "Lieutenant, send your men ahead of the tanks. The houses need to be cleared as we go."

"Can't you just blast them out of there?" Meunch asked.

"No, the tanks have only so much ammunition and the supply column are having problems keeping up. We are advancing too fast. Orders have just come through that most of the division is to keep moving forward. Only one tank battalion will remain to support your attack."

"My attack?"

"Yes, your attack."

Meunch couldn't believe what he was hearing. "I have one hundred and fifty men in my company. Prisoners say there is a battalion of Russian troops inside that village. What does the general expect me to do?"

The tank commander smiled. "He expects you to take the town, Lieutenant."

"Great."

Climbing back down, Meunch turned to his men and shouted, "Follow me!"

He rushed forward from behind the tank, the rest of the company close behind. They crossed the last of the open ground before reaching a stone wall on the edge of the village. Not a shot was fired.

They hunkered down behind the wall, using it for shelter. From his left, Meunch heard Bauer call out, "What do you think the Ivans are up to, Lieutenant? Have they run away?"

"Take your men forward, Hans. Start clearing the houses."

"Yes." The Unteroffizier turned and shouted, "Follow me, you sons of Satan. Death or glory awaits us."

He leaped over the wall, followed by thirty Wehrmacht soldiers, all shouting as though it would keep them safe from fate. Meunch then ordered his own section forward. It was time for the dying to begin.

CHAPTER TWO

Leningrad Russia, January 1941

ANATOLY'S MOTHER BROUGHT HIS HEAD DOWN WITH BOTH OF *her hands so she could kiss him on the forehead. Behind him sat the train as it waited for the last of the passengers to climb aboard. "You be a good boy, Anatoly. Make your mama proud."*

He kissed her on the cheek and promised her he would be. She brushed his uniform with her hand. Then he turned to his sisters. Eva, the youngest. The one who loved life as though she was still a child. Her eyes were filled with tears as she hugged her brother. "Be careful, Anatoly. I want you to come back to us alive."

He hugged her hard. "I will be fine."

Next came Katya. She was twenty and had her mother's long dark hair. She was the dreamer of the family. She would often journey outside of Leningrad to watch the planes at the airfield. He took her in his arms and felt her slight frame through her clothing. "You need to eat more," he told her.

"I will try," she said weakly.

Lastly, Marya. She was the strongest of all the girls. She worked at a factory in the city as a welder. And she was good at it. But even she had a tear in her sparkling blue eyes. "Touch me and I'll knock the hell out of you," she growled.

"Marya," her mother gasped. "Such language. I don't know why you work in that place. You have changed."

Anatoly winked at his sister. She smirked at him and came into his arms. "Look after them," he whispered into her ear.

"I promise."

The train whistle blew, and he looked again at his mother. "I must go, Mama."

"Yes. But you will come back to me. To us."

"I promise."

Anatoly climbed onto the train and sat in a carriage where another soldier was already seated. He made to get up and salute the young officer, but Anatoly said, "Please, don't."

"But, sir—"

"There will be time for it later. My name is Anatoly Kozlov. What is yours?"

"Corporal Nicolai Sobol."

Anatoly held out his hand for Nicolai to take. "Pleased to meet you, Corporal Sobol."

The train shunted and then started to move. Anatoly sat down and asked Sobol, "Where are you bound?"

"The Hundred and Twelfth Rifle Regiment, sir."

"Me too."

There was an awkward silence followed by the question, "Do you think we'll return, sir?"

Anatoly nodded. "Yes. I promised my mother."

————

Korkino, June 1941

Anatoly looked at Sobol who was hunkered down in the rubble to his left. Smoke from various fires drifted across the debris littered square, some of it thick and choking. Russian bodies lay where they had fallen from the first assault. Shadows started to appear to their front, coming in along the main road through the smoke which blanketed out the last of the retreating daylight, adding an eerie glow.

The Russians had held their own so far against the German onslaught. Even with their heavy casualties. But the enemy hadn't gotten off lightly either.

Sobol reloaded his PPD-34 and wiped at the sweat on his face. An orange glow from a fire at the edge of the village illuminated the German soldiers who ran from one side of the debris-strewn street to the other.

The blackened and burned-out hulk of a Panzer IV stood like a monster in the darkness of the side street where one of the anti-tank guns had stopped its advance. But they were no more. They'd been destroyed by a couple of well-placed tank shells just before dark.

So far, the battalion had held but in doing so, there remained only seventy of the three hundred plus men Anatoly had brought into Korkino.

"Comrade Colonel?" Sobol said.

"Don't call me that," Anatoly snapped curtly. "I'm no colonel."

"Yes, sir."

"What is it?"

"I don't want to die here for no reason."

There it was, out in the open. But instead of castigating his sergeant for voicing his thoughts, he nodded and said, "Neither do I, Nicolai."

"Then what are we doing? Almost all the battalion is gone. We're surrounded and cut off. If we wish to get out of this godforsaken place it needs to be under the cover of darkness. Come tomorrow the Germans will roll over us and there will be nothing left."

"What of the wounded, Nicolai?" Anatoly asked. "Am I to leave them behind?"

"We cannot help the wounded. The rest we can help."

"Comrade Colonel," one of the other officers said as he scrambled to where Anatoly and Sobol were sheltering.

"What is it, Sergei?"

"My men are almost out of ammunition and my lookout tells me that the Germans are amassing for another attack."

"Get what you can off the dead, Sergei, and distribute it amongst your men."

"Yes, sir, but—"

"But what?"

"But what is the point of staying, sir? The Germans will slaughter us in the next attack. I have had one of my men search the town where he can and the drainage system under the village will allow us to escape this pocket."

"See to your men, Sergei."

"Yes, Comrade Colonel."

The officer disappeared into the darkness. Anatoly looked at his sergeant. "Say it, Nicolai."

"He is right, sir."

The man acted as his conscience. Any other officer

would have shot both men for what they had said. But not him. "All right, Nicolai. Gather the men; we're leaving. And God help us when the generals find out."

––––––––

THE UNDER-VILLAGE DRAINAGE system smelled of ammonia and shit, the stench so strong that it felt as though it was suffocating those who were in the narrow tunnels. The men moved slowly on hands and knees, their hands and fingers buried wrist deep in the stinking slime. From behind Anatoly Sobol said, "I'm thinking we should have stayed and died."

"Shut up and keep moving," Anatoly snapped.

The inky black darkness of the tunnels was terrifying and the worst fear that Anatoly had was that they would get lost and become entombed under the Russian soil.

Ahead of him a soldier wretched and emptied his stomach, making his own contribution to the foul mess. Anatoly wrinkled his nose in disgust once more and kept moving.

Their progress was slow, almost torturous. Another soldier started yelling in the darkness, screaming about how he was going to die. His shouts became hysterical and other men cursed him. The cries ended abruptly, and Anatoly realized what had happened to him when he crawled across a still-warm body in the dark.

Then a short time later word drifted back to the men in harsh whispers. Those ahead of them had found an exit.

Ten minutes later, Anatoly crawled out of the tunnel and into a drainage ditch where those of the battalion who were still alive had started to spread out in a defensive position.

Anatoly found Sergei with a great coat over his head, looking at a map with the use of a small light, the heavy woolen coat keeping the limited illumination from escaping and acting as a beacon to the enemy. Anatoly joined him and said, "I could have used that in the shit tube we crawled through."

"How do you think we got here, Comrade Colonel?"

Both men looked at the map. Anatoly said, "The Germans will have pushed ahead using the main road. Their target will be Minsk where the rest of the army is. If we cut across here through the forest, then we should be fine."

Sergei nodded. "Allow my men to take point, Comrade Colonel," he said with a hint of pride in his voice. "We will guide the battalion."

For a moment Anatoly let his temper get the better of him. "There is no battalion," he hissed.

"I'm sorry, sir."

Anatoly placed a hand on his arm. "No, Sergei, it is I who am sorry. You led us out of Korkino, now lead us to Minsk."

"Yes, sir."

From behind them in the direction of the village the sound of gunfire could be heard. Sergei said bitterly, "They are shooting the wounded. The bastards."

"We can't help them. Take your men, Comrade Captain, lead us to Minsk."

"Yes, sir."

———

Outside of Minsk, July 1941

To say that Minsk was a key city for the German advance was an understatement. The city was a key strategic railway junction and thus a key defensive position because it was also situated on the main highway to Moscow.

Elements from Army Group North and Army Group Center had closed on it in a pincer movement and were fighting hard to surround it. The horizon was obliterated by the smoke of fires as the Russian Army burned everything that they could to slow the German advance.

Above Minsk, German bombers were unleashing another raid, the third for the day, and it was still before noon. Behind the German line, artillery brought up more shells ready to start their bombardment once the bombers were clear.

"Sir," a young, dirty-faced private said to Anatoly from behind him.

"What is it?"

"We are still able to get into the city from the southeast," he replied. "I was just in contact on the radio with another radio operator from the Fifty-Sixth Regiment and that is what he told me. The Germans are still trying to encircle the city, but they haven't closed the trap as yet."

From where he knelt on the rise looking at the distant city, Anatoly was in two minds. Join the army in Minsk to be trapped by the Germans or bypass it and keep going east to join up with another division. Beside him the dark-haired Sergei waited for his decision.

Finally, he spoke. "We keep going east."

Sergei opened his mouth to speak but Anatoly

stopped him. "Our armor has been all but destroyed. The city will be surrounded within hours, and the noose will be tightened. Once the retreat is cutoff, the Nazis will drive their tanks into the city and slaughter the defenders."

"There are thousands of men in the city," Sergei pointed out.

"And there they will stay once Guderian and Bock close the net. Don't you understand? Get your men moving. We keep going east."

The City of Minsk fell within days.

————

Moscow, Russia July 1941

Joseph Stalin stroked his thick mustache and stared at his chief of the general staff, Georgy Zhukov. The movement was calm, relaxed, but to look into the leader's cold dark eyes one could see that it was anything but. "Why am I only just learning of this, Georgy?"

"The situation is fluid, Comrade Leader."

Joseph Vissarionovich Stalin was born in 1878 and rose to become the ruler of the Soviet Union in 1927. He ruled with an iron fist and watched on as his nation suffered a catastrophic famine in the years of 1932 and 1933, in which over 5,000,000 people died.

He imprisoned many of his so-called enemies, had others executed. He initiated ethnic cleansing of non-Soviet ethnic groups and thus had another 700,000 shot. The NKVD, or People's Commissariat for Internal Affairs operated on home soil and abroad, assassinating defectors and opponents which culminated in 1940 with the death of Leon Trotsky in Mexico.

Also in 1940, he started to purge his army. Anyone who was considered a threat, died.

Like Stalin, Georgy Zhukov was brought up in poverty. In 1915 he was conscripted into the military, was wounded in battle and awarded the Cross of St. George twice. Then promoted to a non-commissioned officers' rank for bravery.

After the war he stayed in the military and worked his way through the ranks to where he was now.

Stalin stared at Zhukov. "Did anyone not think that it was important enough to tell me that Minsk has fallen?"

The last words were shouted and echoed throughout the office.

"Sir, I have been busy trying to stop the Germans from—"

"And failing miserably at it," Stalin seethed.

"Whenever we put up a defense, they surround our soldiers in pockets and annihilate them while other divisions continue their advance. Men are deserting in their thousands; others are shooting themselves just to get into overflowing hospitals. There are other rumblings of dissent emanating from within the army. Now they close on Smolensk."

Stalin rose from his seat and placed his hands on the polished wood of his desk. "Then do something about it, Georgy. Do something!"

"Yes, Comrade Leader."

"I will have Beria put NKVD men in every damned military unit that needs it and have the dissenters weeded out. Executed. Any man who has self-inflicted wounds will also be shot. Commissars will now command with generals in a dual role, and anyone found deserting will face a military tribunal with the option of being *shot!*"

"Yes, sir."

Stalin took a couple of deep breaths to allow his heart rate to settle some, along with his blood pressure. "I'm not done yet. Anyone who is captured or surrenders to the enemy will be classed as a traitor to Mother Russia. Any officer who retreats will be executed on the spot and their families imprisoned. Am I clear, Georgy?"

"Ah, yes, sir," Zhukov stammered.

It hadn't gone unnoticed, and Stalin said, "What is it?"

"Yakov was captured two days ago, sir."

Stalin hesitated, his mind whirling. His own son. Captured? He straightened and looked Zhukov in the eye. "Have his wife arrested immediately and taken to one of the labor camps."

"But, Comrade—"

"What good is an order if I'm seen to be favoring some and not others. Yes, he's my son. And she is his wife, but orders are orders. Lock her up."

"Yes, sir."

"Do you have a list of our losses, Georgy?"

"Yes. We've lost over four-hundred thousand men so far in the past three weeks. Almost five-thousand tanks, plus other heavy equipment."

"What about planes?"

"Just under two-thousand."

"Reserves?"

"As you know we activated them all at the end of last month. All five million of them."

"Will it be enough for you?"

"I do not know."

"Then lower the age of conscription. Make it eighteen."

"Sir."

The figures were grim. Stalin remained silent for a moment as he thought. He sat back in his chair before looking at Zhukov. "If we can't outfight them, we will out-manufacture them. If they build one tank, we will build five. If they make one rifle or artillery piece, we will make six. I want every factory in Moscow, or any other regional city and town, moved east. They must be safe."

"How far east, Comrade leader?"

"One thousand miles."

"Yes, sir. Is there anything else?"

Stalin nodded. "Don't let the numbers of losses get out. I don't want any of the civilians to know how dire the situation is."

"What do we tell them?"

"That their country needs them, I need them, and that to fight for Mother Russia is the greatest honor any of them could do. We need more volunteers to build defenses."

"And if they don't volunteer, comrade Stalin?"

Stalin's gaze hardened. "Then make them volunteer, Georgy. Make them."

———

Leningrad, July 1941

Anya Kozlova felt tears well in her eyes. They were of both pride and sadness. Before her stood her daughters. Two had broken the news to her that they were being called away to do service for their beloved country. "When do you leave?" she asked then, dabbing at the corners of her eyes with her apron.

"Tomorrow," Marya said. "Katya will be working with me."

"Where—where are you going?"

"To Moscow and then further east," Katya explained.

"But, why?" Anya asked, confused.

"Because all of the men are going to fight, Mama," Marya replied. "We will be the ones to manufacture things now."

"Can't you do that here? Much of the population are already building fortifications."

"We don't have a choice. We go where they send us."

Anya tried to speak but no words came out, just tears and weak sobs. Her daughters stepped forward and embraced her. They stood like that for a few minutes before Anya stepped back and looked around her sparse kitchen. "Well, if you are going to be leaving so soon, the least I can do is cook you some decent food."

She started to busy herself with preparations for the meal. Marya walked over to her youngest sibling and said, "Look after her, little Eva. Make sure she is taken care of while we are gone."

"Mama will be fine. Besides, who knows how long before I'm called up like you?"

Katya overheard her. "What do you mean?"

"Oh, come on," Eva whispered harshly. "We all know that you volunteered to go."

Both sisters looked guilty. Marya said, "Don't tell Mama."

"I wouldn't. It would break her heart."

Later while they ate, the radio was turned on. The broadcast started with a speech from Stalin and then went on to say that the German forces were still advancing across all fronts and that the brave soldiers of the glorious Red Army were fighting with the utmost bravery.

Eva looked at her mother and said, "I hope Anatoly is all right, Mama."

"Your brother will be fine. He promised me he would be."

Her words sounded hopeful, her stare, skeptical. They hadn't received word from Anatoly since the fighting had started and had no idea if he was alive or dead. To them, no news was good news.

CHAPTER THREE

Northeast of Minsk, July 1941

MEUNCH MARCHED AT THE HEAD OF HIS MEN THROUGH the village which held a name that he couldn't pronounce. Their uniforms were dirty, and the men were all hungry, but still they pressed forward. Somewhere ahead of them were the advance armored divisions as well as the regiments that were in trucks trying to keep up with General Heinz Guderian's 2nd Panzer Group as it began its attack on Smolensk.

The village was partially destroyed. The tanks and Wehrmacht soldiers had taken it within a couple of hours. Up ahead of Meunch's company he could see a makeshift scaffold. From it hung five bodies. All were male. As the column grew closer, Meunch could see that their faces were grotesquely swollen, and a blackened tongue protruded from slack lips. To their clothes were pinned small hand-scrawled signs. Written was one word, Partisan. Already the Russian civilians were organizing a resistance.

"Keep your men moving, Herr Lieutenant," a voice called out to him from across the street. "The war will not wait for stragglers."

Meunch stared in the officer's direction. He was an SS-Standartenfuhrer, or colonel. He was dressed in the black SS uniform with a peaked cap with the silver skull pinned to the front of it. Then he understood, the hanging was of his doing. Him and all his followers.

Ignoring him, the lieutenant kept his men moving towards the other end of the building. A truck bounced past them, followed by a halftrack. Both were filled with Wehrmacht soldiers. As Meunch and his men passed a side street he caught sight of more SS. This time they were lined up, side-by-side. In front of them were perhaps five or six villagers. The soldiers were under the command of an SS-Unterscharfuhrer or sergeant. Meunch heard him bark an order. The MP40s in his men's hands came up. Another order and the weapons chattered with their staccato sound. The prisoners jerked before collapsing to the street.

"Bastards," Meunch heard Bauer say from behind him. "That's no way to fight a war."

"Silence in the ranks," the lieutenant snapped hoping that his Unteroffizier had not been overheard. Then he dropped back so he was walking beside Bauer. "If you must say something like that at least make sure that you cannot be overheard."

"Black hearted shit eaters they are, sir," the Unteroffizier said out of the corner of his mouth.

"As you were, Unteroffizier Bauer."

"Yes, sir."

They marched on, clearing the village. Ahead on the right side of the road was a small forest, on the left, an open field. In it were the remnants of a destroyed Panzer III tank, beside it a halftrack. A Wehrmacht soldier hung over the side of it, arms dangling down past his head. Another lay on the churned-up soil, the lower half of his body gone.

The tank had burned and as they walked past it, Meunch could detect the scent of scorched flesh carried on the gentle breeze. It was a smell they were now well used to.

As they grew closer to the trees the lieutenant thought he saw movement. He stared at the shadows in the woods and saw nothing more. It wasn't until the gunfire erupted from within the trees that Meunch realized what he'd seen.

"Get down!" he shouted at his men. Some of them dived into the ditch which ran alongside the road while others dropped where they stood. Bullets found flesh and screams erupted from the wounded and dying.

An explosion flung debris skyward. Amongst it was the leg of a German Fusilier. Another grenade landed close to their position and Meunch felt the concussive blast batter his body. His ears rang, and his senses were stunned. Beside him, Bauer was up on one knee, firing his MP 40 and barking orders.

"Anton, Boris, push forward with your sections. Show these Ivan bastards how to fight a real war. Move!"

More men buckled under the enfilading fire. Meunch felt a hand grab his uniform. "Are you all right, sir?"

He looked up and saw Obergefreiter Felix Glass looking down at him. "I'm fine. That last grenade landed too close."

"At least you're still alive, Herr Lieutenant," Glass

allowed. "Get into the ditch, sir, while we fix these Ivans."

Meunch watched as Glass motioned to his section and they started forward. Bauer shouted at him, "Where are you going, Glass?"

"To kill the enemy, Unteroffizier Bauer."

"Get your men back under cover. Anton and Boris have got this."

"They couldn't win crotch rot in a whore house if they were the only two there, Unteroffizier, let alone a battle."

With a shout he led his men forward into the trees and amongst the Russian ambushers. The fighting quickly turned to hand-to-hand and with it came a monstrous brutality of men doing whatever it took to survive.

Although Meunch disagreed with Glass disobeying orders, he knew he was the best NCO, apart from Bauer, for the job. Feeling better now, he rose to his feet and waved his arm in the air. "Forward, men. Push forward."

The soldiers came out of the ditch and entered the trees, joining battle with their comrades. More men died on both sides; others were wounded. Meunch saw one of his men fighting with an entrenching shovel. He swung it viciously and it hit a Russian's head, cleaving it open. The man never made a sound as he dropped at the German soldier's feet.

Meunch ducked under the swing of a Russian rifle and shot the attacker with a short burst from his MP 40. The soldier cried out and dropped to the damp earth of the forest.

The lieutenant looked about and saw that his men had gained the upper hand and the Russian survivors were starting to surrender. Taking in large gulps of air, Meunch called to Glass, "Gather all of the prisoners out on the road, Obergefreiter Glass."

"Yes, Lieutenant."

Ten minutes later, the surviving Russians were out on the road. "What do we do with the wounded?" Bauer asked Meunch.

"Ours or theirs?"

"Theirs."

"Do you have a casualty report?"

"We lost eight killed and five wounded," Bauer replied.

"What about them?"

"Twenty dead and another ten wounded. Our medical officer is tending them."

"Send a runner back to the village and see if we can get a couple of trucks out here for them."

"Sir. And the Russians?"

Meunch nodded along the road. "I think that will be taken out of our hands."

Bauer looked and saw a small squad of SS coming towards them, being led by a young SS-Obersturm-fuhrer, or lieutenant.

He called a halt where the prisoners were gathered under the watchful eye of Glass. "Who is in charge here?" Meunch heard him ask stiffly.

"I am," Glass replied.

"You will turn these prisoners over to me at once."

"I'm sorry, Herr Obersturmfuhrer, I can't do that."

"Why not?" he asked indignantly.

"Because my lieutenant told me to keep an eye on them."

"Where is your lieutenant?"

"I'm here," Meunch replied.

"You will hand these prisoners over to me at once by the order of Standartenfuhrer Klein."

"Where is the Standartenfuhrer?" Meunch asked.

"He is back in the village."

"What does the Standartenfuhrer intend to do with the prisoners, Obersturmfuhrer?"

"Shoot them, of course."

Meunch looked at Bauer and then Glass. "Obergefreiter Bauer, fall the men in; we've got some marching to do."

"What about our wounded, sir?"

"Leave the medical officer here with them. He can catch up to us. Along with the runner who was sent back to the village."

"Yes."

Meunch looked at the SS soldier. "They're all yours."

———

Smolensk, July 1941

The general looked at Anatoly and said, "It is the first time I've seen a colonel wearing a lieutenant's uniform."

"I'm sorry, sir, but the duty was thrust upon me by another officer outside of Korkino," Anatoly replied.

The sound of bombs exploding in the south of the city reverberated across Smolensk and a glass of vodka trembled on the desk beside the papers General Boris Fedorov was reviewing. "Tell me, what am I to do with you, Lieutenant?"

"Sir?"

The general held up a piece of paper. "Do you see this?"

"Yes, sir."

"These are orders that have come straight from Moscow. They are addressed to all officers. What it basically says—"

"You deserted in the face of the enemy."

Anatoly's heart lurched as he looked at the man standing behind Fedorov. "What?"

"You heard me. You deserted your post in the face of the enemy."

"This is Comrade Popov. He is from the NKVD," the general explained.

"I did not desert in the face of the enemy. We were driven back. The battalion I commanded has been almost wiped out. Hell, the regiment is all but gone. What—"

A volley of gunfire sounded from nearby. Popov nodded grimly. "That was the commanding officer of the Four-Forty-Fifth Regiment departing this world. He too was *driven back* by overwhelming numbers."

"So it was better we stayed there and die, not save as many of my men as I could so they could fight another day?"

"Yes," Popov replied. "For the glory of Mother Russia and Comrade Stalin."

Anatoly looked at Fedorov as another stick of bombs fell in the city. "General?"

"I'm afraid that my hands are tied, Lieutenant. You and the other officers and NCOs who are left shall be tried for desertion as soon as possible and then punishment will be carried out swiftly."

"You mean we will be shot?" Anatoly asked incredulously.

"That remains to be seen." Fedorov waved at the two guards standing near the door. "Take him away."

Anatoly was locked in a basement with other officers who had fallen foul of Stalin's new orders. Soon Sobol and Sergei, along with a few more NCOs joined them.

"What is happening, sir?" Sobol asked. "From what I was told we're to be—"

"Tried for desertion in the face of the enemy," Anatoly finished for him.

"This is horseshit," Sergei snarled. "What we did was save as many as we could."

"New orders from Comrade Stalin," Anatoly stated.

"To hell with him," Sergei snarled. "The son of a bitch sits on his fat ass behind his desk and does nothing except have men shot because he's afraid of them."

"Shut up, Sergei," Anatoly whispered harshly. "Do you want to be shot?"

He mumbled something in reply before withdrawing into himself. Sobol looked at his commanding officer. "It can't get much worse, can it, sir?"

"I'm not sure, Nicolai. I'm not sure."

———

THEY TRIED Anatoly and Sobol together which turned out to be advantageous for them both. The presiding officer was Fedorov. Either side of him sat a general. Fedorov stared at the two men through alcohol glazed eyes and asked, "What do you have to say for yourselves?"

Anatoly said, "What I did was save all of the men I could so we could fight another day at a better place. Before that, we stood at Korkino where the battalion lost its commanding officer and hundreds of its loyal sons. We held the Germans until we could hold no more, and I ordered those that were left to retreat."

Fedorov grunted. "Fine. You're both guilty of the charges and will be sent east to be incarcerated in a labor camp for twenty years."

"Twenty years!" Sobol exclaimed.

Fedorov narrowed his eyes. "You're right, Sergeant. Thirty years. Be thankful you're not being shot."

Anatoly was stunned. Thirty years? He'd never see his mother again. Most likely he'd never see his family again. All because he wanted to save the last of his men from massacre.

He opened his mouth to speak but nothing came out. Instead, he heard Fedorov say, "Take them away. Next case."

———

Over Moscow, July 1941

The Heinkel He III lurched again, buffeted by anti-aircraft fire from below. Hauptmann Edmund Wagner breathed deeply through his mask and looked out of the Perspex window at another bomber in his formation. Its port engine was on fire, and it was starting to roll lazily as the pilot lost control.

He said a brief prayer for the crew and then focused

his attention forward as he tried to keep the plane level. In his radio he heard Rudi, his bombardier say, "One minute to target, Herr Hauptmann."

One minute, it felt like an hour. Black balls of cottonwool laced with deadly shrapnel dotted the sky. A Heinkel fell away from another formation to starboard, both engines aflame. Two parachutes appeared and Wagner wondered briefly if maybe they would be better off dying on their plane. Suddenly he heard his dorsal gunner open fire. "Planes coming in—"

The thin skin of the Heinkel was violently battered by gunfire punching holes in it, admitting streams of sunlight from outside. One of Wagner's men cried out, hit by a round but the pilot ignored it. They were only seconds out from dropping their bombs.

———

LIEUTENANT IVAN SAFONOV depressed the firing button of the Yakovlev Yak-1fighter and felt it shudder as its weapons expelled their deadly loads. Around him the flak burst but he ignored it as did the other pilots of his flight. Their mission was to shoot down the enemy, not worry about getting shot down.

Within the first days of the German invasion the Red Air Force had been decimated by the Nazi planes. The ones he and his men were flying now had fewer than ten hours' flight time.

"Der'mo," one of his pilots blustered over the radio. "Shit."

"What is the problem, Igor?" Ivan asked as he started to pull up from his last attack.

"My guns have jammed, Lieutenant."

"Both of them?" The Yak only had two.

"Yes, both of them."

"Go back to the field."

With Igor's departure the flight was left with three planes. No, two. Ivan muttered a curse as another of his flight, a young pilot who'd joined them only the day before, was knocked out of the sky, hit by flak from below.

Ivan pulled up into an almost vertical climb. Once he hit a thousand feet above the bombers, he cut the throttle, let the machine lay over, and put it into a free fall type roll. Once its nose was pointed back down, he opened the throttle once more and pointed it at the lead plane in the formation.

Ivan fired once more, and he saw the tracers reach out across the sky. He saw the rounds impact the bomber halfway along its fuselage. The Heinkel started to roll lazily onto its side, the port wing dipping, motor trailing black smoke.

Then he was through, the screaming Klimov M-105PF V-12 liquid-cooled piston engine powering the Yak into the narrowest of gaps in the formation. His remaining wingman tried to follow him and screwed it royally, his starboard wing shearing through the last third of a Heinkel's fuselage, separating it from its tail.

The lieutenant pulled back on the stick, the nose of the plane responding and coming up. He looked at his fuel gauge. It was almost empty. Ivan looked up and heaved on the stick, working the rudders with his feet. He hissed out loud as his port wingtip just missed the falling stick of bombs from a Heinkel somewhere above. "Careless, Ivan," he growled.

Twice more he had to perform the maneuver before

he was out from under the bomber formation. He put
the Yak into a turn and looked out through the Perspex
cockpit cover. Below he could see the dark smoke and
flames rising from the city. This was the second raid
from the Germans, and it was only noon. They would
probably get another two in before dark which meant
he had to get down, refueled, rearmed, and ready for
the next one. And he was two planes short.

Moscow, July 1941

Stalin tried to ignore the sound of the bombs but the
vibrations rattling his office was distracting to say the
least. There was a knock at his door and Zhukov
entered. Stalin looked up and waved him in. "What is it,
Georgy?"

"I have the latest reports from the front."

"What is the news?"

"Smolensk has been surrounded. The German
pincer movement has closed around it trapping the
soldiers we have there."

Stalin's eyes darkened. "How many, Georgy?"

"It is estimated we have seven-hundred thousand
men inside the perimeter, sir."

"Mother of God," Stalin growled. "What are we
doing about it?"

"They have been ordered to break out, if possible,
sir."

"Can't they stand and fight?" Stalin asked. "That
amount of men—"

He stopped as Zhukov shook his head. "We have no

way of resupplying them, sir. They could stand and fight but eventually they would run out of ammunition and then have to surrender. If they can break out, we'll be able to use them in the defense of Moscow."

Stalin's eyes narrowed. "What do you mean, the defense of Moscow?"

"At the rate they are pushing our troops back, sir, they will be outside the city within a week or so."

"Every time I see you, Georgy, it takes me all of my will not to have you shot. You always bring me bad news; what about some good news for a change?"

"I'm sorry, sir, there is no good news. We are being pushed back across the whole front. We lose thousands of men every day along with desperately needed equipment. We may lose Leningrad soon and Kiev as well if we cannot stem the flow."

"What about our air force, Georgy?"

"What air force?"

So there it was, laid bare. "Can we reinforce Kiev? Leningrad? Moscow?"

"We can divert reinforcements to Moscow. Leningrad will have to fend for itself. There is a trainload of troops which could be diverted to Kiev."

"What troops?"

"Ones that were to be sent to labor camps."

"Will they fight?"

"If we give them no alternative, I believe so."

"Then do it, Georgy. Do it now."

CHAPTER FOUR

Army Group Center, HQ Meeting, July 1941

GENERAL HEINZ GUDERIAN COULDN'T BELIEVE WHAT HE was hearing. "No," he growled as he stared back at his narrow-faced commander with ears that stuck out. "No, no, no."

General Moritz Albrecht Franz Friedrich Fedor von Bock, commander of Army Group Center stared stoically back at his subordinate. "Explain, Heinz."

Guderian looked at the other officers. Geyr von Schweppenburg, von Vietinghoff, Hoth from the 3rd Panzer Army, von Kluge from the 4th Army, and Strauss 9th Army, among others. "Sir, you are taking my 2nd Panzer Group out of the line and turning us back to Germany."

"That is a little over dramatic, Heinz," Bock said.

"It might as well be sending me back. You're taking one of your strongest forces out—"

"You've been beat up worse than any of us, Heinz."

"And still I got my mission completed. If you take

me out now, you're killing any chance of reaching your objective inside the time frame. Ask Hermann."

Bock looked at the shorter, gray-haired general. Hoth nodded. "He's right."

The others murmured their concurrence, but Bock wouldn't be persuaded otherwise. "The order stands, Heinz. You will be reinforced and resupplied within the next few days."

"Damn it, Fedor!"

"Enough!" Bock snapped. "If you would like me to relieve you of command, just say so."

"That won't be necessary," Guderian said bitterly.

"Fine. Dismissed."

As they filed outside into the Russian sunshine, Hoth pulled Guderian aside. "Don't let it get to you, Heinz. He will be recalling you before too long. Once Adolf hears that his finest Panzer general is being taken out of the fight, I'm sure the order will be reversed."

"Why can't he see that it is a mistake, Hermann?"

"He commands an army driving deep into Russia with his supply lines stretched so thin that it only takes just a little snip, and they will be severed. He's under a lot of pressure from Berlin, Heinz."

"I suppose. I just hope he realizes that it is a mistake and reverses the decision."

———

Kiev, July 1941

Anatoly and Sobol climbed from the freight car and stepped down onto the hard ground beside the rail line, thankful for fresh air after being packed tight within the railcar's confines with other soldiers and officers who shared their plight. "Sir," Sobol said, pointing at the sign on the station wall. "We're in Kiev."

"All right, you weasel bastards, get into ranks," an NKVD officer roared.

"Where are we going?" a soldier asked.

The NKVD officer, a large man with dark hair stepped in so close that his nose was almost touching the man he stood in front of. "Wherever I tell you, you piece of cowardly shit."

"Is that really necessary?" another man asked. He wore the uniform of a colonel.

The NKVD man sidestepped and headbutted him in the face, shattering his nose. "Shut up," he growled menacingly.

A murmur ran through the onlooking prisoners. The NKVD officer looked up and down the line. "Move. Do as you are ordered."

The prisoners formed up into ranks. Along with them were men from the various other railcars. From what he could see, Anatoly figured there were upwards of 1,500 men all told. Before they could move, a fat Red Army general appeared and stood on a crate so he could be seen. Anatoly recognized him immediately. He looked them over and said, "Listen to me, cowards of Mother Russia. You have been ordered here and given one last chance of proving yourselves. From now on you will be known as Punishment Battalion Three Sixty. You will be divided into six companies."

The general looked around the lines in front of him. He pointed at a young man wearing a lieutenant's uniform. "You, step forward." He then picked out four more before pointing a finger at Anatoly. "And you."

All six of them stepped forward. "Each of you will now command a company in the battalion and be given the rank of captain."

They looked at each other, confused. The general continued. "You will be under the command of a colonel."

Once more the general looked around. He then pointed at the man with the bloodied face. "You. You will command them, and you will answer to me. My name is General Yevgeny Serov. You will fight when you are told to, stand when you are ordered, and run like hell when the time comes. You will also dig. Dig, dig, dig. Until you can't dig anymore."

"What are we digging for, General?" a soldier called out.

"You men are going to be in the front line when the Nazis come, along with many others."

"With what do we fight, Comrade General?" Anatoly asked.

The NKVD officer glared at him, but Anatoly ignored him. Serov nodded. "You will be issued with weapons when they arrive, Captain..." Serov paused after using Anatoly's new rank.

"Anatoly Kozlov, sir."

Recognition registered. "Yes, I remember you. The lieutenant I promoted to battalion commander outside of Korkino."

Anatoly smiled inwardly as he realized that this command was Serov's punishment for the farce. "Yes, Comrade General."

"Too bad, you're now a captain." He then stared at all the new company commanders. "Pick your men.

Make them as even as possible. Your work starts today, for the German army is coming."

Anatoly walked over to Sobol. "You're now my second in command, Nicolai. Let's find some good men."

It took time but Anatoly soon had a company of 246 men. He chose more NCOs and then divided them into squads. Once everything was done, a truck rumbled into view, leaving a trail of black diesel smoke in its wake. The NKVD officer walked over to the back of it and pulled back a tarp. He pulled out a shovel and held it at shoulder height. "Come on, you cowardly bastards, come and get your weapons."

Moscow, July 1941

"What is this, Georgy?" Stalin asked holding up a sheet of paper. "Please, tell me before I take it to wipe my ass with it."

Zhukov remained silent. He knew what it was and had expected a reaction but not quite the one he was getting. "It is my recommendation, sir. That was what you asked for."

"You call this a recommendation?"

"Yes, sir."

"You want to withdraw the southwestern front beyond the Dnieper and surrender Kiev to the Nazis? Am I right?"

"I need more troops to bolster the front west of Moscow, Comrade," Zhukov explained.

"Didn't you already do that?" Stalin asked.

"Can I show you on the map, sir?" Zhukov asked.

Stalin came to his feet and walked over to where the large map of Russia hung on the wall. Using his finger, the chief of staff pointed out the situation.

"I need more, sir. Kleist, here, is pushing hard in the south towards Kiev and I have intelligence that suggests that Guderian's Second Panzer Army is preparing to push south to link up." He traced a path on the map. "If they do that, we will lose upwards of one-hundred thousand men. They will be encircled and slaughtered. Kiev must be considered a lost cause, Comrade."

Stalin shook his head. "No. The armies there will stand and fight."

"But, Comrade..." Zhukov looked exasperated.

Stalin held up his hand, a look of cunning hidden deep in his dark eyes. "It is time you had a change, Georgy. I'm relieving you of command—"

"Comrade, I—" Zhukov blurted out.

"The decision is made, Georgy," Stalin said firmly. "You will leave tomorrow and take command of the reserves you have placed there." It was Stalin's turn to poke at the map. "Upon your arrival you shall assess the divisions which you have and then you will attack, Georgy. *Attack!*"

———

WITHIN THE NEXT MONTH, Zhukov's fears were realized. In the south, Kleist's Panzers encircled twenty divisions near Uman. Guderian's 2nd Panzer Army was indeed deployed south to link up with Kleist. It smashed through all that stood in its way, Guderian's army taking casualties but never slowing its progress.

Boris Shaposhnikov the new Chief of the General Staff who replaced Zhukov, recommended that the southern troops be withdrawn to Kiev and beyond. The commanding officer at Kiev assured Stalin that his defenses would hold the German onslaught.

Stalin ordered them to stand.

———

Guderian's 2nd Panzer Army, August 1941

Meunch glanced at the bloated Russian soldier's corpse as he and his company drove past it in the trucks. Up ahead lay the front but he guessed that it would be moved further on before they reached it. Columns of smoke rose into the sky, turning it brown. The distant rattle of gunfire could be heard, punctuated by the crump of artillery or the main gun of a tank.

They had not long passed through some nameless village. Most of it was burned to the ground. Dead horses and cows lay in paddocks, burned out vehicles as well. At one point they had driven past the wreckage of a Russian bomber in a field beside the road.

They had been fighting now for days and Meunch's company was down to seventy men. He'd been told by his commanding officer that more replacements were on the way, but he was yet to see any.

Suddenly the trucks stopped, and a major appeared. "Out, everybody out of the trucks. ieutenant Meunch, with me."

"Take over, Bauer," Meunch said as he hopped over the tailgate. He followed the major towards the rear of the column. He wasn't alone; other officers followed suit.

The major's name was Fischer. He'd taken over command of the battalion after the Oberst had been killed three days before.

The officers gathered around him at the rear truck, and he said, "Up ahead there is a crossroads. This side of it is a bridge over a creek. It's a natural defensive position and the Ivans know it. They've got a battalion dug in on the other side and one of our tanks is blocking the bridge. It can't be moved until the Ivans are routed on the other side."

"So it's up to us to persuade them to move," Meunch said stoically.

"Exactly. It seems we've become the general's favorites at getting things done."

Meunch knew what the major meant. They'd cleared a village along the route and another strongpoint thirty miles back along the same road. The problem was that every time they went into combat they came out with fewer men. Now they were down below half strength. "I wish that another battalion would become his favorite," a dirty-faced Hauptmann said.

A dry chuckle emanated from the other officers, including Meunch. Then he looked at his watch.

"Am I keeping you from something, Lieutenant?"

"I was just looking at the time, sir. Seeing how much light we have left in the day."

"You have a plan?"

"I was thinking we could cross over after dark, sir. Ford the creek and hopefully surprise them."

The major nodded. "That might be a good idea, Meunch. Your company will cross first."

"Me and my big mouth."

"Don't worry, you will have artillery and tank support."

"My heart is filled with joy, Herr Major."

"And so it should be; leading the battalion across is a great honor."

Meunch gave him a mirthless grin. "Honor comes to fools and dead people, sir. I'd rather not be any of those."

———

BEFORE THE SUN was even close to going down, the orders changed. They were to go immediately. Meunch shook his head upon hearing the news. Attacking an entrenched position head-on in broad daylight wasn't ideal. It was a downright shit show but there it was.

He turned to Bauer. "You take your section in during the right, I'll go up the middle, and Felix will go left. I've asked for smoke as well as high explosive rounds."

"Let me go up the middle, sir," Bauer said.

"No, my company, my decision."

"Yes, sir."

Suddenly the air above them seemed to be torn apart as the shells from the artillery bombardment commenced. Meunch looked at his watch. "Right on time. Get Felix, it's time to go."

"Good luck, Lieutenant."

"You too, Hans."

They moved into position and went forward under the cover of the artillery. Smoke shells covered their advance and as they slipped into the creek, it was like a dense fog overhanging the water. The good thing about the German advance was that the Russians had no artillery, just anti-tank guns.

The three tips of the spear sheltered under the bank as they waited for the artillery to stop. Meunch turned to a young Obergefreiter and held out his hand. The young soldier handed his commander a stick grenade then took one himself.

Meunch looked once more at his watch and on cue, the shelling stopped. Then he primed the grenade and threw it. The Obergefreiter did the same.

Two explosions sounded which was the signal for the attack to begin. Meunch and his men came out of the water, scrambling over the edge of the creek bank. Once on top he could see that the smoke screen was already starting to clear which gave him a first look at what he and his men were facing.

A DP-27 light machine gun opened fire and the air was instantly filled with bullets. Meunch brought up his MP40 and opened fire. Beside him the young Obergefreiter cried out and fell forward. Beside him another of the assaulters grabbed at his throat, his life-giving blood running thick between his fingers. He too fell to the ground.

Bullets kicked up dirt around Meunch as he tried his best to silence the savage weapon. All along the line now, Russians and Germans alike were engaged in heavy combat. The machine gun fell silent, but it was like swatting a bee in a swarm as the outgoing Russian gunfire intensified.

The company commander saw a Russian soldier rise and pull his arm back to throw a grenade. Meunch shot him but was too late to stop the release of the small high explosive.

He dived to the ground just before the grenade exploded. He felt the heat of the blast and heard one of his men cry out as razor-sharp splinters and shrapnel bit deep and ended his young life over eight-hundred miles from his home.

Meunch's magazine ran dry, and he replaced it with a fresh one. Coming to his feet he shouted, *"Forward! Press Forward!"*

He started to run towards the Russian trench; beside him and behind, his men followed. When he'd first become an officer, a seasoned Hauptmann had said, "If you want respect from your men, lead them, don't drive them." That same man had died on the second day of Operation Barbarossa. But here was Meunch, leading from the front.

The German infantry pressed home their attack using heavy fire and grenades. Men fell on both sides, maimed and dead.

Then they were there; on the edge of the trench. Meunch raked the trench with fire from his MP40. Defenders fell under the onslaught. Soon the survivors were either throwing up their hands in surrender or running across the road behind them and into the field beyond.

Meunch looked around behind him and saw the next company of soldiers crossing, behind them another. He looked along the line of the defensive position and saw some of his own pushing forward after the fleeing Russians.

He grabbed a young gefreiter, lance Corporal, from beside him. "Bruhn, run to Unteroffizier Bauer and tell him to pull his men back to this position, now."

"Yes, Her Lieutenant."

The man jogged off holding his rifle in his right hand. Meunch turned away and looked for Glass. He found him nursing a bullet wound to his arm. "Are you all right, Felix?"

"Never better, sir," he replied shrugging his shoulders. "Just a scratch."

"Get the medic to have a look at it. What are your casualties?"

"Four dead, five wounded."

Meunch nodded. "Hold here. We'll let the other companies pass through us and—"

BOOM!

Earth leaped skyward short of the trench the Russians had used. Meunch looked to the low hill to the rear and saw three tanks. T-34s.

"Get into the trench!" the company commander shouted.

His men took cover just as a second high explosive round came in. The earth shook as it exploded amongst the men of the follow up companies. Shouts of pain accompanied the blast, and the orders of NCOs filled the air.

Wehrmacht soldiers started leaping across the trench and took cover on the other side of the road in a drainage ditch. Behind the defensive position others used the creek bank. More rounds came in, one close enough that Meunch felt clods of earth rain down upon him.

He raised his gaze over the lip of the trench and saw the three tanks moving down the slope towards their position. If they got much closer, they would cause untold chaos amongst the German soldiers, forcing them back and their assault on the crossroads would be all for nothing.

There was a crash from his right and Meunch turned his head to find the source. It had come from the bridge where a Panzer IV tank had battered into the remains of the destroyed MK III Panzer and was pushing it off the bridge.

Behind where this was happening, another Panzer IV sat on the road. Meunch saw its main gun traverse. It stopped for a moment and then the whole tank rocked violently as it fired.

Meunch's head whipped around to see an eruption of earth beside one of the three T-34s. The three of them separated to confuse the enemy. One of them fired and Meunch heard the loud clang as the shell from the Russian tank skipped off the Panzer's armor.

The Panzer traversed its turret once more and fired. The Russian T-34 which had fired the ricochet had its turret lift of in a flash of orange. It seemed to hang in the air before crashing down beside it. Black smoke started to pour from the remainder of the tank and Meunch thanked God that he wasn't inside.

By now the second Panzer had cleared the bridge and it was coming off the other end. Its main gun traversed right to come to bear on a T-34 hurrying across its bow, its own weapon coming around to fire at the German tank.

Both fired at the same time. The armor-piercing round from the Panzer passed through the side of the T-34 and turned flesh to mush on the inside. The Russian shell hit the German tank in the tracks, blowing them off. The tank lurched to a halt. The crew scrambled from the steel beast and ran towards the creek where they took cover behind the bank. This left the lone Panzer against the remaining two T-34s.

The German tank's main gun fired. The armor-piercing round reached out and touched the T-34 where the turret attached to the hull of the fighting vehicle. The effect was cataclysmic. The shell struck the ready use ammunition inside the Russian tank making it detonate immediately. The T-34 exploded in a fireball, its turret dislodged and parts of its hull steel peeled back.

The remaining Russian tank reversed suddenly, heading for the rise it had not long crested. It kept its front facing towards the enemy so that its main armor could afford it some protection.

That was the theory anyway.

However, when the Panzer IV fired once more, the T-34 stopped its maneuver and smoke began pouring from it. In just moments it was ablaze and all within it were dead.

"Remind me never to become a tank commander," Meunch muttered to himself.

The two fresh companies came to their feet and under orders of their commanders moved towards the hill where the Russian T-34s had appeared. There they would take up positions that could overlook the crossroads and watch the approaches.

Meunch looked for Bauer, locating him as he was seeing to his wounded. "I just received word that we're moving out in thirty minutes. Make sure everyone able to is ready."

"Yes, sir."

The company commander hesitated before saying, "Good work today, Hans."

CHAPTER FIVE

Leningrad, Russia, August 1941

ANYA KOZLOVA GRASPED HER DAUGHTER'S HAND AND pleaded with her. "You must leave today, Eva, before the Germans cut the city off completely."

"But, Mama, I cannot leave you here on your own?"

"I will be fine. Go with your cousin, Kolya." She pointed at the bearded young man. "He will get you to safety."

"No, Mother. Not unless you come with us."

Anya looked at her nephew with desperate eyes. "Please, Kolya, help me."

"Your mama is right, Eva. If we don't leave today, then we will be stuck here."

"But where will we go?"

"I have people to the south, behind the German lines. They are fighting them while they look the other way. Partisans."

Anya said, "Or maybe you can go to Moscow, find your sisters. Join them."

"Yes," Kolya said. "I can get you there."

Eva nodded. "All right, I will go with you."

Relieved, Anya tried to smile but her eyes belied her feelings. "Take her now, Kolya."

"I don't have any clothes."

A truck filled with Russian soldiers drove past them at speed. It was followed by another, and yet another as the front around Leningrad was being reinforced.

"Forget your clothes," Anya hissed at her youngest. "Just go, go now."

Eva wrapped her arms around her mother, eyes filled with tears. "Be careful, Mama. I will write to you."

She drew back and saw that her mother's eyes were like her own, her cheeks wet. "I'll be back, Mama."

"I know you will, sweet. Go, don't look back."

Eva and Kolya made their way through the busy streets until reaching the outskirts of the city. Eva cried silently most of the way. Leningrad itself was teaming with soldiers and civilians. Once they had bypassed a military checkpoint, they were met by two more men. Pavel and Boris. Both men were armed and handed Kolya over his own weapon. Pavel looked at Eva and asked Kolya, "Where are we going?"

"To Moscow."

"For her?"

"That's right."

"Why?" Boris asked scowling at Eva.

"Because I said I would. Do you have a problem with that?"

"What about the Germans?" Pavel asked.

"There will be more than enough to go around."

"Can she shoot?"

"I guess we'll find out. Let's go get the truck and join the others."

———

"THAT EVENING, twenty miles southeast of Leningrad, they stopped at a farm which was occupied by the small partisan band Kolya commanded. There were ten more men and three women, and all looked upon Eva with distrust except for Irina. She was around Eva's age and seemed to warm to her right away. She brought Eva some food later that night. Handing her the plate, she said, "I'm Irina."

"Eva."

"I know. Kolya told me."

"Are you really partisans?"

"Yes."

"But you're all so young."

"Like you?"

"Yes. How did you all come to be together?"

"We are all from the same town, further west. When the Germans came, they killed most of our families. We managed to escape from them. Everyone here has lost people they love. What about you?"

"My brother is away fighting. I'm going to Moscow to join my sisters."

"What are they doing?"

"I'm not sure? Whatever they are told to do, I guess."

A deep booming sound filtered into the farmhouse from outside. Eva frowned. "What is that?"

Irina grabbed Eva by the hand. "Come, I'll show you."

They went outside and climbed onto the back of a

truck. Once aboard, Irina pointed to the southeast. "There, see it?"

On the distant horizon came the flashes of yellow light. Every one of them was followed by the deep crump of an explosion. "It is the German artillery shelling the lines. They do that of a night before an attack. They were further away last night. Now they're closer."

Eva felt a chill run down her spine and shivered. Irina sensed it and put an arm around her shoulders. Eva said, "I'm scared."

"It starts like that. But in time it will go away."

"Have you—have you killed Germans before?"

"Yes."

"What's it like?"

"Terrible."

A bigger flash lit up the horizon. Eva waited for the sound to reach them. When it eventually did, it was deeper and seemed to buffet her.

"You should stay with us, you know," Irina said.

"What?"

"Stay with us. We need as many people as we can get to help fight the invasion of Mother Russia."

"I-I don't know."

"Think about it."

"All right."

Eva thought about it all night and by the next morning, when it came time to leave, she said to Kolya, "I want to stay."

"Are you sure?"

"Yes."

"What about your sisters?"

"I don't even know if they are still in Moscow," Eva replied.

"Alright, then, let's see about getting you a weapon."

Over Kiev, September 1941

Bullets rattled along the port wing of the Yak-1 bringing a curse from Ivan Safonov's lips. "Shit!"

He immediately put the Yak into a roll to starboard as the BF-109 blasted across the top of him, no more than forty feet above. Ivan kept the roll going and tried to bring his plane back level, hoping to get onto the German fighter's tail. Stunned by being jumped by the enemy planes, he fought to regain his composure, gasping in great lungsful of air from his oxygen mask.

"Ivan, are you all right?" he heard the voice in his ears ask from his flying helmet.

"I'm fine, how many?"

"Six of them, they're coming back around."

"Break and engage," Ivan said to his pilots.

The three Yaks flying on his wing broke and climbed steeply to meet the returning enemy. Six 109s was bad odds when it came to dogfighting, but his pilots needed to learn what it was all about. Besides, when the Nazis came calling, there was never anything such as an even fight. He'd heard some figures just the day before and the Red Airforce had already lost three-hundred planes in the skies over Kiev[1]. They took the 109s head on as they came at them. A Messerschmitt filled Ivan's sights and he depressed the firing button. The Yak vibrated and pieces flew off the attacking German plane.

The pilot of the 109 broke to his right and dived towards the city below. Ivan put the Yak into a roll and followed it.

Above Safonov the other pilots engaged the German planes. He could hear them talking over the radio, calling out their targets. The 109 in front of Ivan pulled up suddenly and rolled to flatten out. Ivan tried to follow him, but the Messerschmitt had the tighter turning circle.

The 109 disappeared and Ivan's head swiveled left and right as he tried to find it. He put his Yak into a turn to port trying not to remain on a steady heading.

Once more he heard and felt the impact of German rounds as the 109 came in from behind. The engine of the Yak coughed and started belching black smoke. Ivan cursed. This was the second plane he'd lost inside a week, and the Yaks, at that point in time, were few and far between.

The plane started losing altitude rapidly as its power drained off. Ivan tried to open the canopy and found that it was stuck. "Damnit."

He was going to have to ride this one in and hope for the best.

Through the side of the canopy, he saw an open field at the edge of the city. He worked the rudder and stick and managed to get the plane turned. The engine had lost even more power now and was barely running at all. Ivan cut the power and fought to keep the nose of the Yak up just enough so it wouldn't stall.

The ground came to meet him almost quicker than he anticipated. Ivan moved the Yak left and right as he tried to bleed off speed. Once he figured he'd done enough, Ivan straightened the plane out and prepared to put it down.

AFTER THE FACT, Safonov couldn't recall much at all. The wooden wings ripped from the fuselage, the crunch of the Yak hitting the ground. Then things went black for a time after he hit his head. The next Ivan knew was he had hands roughly manhandling him from the cockpit as soldiers working on the defenses of Kiev pulled him from the wreckage.

It took a few moments before he realized that he was actually in pain as it ripped through his back and his legs. Voices called out and then he was on a stretcher.

Then the unthinkable happened. The useless bastards dropped him. Just like that. This time more excruciating pain tore through his body and everything went black once more.

Kiev, September 1941

"Do you think he'll be all right?" Sobol asked Anatoly.

"He was a little banged up but I'm sure he'll be flying again in no time."

"He sure hit the ground hard."

Both men looked back at the aircraft. The propeller was bent back, the wings were gone, even the tail had come away from the rest of the fuselage. Anatoly and his company had watched the dogfights above from the ground where they had been digging a tank trap in the outskirts of the city. Even the civilians had been roped into helping all of the soldiers dig.

Anatoly looked up and saw Serov coming towards them. He stopped and stared at Anatoly. "Have you had enough of digging, comrade?"

"Yes, sir."

"Good. Get your men ready, we're leaving."

Anatoly frowned. "Why?"

"It seems Comrade Stalin is starting to shit his pants. We're joining the front outside Moscow."

"When do we leave, General?"

"As soon as the battalion is on the trucks."

———

Leningrad, September 1941

Georgy Zhukov arrived in Leningrad on the 11th of September, three days after the land encirclement of the city was complete. To the north were the Fins, while to the south was Army Group North, commanded by Feldmarschall Wilhelm Ritter von Leeb. Zhukov set about immediately rectifying the city's defensive needs after having toured them, and now, on the 12th he had brought everyone together. While calling the meeting of his staff he received news that Kiev was almost completely encircled by the First and Second Panzer Armies. Another week and it would be complete, and the Russians would lose four more armies. A total of over 400,000 men, not to mention equipment.

A large map was unfurled on a table around which Zhukov and his commanders stood. He stared at the map for a moment and stabbed a finger at it. "Listen carefully and I shall tell you what I want, Comrades."

In the distance could be heard the crump of incoming shells from the German front. The Red Army was holding the advance for the time being but if they didn't get the defenses squared away then it would only be a matter of time before the Nazis overran the city.

"I want concrete bunkers here, anti-tank ditches here, and an inner ring of fortified defenses here," Zhukov said. "We will barricade the roads, fortify houses at certain streets inside the city, and have bridges, factories, and other buildings set for demolition."

"What about the civilians, Comrade Zhukov?" one of the generals asked.

"Those that have not been evacuated, and can, will be put to work."

"What about food?"

"Once the defenses are prepared, we shall mount a counterattack and hit the Nazis hard. We will concentrate on one section of the line. I'm hoping we can break through and make a corridor that supplies can be brought in on."

Every man there knew it was a fanciful idea, but at least it was a plan. And any plan was better than no plan at all.

ANYA LOOKED at her food cupboard. It was empty. It had been three days since the largest food storage warehouse in Leningrad had been hit by German shells and been destroyed.

A noise outside of the house drew her attention and she looked out of the window and saw NKVD officers and soldiers gathering civilians onto the street. Anya frowned as two soldiers came through her gate and up the short path. She hurried to the door and opened it before they could knock. One of the soldiers, a stern-faced young man, stared at her and said, "You will come with us."

Anya was confused. "Why must I?"

"Because you have work to do." He grabbed her by the arm and started to drag her from her home.

"Let me go," she pleaded.

"Stop."

Both soldiers did as they were ordered. Anya shook her arms loose of their grasp and saw an officer walking towards her. "I'm sorry for their over exuberance, ma'am. We need all civilians who are capable to help us with the fortification of the city."

Anya straightened. "What do you expect me to do?"

"I'm sure we could find you something."

Anya nodded. "I can help."

"Thank you."

———

THEY GAVE Anya a shovel and put her in the bottom of a tank trap outside of the city where she worked along-side a hundred other women. The dirt and rocks were either loaded into sandbags or small boxes attached to ropes which were then hauled out of the ditch to be dumped on top. They all worked steadily under the watchful eye of and officer and an NKVD representative.

Anya stopped work, putting her shovel aside while

she looked down at her hands. What started out as blisters had now burst and were sore to the touch.

"Keep working there, the Nazis wait for no one."

She looked up at the officer. "My hands hurt."

"I don't care. Keep going."

"Here, let me help," a woman beside Anya said.

When Anya turned to look at her, the woman was tearing a strip from her petticoat, and waved the fabric in front of her, indicating her intentions. "Give me your hand."

Anya held it out and the woman wrapped it around the hand, covering the blisters. Without hesitation the woman said, "Now the other."

Within moments it too was wrapped. Anya looked at her. "Thank you. I don't even know your name."

"Olga."

"I'm Anya."

"Check to see how your hands are."

Anya checked and the hard wood of the shovel's handle felt a lot better. "They're good, thank you."

"Samolet! Samolet!" (Plane! Plane!)

Alarm filled Anya as she looked up at the soldier standing on the lip of the tank trap. He was pointing at the sky to the south. Anya glanced in that direction and at first saw nothing. Then she saw the black spots against the high cloud cover. There were indeed planes coming their way.

"Take cover!" the officer overseeing them shouted.

Anya, Olga, and others along the ditch pressed themselves against the front wall, folding their arms over their heads as a form of protection. Shouts and cries of alarm sounded from somewhere outside the trench. A couple of women ran away along the tank trap.

Somewhere anti-aircraft guns opened fire. Black puffs of flak appeared around the planes. They were JU-87, or Stuka, dive bombers. Anya stood up for some unknown reason and stared at the planes way up in the sky. While she observed them, she noticed the lead plane roll into a steep dive.

The scream of the siren fixed underneath the fuselage reached her ears. The bomber hurtled towards the ground.

"Get under cover, you silly cow!" the NKVD officer roared at her.

Snapping out of her trance, Anya sought the refuge of the steep wall of the tank trap again.

The screaming of the bomber grew louder until it suddenly pulled up out of its dive. Just before the pilot did so, he released the bomb beneath the Stuka, letting it fall free.

The ground above the trench shook violently as the bomb exploded. Earth rained down on the cowering women, a clod hitting Anya on her back while others fell around her.

The plane howled over the tank trap, low enough that Anya thought that if she reached up she might be able to touch it.

Then came the others. Screaming banshees that delivered explosive death. Another bomb landed close, and something fell into the tank trap beside where Anya crouched with the other women. Anya glanced sideways and saw the top half of a soldier lying nearby. Guts hanging from what was left of the torso, an arm missing as well.

Recoiling in revulsion, Anya closed her eyes tight trying to block out the sight that was now seared into her soul.

More bombs followed and then the drone of the planes started to fade into the distance. Up above, out of sight of those below, two trucks were on fire, and the bodies of soldiers were visible, some in craters, others dismembered and scattered to the four winds.

The officer reappeared and stared down at the distressed women in the bottom of the tank trap. "Get up," he ordered. "Get back to work."

Protests came from some of the women but they were quickly quashed as the officer barked more orders. He pointed at Anya and Olga. "You and you. Get up here. I have something for you to do."

The two women made their way up top and immediately saw firsthand the devastation of the bombing raid.

Soldiers cried out from their wounds as they were being helped by their comrades. A sickening sound which from most sounded like a wail. Then they saw the civilians. Women and men both, chopped down by shrapnel, limbs missing, insides now on the outer.

Anya paled at the sight, her bottom lip and hands trembling.

"You there," a sergeant called over to Anya and Olga. "Take this one."

He was pointing at a dead civilian, a man with no legs and a gaping hole in his chest. Both women hesitated. The sergeant said, "Hurry up before Nazi Goring's flyers come back for another go. Move."

Olga said, "I will take the legs. It's all right."

"I—I don't know if I can do it," Anya stammered.

"Sure you can. Just follow me."

They walked over to the dead civilian and struggled to pick him up. They went a few steps before Olga dropped his lower portion, her hands slipping in all the blood. She grunted and tried again. Anya said, "Come grab an arm and we'll drag him."

Olga moved to join Anya and took an arm. The pair made better progress this time and dragged the partially dismembered corpse to where the others were being left for collection. When they let him go, he flopped down then suddenly sat up and screamed.

Anya and Olga fell back, scrambling to put some distance from the horror which now faced them. Part of the man's guts slipped out and suddenly his screams ceased and he fell back. Olga looked at Anya. "So much for being dead."

Still pale, Anya gave a quick nod and leaned to the side, emptying the contents of her stomach onto the ground.

"Get up!" the sergeant shouted at them. "There are more—"

It sounded like a freight train coming in at speed. The air was torn apart and suddenly the shouting sergeant disappeared in a violent explosion. Anya was jolted by the shock and sound of what she'd just witnessed. However, there was no time to comprehend what had happened, for the first artillery shell was followed by another.

Olga grabbed her by the arm. "Quick, this way."

Anya came to her feet just as a third shell landed and they were soon running through what was akin to a severe hailstorm only these stones didn't have to hit you to kill you.

They ran as fast as they could, the shells raining down, guiding their movements with each explosion. Anya suddenly realized that she was screaming, her throat starting to hurt with her efforts. Beside her, Olga was doing the same. The latter tripped and fell, dragging Anya with her. They tumbled into an open crater and rolled to the bottom. They lay there, hands over heads as more shells landed. With each explosion Anya's body stiffened with fright.

The shelling continued for the next twenty minutes without reprieve. By the time it finally stopped, Anya couldn't figure out how she was still alive.

On trembling legs both women emerged from the shell crater and looked at the moonscape around them. Numerous fires were blazing, and the number of bodies had multiplied. They looked towards the anti-tank ditch they had until recently occupied and saw that part of the side had been blown out. Walking towards it, they peered into the trench, aware of the multitude of voices calling out.

In the bottom of the ditch was a scene of horror. A shell had landed amongst those sheltering there and exploded, blowing them apart.

"Good Lord," Anya breathed. "That could have been us."

Behind them a voice said, "Back to work."

They turned and stared at the corporal who'd replaced the sergeant. He wasn't much more than a boy. "Move," he snapped. "Comrade Stalin needs your help to defend the Motherland."

CHAPTER SIX

Outside Vitebsk, October 1941

EVA SLID HER MOSIN-NAGANT RIFLE FORWARD AS SHE waited for the small German convoy to come within range of the ambush. During her time with the partisans she had discovered a prowess with a rifle which she'd never thought possible. Within those couple of months, she'd become quite a capable marksman, killing six men so far; which was why, even at nineteen, Eva was given the important job of taking out the lead car of the convoy.

The staff car carried a general sequestered in the comfort of the back seat. The driver, a lowly obergefreiter, or corporal. Behind them came seven trucks. One was filled with Wehrmacht soldiers, the rest with supplies. Food, ammunition, and other such things. This would be the third convoy the partisans had ambushed that week. Some were against it reminding Kolya that it would be better to move to new hunting grounds because of the buildup of SS soldiers hunting them.

Kolya had replied that they would move on after the success of this mission. Grudgingly the others had agreed to his plan for one more. Now that time had come.

Eva took a deep breath and sighted through the scope at the staff car. It rocked and rolled along the churned-up dirt road. Eva waited patiently for the right time. As time seemed to slow, she became aware of the smells around her. The damp earth upon which she lay, decaying leaves that had fallen from the trees as winter approached. Beside her, Irina touched her shoulder. "The road is too bad. You cannot make that shot."

Eva looked at her. "If I cannot then I will give you my ration of schnapps when we get back."

"And if you can?"

"I will think of something."

"Fine," Irina said with a smile. "I agree to those terms."

Eva looked back through her scope, sighted on the driver, and squeezed the trigger. It all took a matter of seconds.

A bullet hole appeared in the windscreen of the staff car and the driver jerk under the impact of the round. The vehicle swerved on the road before hitting a small embankment and blocking any further passage of the trucks behind it. "Seven," Eva said.

The shot was the signal for the rest of the partisans to open fire. All along the road gunshots erupted. One of the attackers threw a grenade which rolled beneath the truck carrying the Wehrmacht soldiers. When it exploded the Krupp Protze dual rear axle truck seemed to lift in the middle. Flames shot upward engulfing all within it.

German soldiers leaped from the back, flames feeding upon their clothing. Shrieks of pain pierced the constant gunfire as they tried to escape the burning death. Eva worked the bolt of her rifle and shifted her aim. She waited for the officer to appear, whispering to him to come out and show himself. When he did, she took another breath and squeezed the trigger.

This time her kill was more visible than the last. The general's hat flew from his head and a mist exploded from his shattered skull. "Eight."

To Eva's left she saw Kolya lead the others from their ambush positions and assault the column. Many Germans died until, realizing the futility of continuing to fight, those who remained threw down their weapons and surrendered.

Eva didn't have to watch to know what was about to happen. She looked away before more gunfire sounded and Kolya, along with several of his followers killed the prisoners.

"I don't know why he has to do that," she muttered to Irina.

"They are all Nazi scum. They deserve what they get," Irina spat. "You kill them, or do you forget?"

"That is war."

"So was that."

Eva glared at her but said nothing.

Irina continued. "If you had been witness to what we saw before you joined us you would understand."

"Whatever," Eva replied and got to her feet.

Already the looting of the trucks had begun. They had to be quick before more Germans came along. They only took what they could carry and destroyed the rest.

Kolya looked at her as she approached. "Do you ever miss?"

"Not if I can help it," she replied.

"Get whatever you need. We will leave shortly."

"Where are we going?" she asked inquisitively.

"South."

"Kolya! Kolya! The SS. They—argh!"

Gunfire erupted as black uniformed soldiers appeared. Kolya's eyes widened as bullets ripped through the partisans. Eva dove to the ground, dropping her rifle. More rounds kicked up the dirt beside her and she heard Kolya start to bark orders to his people, but they were cutoff abruptly and he dropped where he stood. His face was turned towards Eva and as she stared into his sightless eyes blood ran from his slack lips.

More shouts and screams filled the air of the surrounding woods. A German officer barked instructions to his men and the firing stopped. Eva trembled where she lay, each breath came fast and labored. A pair of dark boots appeared before her, and a hand grasped a handful of her hair. She was dragged harshly to her feet where she stood facing an SS officer. An SS-Hauptsturmfuhrer, or captain. His dark hair tucked under a black officer's peaked cap, his stare the temperature of ice.

"Who are you?" he asked.

Eva said nothing.

He struck her with an open hand. "Talk."

Eva glanced left and right. She saw other soldiers

gathering the survivors together. Amongst them was Irina. Her eyes widened and the Hauptsturmfuhrer saw. "Is there something the matter?"

Eva looked away.

The officer grabbed her arm and marched her over to the main group. There were ten of them altogether. Irina caught her eye, but Eva refused to look at her. Not that it mattered. The Hauptsturmfuhrer had all that he needed to know.

With fluid movement he took out his Luger and pressed it against Irina's forehead.

"No," Eva gasped.

"Name?"

"Eva."

"Eva who?"

"Eva Kozlova," she replied, tears starting to run down her dirt-stained cheeks.

"Where are you from?"

"Don't tell him," Irina asked.

The officer shrugged. "It doesn't matter. You will tell us anyway."

And with that he shot Irina in the head.

"No!"

"Kill the rest of them and bring her with us."

Gunshots rattled and the rest of the partisans died where they stood. All except for Eva who was taken away by the SS.

———

The Moscow Front, October 1941

The Russian army was in retreat once more under the orders of Stalin. As usual he'd waited too long to give it and the Russians had lost the best part of four armies while the Germans advanced almost a hundred and thirty miles towards Moscow.

Anatoly and what remained of his company of so-called criminals were holed up in an abandoned farmhouse, waiting for dark so they could pull out once more. He was down to fifty men after the last German attack where men and armor rolled over the top of them. There was nothing they could do except fall back.

General Serov was last seen at the head of the column moving faster than anyone else. The colonel he'd put in command had his brains blown out by a sniper in the previous village they'd passed through.

Sobol placed a bottle in front of Anatoly, the thud awakening him from his thoughts. "Wine, Comrade Captain?"

"Where did you find that?" Anatoly asked his sergeant.

"In the cellar with the moldy cheese you were eating."

"Share it with the men."

"I already gave them a couple of bottles to help with the march tonight."

Anatoly took the bottle and drank. He pulled a face and looked at Sobol. "It tastes like you pissed in it."

The sergeant frowned. "Shit, did I give you the wrong bottle?"

His captain glared at him, and he smiled. "You're right, it is bad."

"How are the few wounded?"

Sobol shook his head sadly. "One has died and the other won't make the journey."

"Who?"

"Pavlov died and Federov is almost there. The others will be fine."

Pavlov had a chest wound while Federov caught some shrapnel in his guts. Anatoly nodded and made a decision. "We can't take Federov with us and we can't leave him for the Germans."

"What do you propose?"

"There's only one thing to do, wouldn't you agree?"

Sobol nodded. "Who's the lucky person?"

"I'll do it. I won't ask my men to do something that I wouldn't do myself. Once it's done, we'll put them in the barn and burn it. Burn the farmhouse too."

Bear appeared in the doorway of the kitchen. "There is dust. The Germans are coming."

"Get the men organized, Nicolai. It's time we left."

"Yes, sir."

Ten minutes later, against a backdrop of orange from the sunset stained with black smoke, Anatoly led his men into the forest near the farm. They would use it for cover and keep pushing west towards Moscow.

Moscow, October 1941

If Stalin looked tired, Georgy Zhukov looked dead on his feet. He'd not long arrived back in Moscow from strengthening the Leningrad defenses and now the supreme leader was demanding that he do the same for the country's capital.

"You must strengthen the defenses, Georgy," Stalin demanded. "The Germans mustn't take the city. We must hold."

"If you want to do that, Comrade Stalin we need to bring in more troops."

"What troops?" Stalin spat. He drank more vodka from the glass in front of him. He'd been doing a lot of that lately. "The cowards who refuse to fight when ordered?"

"Use all of the reserves, shift other regiments, divisions into the line. But it must be done now before the Germans gain much more ground."

Stalin reached for the bottle on his desk, picking it up and filling his glass. He took a long drink and gave Zhukov a disdainful look. "All right, Georgy. Have your men. But I warn you, I want results. The Nazis must be stopped."

"All I can promise you, Comrade Stalin, is that we will try."

———

Borodino, 77 Miles from Moscow, October 1941

Meunch stared at the horizon. Beyond it was the Village of Borodino, roughly where the columns of black smoke were rising against the sky. An Me109 flew low over head towards the rear of the German lines. Army Group Center was going to push hard today and try to break through the lines once more.

Bauer and Glass handed the spare ammunition out

to the company while Meunch waited for the order to advance. Up ahead the 346th and the 251st Regiments were already heavily engaged with the Russians. The 45th and 67th Panzer Regiments were also pressing hard. Reports were coming back from the front of heavy losses in both men and machines. The Ivans had brought in extra troops and tanks to prepare for the onslaught as well as field guns.

Meunch was suddenly aware of a man standing beside him. He glanced to his right and stiffened. "Good afternoon, Herr General."

Guderian turned his head and looked at the Lieutenant beside him. "Good morning, Lieutenant..."

"Meunch, sir."

"Meunch. Are your men ready for the coming battle?"

"I guess so, sir. Although..." his voice trailed away before he said too much.

"Although what?"

"More supplies and ammunition wouldn't go astray, sir."

"The same thing my commanders are crying out for, Meunch. We'll just have to do with what we have."

"Yes, Herr General."

"Relax, Meunch."

"Sir. Is it true that we are taking heavy losses around Borodino?"

Guderian nodded. "Yes. The Ivans have dug in like a tick on a dog's ass. But we will carry the day. Have no fear."

"Sir."

"Prepare your men, Lieutenant Meunch. And good luck."

"Thank you, Herr General."

He watched as Guderian walked back to the rear where his headquarters was set up. Meunch started to hear raised voices and then the motors on the Panzer IIIs start up. He nodded to himself as he gripped his MP40 tight in his right hand. Once more it was time to go to war.

CHAPTER SEVEN

Borodino Village, October 1941

ANATOLY REPLACED THE SPENT MAGAZINE IN HIS WEAPON with a fresh one and turned to look at the village behind him. The word shattered was too kind a word to describe the way it looked. Buildings burned while others were completely decimated. Bodies of the dead lay where they had fallen, while the wounded were shuttled back to the hospitals in trucks.

The Germans had thrown a lot at them during the last attack, but the Russian line had held. The wrecked tanks and dead Wehrmacht soldiers attested to that.

General Yevgeny Serov appeared out of the smoke to the rear, his hat gone and his clothes dirty. Sobol nudged his commanding officer. "Get a look at the runaway general. He's crawled out of his hole."

"The backbone of the Red Army," Anatoly sneered and then regretted his words. His job was to lead, not criticize.

"Captain, Kozlov, I have found you," the red-faced

general panted. "More replacements are coming in. They are down by the village. You'll need to fetch them forward."

Great, thought Anatoly. *More lambs for the slaughter.* "Yes, sir, I will fetch them forward immediately."

"What are your casualties from the last attack?"

"I'm down to thirty men, sir."

"Then the replacements will be welcome, Comrade."

"Yes, sir."

"Have you seen Colonel Orlov?" Serov asked.

He'd seen him. Or rather parts of him after a shell from a Panzer III had finished with him. "No sir, not since the last attack."

"Where could he be?"

"I'm not sure, sir."

"All right, Captain, get your reinforcements. Word is that the Germans are massing for another attack before dark."

"Yes, Comrade General."

Serov disappeared through a swirl of smoke coming from a burning tank. Anatoly turned to Sobol. "Come with me, Nicolai."

The pair headed back towards the village where they found a huddle of reinforcements. A quick count told Anatoly there were somewhere in the vicinity of thirty men there. However, they weren't just political prisoners and cowards anymore. There were also layabouts, men whom officers didn't like, or ones who had dirty weapons which NCOs took as an excuse to get rid of the ones they didn't like.

Anatoly sighed as he ran his gaze over them. Officers, NCOs, normal enlisted men. His eyes stopped on a stern looking major. "You, step forward."

The major did so. "Who are you?"

"Major Ilya Zorkin. Formerly of the—"

"I don't care who you were or where you come from," Anatoly said harshly. "My name is Captain Anatoly Kozlov. I need a new lieutenant for the company. You're it. Understood?"

The major ground his teeth together. "I suppose it will have to be."

"Lieutenant," Anatoly started. "To get through this war we will have to work together, not against each other. I don't like being here any more than you do, but this is where we are and where we'll stay, unless we wind up dead like your predecessor. Do you understand me?"

"Yes, sir."

A shell ripped overhead and landed in the village. Many of the replacements ducked reflexively. Anatoly and Sobol stood erect. They had learnt already that if a shell had your name on it, there was no getting away.

Anatoly said loud enough for everyone to hear, "One more thing. Sergeant Sobol answers to me, and only me. Now, fall the men in."

"Yes, sir."

———

Borodino Village, October 1941

An explosion to his left caught Anatoly by surprise as he ducked down behind what was left of a stone wall. Beside him, Sobol placed a dirty bandage around his own arm where a German bullet had dug a furrow through the soft flesh.

Anatoly cradled his PPD-34 submachine gun as bullets from an MG 34 peppered the wall behind him.

"We need to shut that machine gun down," Sobol growled.

The sergeant was right. The weapon was taking its toll on the defenders and allowing the enemy to start flanking their position on the right. Anatoly looked around. "Lieutenant Zorkin!"

"Sir," Zorkin replied as he slumped down beside his commander.

"We need to silence that machine gun."

"My thoughts too, sir."

Anatoly let the comment go. "Good. Take six men and flank it on the left before the Germans on our right ruin our day."

"Yes, sir."

The Germans had attacked the previous evening just before dark. They broke through the Russian line on the right before driving into the village where they were finally held up. Throughout the night the battle had ebbed and flowed until around three in the morning both sides ceased combat. However, that only lasted until first light for Guderian had been bringing up another tank regiment to throw against the Russian defenses.

"We'll give them covering fire, Nicolai."

"Yes, sir," Sobol said and moved along the line to let a selection of his men know. Once it was finished, they opened fire upon the German position.

On the left, Zorkin and his handpicked men broke cover and ran towards the rubble of what had once been a house. They disappeared into the ruins and Anatoly looked around. To his right one of his men cried out and he saw Sobol drag him behind cover.

There was an explosion, and the machine gun went silent. Zorkin and the others appeared as they over-whelmed the position.

Anatoly waved his company forward and they took up the position the Germans had just occupied. He singled out one of his men. "Get that machine gun turned around before the Germans counterattack."

"Sir."

Zorkin approached him and said, "All present and accounted for, Comrade Captain."

"Well done, Ilya. Get the rest of the company into position. They'll counterattack at any moment."

"Sir."

"They're already coming, sir," Sobol said. "I can see the tanks."

"It was never meant to be an easy war."

———

Borodino Village, October 1941

Bullets fanned Meunch's face, and he ducked back behind the single pillar of stone, the last remnant of what had once been a solid two-floor house. The Russians had captured the machine gun position and now they were ordered to take it back. This time however, they had tank support from the 45th tank battalion.

Meunch looked across at Bauer who was burning through the last of a magazine while covering four of his men who were trying to push forward and knock out an anti-tank gun. All four were mown down by the captured machine gun position.

"Useless horse's asses," Glass shouted at them. He picked out two men. "You and you, come with me. Take out a grenade."

The two troopers did as they were ordered by the Obergefreiter. Glass took a deep breath and said, "Right, stay on my ass."

He leaped over the rubble in front of his position and started running towards the enemy position. As he went, he primed the grenade. Bullets kicked up debris around his feet while others whipped around him. Glass stumbled on a piece of rock and started to fall. However, he managed to throw the grenade at the position before he hit the ground.

Behind him, only one of the two Grenadiers managed to follow his lead, for the other was dead, shot down before he'd even covered ten yards.

The two grenades exploded and knocked out the machine gun. Laying there, Glass brought up his MP40 and sprayed the area ahead of himself with bullets, all too aware that he was in an exposed position and hadn't really thought his assault plan all the way through.

The second Grenadier fell beside him, eyes open, a hole where his nose had once been. "Shit, Felix," Glass growled at himself. "You are a stupid asshole."

The rest of the company moved forward now that the machine gun had been silenced. Meunch directed them towards the anti-tank gun. Within moments it had been overwhelmed and for the third time that day, the position had changed hands.

Glass looked up and saw Bauer standing over him. "Are you in that much of a hurry to die?"

Glass grinned at him. "It seemed like a good idea at the time."

"If you're in a hurry to get the Iron Cross, I'll give you mine."

Bauer dragged him to his feet. The Obergefreiter said, "You keep it."

An explosion erupted close enough to make the two men flinch. They turned and saw two T-34 tanks coming up the road towards them. Bauer cursed. "Looks like we're about to have visitors."

Meunch saw them too and turned to his men. "Take cover! Take cover!"

The T-34s rattled closer, the one in the lead halting as its main gun traversed to the left before belching fire, part of a building further along the German line disappearing under the onslaught.

Meunch saw the main gun move once more. This time when it stopped it was pointed right at his position. The lieutenant took a deep breath and prayed that the gunner was a poor shot.

Just as it seemed about to blowup all around him the T-34 exploded.

———

Borodino Village, October 1941

"Reload, traverse left," SS-Untersturmfuhrer Karl Egger barked into his intercom. "I want that second tank."

The gunner traversed as ordered while the loader reloaded the main gun. Heinrich, the gunner, kept his eyes on the prize and when his sights came on, he stamped on the foot trigger and fired.

The short-barreled 75mm gun roared and the shell bounced off the remaining T-34's armored hull. "Stupid," Egger blurted out as he looked through one of the ports in his cupola. "Hit it again."

Ralf Lehman the loader rammed home another armor piercing round. Meanwhile the driver, Heinz Blumenberg kept the Panzer moving.

From behind them, a second Panzer fired. The result was the same. The armor piercing shell ricocheted harmlessly off the tank.

"Useless piece of shit," Egger snarled. "When will they replace the main guns on these things? Heinz, reverse."

The Panzer stopped suddenly just as Heinrich used his boot to trip the trigger. Once again, the main gun roared but the shell missed by a good margin.

The T-34 fired, and the shell glanced off the front armor of the Panzer. The sound of it was almost deafening from inside the tank.

"Heinz, steer right. Advance."

Heinz changed direction again and the tank lurched forward. The second Panzer was now further away from Egger's and in front. A blinding flash appeared as Egger watched though one of his cupola ports and the second Panzer exploded.

"Get that damned tank," he bellowed.

Once again Lehman rammed an armor piercing shell into the breech. Heinrich traversed to the left and then stomped on the foot trigger. This time it was a solid hit, and the T-34 came to a stop. Smoke began rising from the disabled tank and three of the crew scrambled from it.

"Cut them down, Kurt," Egger snarled.

Kurt Schulman, the radio operator and bow gunner opened fire with the front mounted MG34 machine gun. The Russian tankers staggered and then fell as bullets punched into each of them.

"Good shooting. Kurt. Now, driver advance."

The Panzer rolled forward along the road. A Russian machine gun peppered its hull and Egger looked out through the ports to locate the weapon. He found it almost immediately. The weapon was in the ruins of a house. He said into the intercom, "Heinrich, machine gun on our left in the ruined building.

The turret traversed until the gunner had located it. He said, "Ralf, one round HE."

The loader took a high explosive shell and rammed it into the breech. "Ready."

The tank rocked as it expelled the shell. A violent eruption rocked the ruins and the machine gunner seemingly disappeared with it.

Egger gave a grunt of satisfaction then said into the intercom, "Driver, advance."

———

"FALL BACK!" Anatoly shouted as the tanks came on. He swore bitterly under his breath when the machine gun had disappeared and now, there was only one thing they could do. "All of you move. Ilya, Nicolai, get them moving."

Wehrmacht soldiers appeared and Anatoly opened fire with his submachine gun. Bullets hammered into an approaching German soldier and the man fell amongst the rubble. His comrades opened fire and bullets ricocheted around Anatoly.

Sobol grabbed his commander and said, "Get down, you fool."

Anatoly did as he was told and hugged the rubble. Sobol looked at him. "It is time to go, before we are cut off."

With a nod, Anatoly, agreed. "Lead the way, Nicolai."

Sobol came to his feet, and in a low crouch, started following the rest of the company. Anatoly glanced again at the advancing Germans and saw that an additional two tanks had joined the others. With another bitter curse, Anatoly followed his men.

Borodino had fallen.

———

Vitebsk, October 1941

At first, they had beaten her. Then they had raped her until her mind was numb. Then they had beaten her again. Eva had told them all she knew and more things that she'd made up because that was what she thought they wanted to hear. When they had finished, she had no idea what day it was or where they were holding her.

The door to the cellar they were holding her in opened and she scooted across the floor to the rear wall in a desperate attempt to get away. The SS-Hauptsturm-fuhrer stood in the doorway, holding out some clothes for her. He tossed them on the floor at his feet. "Clothes for you to wear when my men shoot you."

His name was Klaus. That was all Eva knew. She

eyed him warily as she shivered against the cold. Her nakedness exposed to the coming weather. Her flesh was bruised and scratched. She edged across the floor towards the clothes.

Eva reached out with a trembling hand and placed it on the garments. They felt warm to the touch. She looked up at Klaus, wild eyed expecting some kind of trick.

He laughed at her. The kind of maniacal laugh he'd had when he'd taken his turn. His eyes were wide, his head tilted back as the laughing grew louder.

Eva clasped her hands over her ears but no matter how she tried, the crazed cackle still got through.

She looked at him again, he was still throwing his head back in laughter. She could hear him, feel him, and it disgusted her.

When she moved it was like a panther striking at its prey. One moment, Eva was on the floor, the next her face was buried in the Hauptsturmfuhrer's neck, an animalistic snarl escaping his throat as her teeth tore into his flesh.

Klaus howled in surprise and shoved Eva away from him, but it was too late. The damage had already been done. Her face was a mask of cherry red from the warm blood which spurted from the open artery. Klaus, stunned by what had just happened, tried to stem the flow with his hand but it was pointless.

His other hand went to the Luger in his holster but already he was growing weak and instead he leaned against the door jamb and started to slide towards the floor. Eva stood over him and grinned, her face a ghoulish mask.

By the time the guards got to him and dragged him

out of the doorway Klaus was already dead. But at least his maniacal laugh had been brought to an abrupt end. However, it was replaced by a new laugh. This one more a high-pitched cackle. Then, "Bastard! Bastard! *Bastard!*"

———

586th Fighter Aviation Regiment, October 1941

Katya Kozlova climbed down from the back of the truck and stared in awe at the Yak-1 as it hurtled along the rough airstrip and then lifted into the air. She stared after it and didn't notice the senior lieutenant approach.

The 586th Fighter Aviation Regiment had been formed by Marina Raskova who had pleaded with Stalin to allow women pilots to fly. He eventually gave her permission and she formed 588th Night Bomber Aviation Regiment, the 586th Fighter Aviation Regiment, and the 587th Bomber Aviation Regiment which she commanded herself.

Blonde haired Yevgeniya Prokhorova stood beside her and waited for Katya to finish. When she turned to walk, she almost crashed into her. "Oh, God, sorry—Senior Lieutenant. Oh dear."

"I gather you are a new recruit, yes?" Prokhorova asked.

"Yes, Senior Lieutenant."

"Fine, let's get some things straight. My name is Senior Lieutenant Yevgeniya Prokhorova. The five-eighty-sixth is my command. Whatever you are told to do you will do better than any male pilot. Is that understood?"

"Yes, Senior Lieutenant."

"Right, get your things put away and then get back out to the flight line. Your training starts today. You can fly, yes?"

Katya looked sheepish. "Um, no."

"Der'mo. Shit. Well, get going."

"Yes, Senior Lieutenant."

Katya hurried away and suddenly realized she didn't know where she was going. She stopped and looked around. It was then she noticed a young woman watching her. With more than a hint of apprehension, Katya approached her. Before she could speak, the young woman said, "Her bark is much worse than her bite. She just wants us all not to fail. She is like our mother really. I'm Elena. Elena Guseva."

"Katya Kozlova. Are you a pilot?"

Elena shook her head. "Not yet. But soon."

"Do you know where I'm meant to go?"

"I will show you."

With a sigh of relief, Katya said, "Thank you."

———

Vitebsk, October 1941

The SS marched Eva Kozlova into the middle of the town square and tied her to a post. Six men and an officer. She was clothed now, warmer. For the first time in days, she felt at ease. While in the cellar she had always been on edge, unaware what would happen to her from one day to the next. This day, however, she knew exactly what was going to happen and felt at peace.

Eva looked around the square. The Germans had herded civilians around to reluctantly watch the execution. A way of setting an example. Almost every single one dropped their gaze away from hers. All except for an old man who defiantly stuck out his chin and lifted his head a little higher. Eva felt the corners of her mouth turn up slightly in a wan smile. Then they blindfolded her.

Soon it would be over.

She heard the officer bark an order. She imagined the soldiers raising their rifles. Another order, another movement. Then the final order and the rifles fired.

The old man stepped forward out of the crowd. He walked over to Eva as she sagged forward from the post against her bindings. He felt for a pulse and then turned to the officer. "She is dead."

The man nodded abruptly. "Good, get her out of the square before she starts to stink."

The soldiers marched away, and the doctor singled out two men. They untied Eva and lay her on the ground. The doctor looked at the strongest of the two and said in a hushed voice, "Get her to my home. If she is to live, I must work fast."

The man looked surprised. "She is dead, Doctor. Shot six times—"

"Are you a doctor?" the old man hissed.

"No, I—"

"Then shut up and do as I say. Move."

Without another word, the two men picked Eva's limp form up and carried her away.

CHAPTER EIGHT

40 Miles West of Moscow, October 1941

MEUNCH AND HIS MEN MARCHED THROUGH THE worsening rain towards the sound of the guns. Their legs were caked with mud up to their knees as they struggled to advance. The heavy vehicle movement east had almost made the roads impassable. And to go off them was not even an option.

The company slogged past a bogged truck. Hitched to the front of it was a team of horses that someone had found and promptly put them to work trying to pull the vehicle free. Meunch heard Glass say, "Good luck with that."

Army group Center had driven hard to the east, pushing the Russian army back every day. In Moscow as in Leningrad, the civilians were being used to reinforce the defenses of the city. But now the weather had slowed that mighty advance to a mud-soaked crawl.

Like other officers, Guderian had demanded warm

clothing for his soldiers because of the rapidly approaching winter. Berlin, however, didn't have what was needed, or chose to ignore his demands and thus the Wehrmacht suffered.

Up ahead, out of the gloom of the curtain of rain, Meunch saw a barn materialize. He turned to Bauer and said, "Get the men over there where they can get some shelter."

"Yes, Herr Lieutenant."

They came off the muddy road and crossed the muddy field to the entry of the barn. It was only small, and room was at a premium but at least it was dry. Glass managed to get a fire going and soon the barn was full of smoke and limited warmth. But no one cared. They were out of the rain.

Bauer sat beside Meunch, listening to the heavy artillery that could be heard in the distance. It sounded like the thunder that usually accompanied torrential rain like that falling outside. "Sir?"

"What is it, Hans?"

"We can't go on like this, Lieutenant. The men need warmer clothing. Winter is just around the corner and many of them will die if we don't get the things we need."

Meunch nodded. "I'm aware of that fact, Hans."

"Just doing my duty to the men, sir."

"I understand."

Suddenly the door crashed open, and a cold wind ripped through the barn. Men grumbled at the disturbance, but Meunch ignored them as he, Bauer, and Glass stared at the figures that stood filling the void.

An SS-Hauptsturmfuhrer stood flanked by two SS-

Scharfuhrers, or sergeants. "What is this?" the SS officer demanded.

"A church meeting for real soldiers," Glass muttered.

"What?" the officer demanded. "Was that insolence I heard?"

"What do you want, Hauptsturmfuhrer?" Meunch asked wearily.

"Are you in charge of this rabble?"

"These are my men, yes."

"Then you will get them out of here and keep moving."

Bauer leaned close to his commanding officer. "It would seem that Himmler's ass lickers want our barn."

Meunch said to the Hauptsturmfuhrer, "I think we shall stay here for the time being."

"Do you know who I am?" the officer demanded.

"A toy soldier who humps whores because he can't get it from his mother?" Glass guessed.

A chuckle ran through the rest of the men inside the building.

"How dare you?" the officer barked. "I'm Hauptsturmfuhrer Walther Huber. I'm here in the east under the direct orders of Himmler himself to bring the Communist partisan rabble to heel before they can do too much damage to our supply lines."

"How many times did you suck his dick to get that posting?" Glass asked.

"Arrest that man!" Huber roared.

The two Scharfuhrers moved but Bauer's MP40 stopped the dripping men in their tracks.

"What is the meaning of this, Lieutenant?" Huber demanded.

"Let's get to the point, Huber." There was no time for niceties. "You want this barn for yourself, but we beat you to it. Now, take your two pets and leave us alone before I let my Unteroffizier shoot you."

"I will not forget this."

"Good. Now go."

The three men disappeared into the curtain of rain outside. Meunch turned to Glass who was grinning. "Felix, a word."

"Sir."

As Glass walked past Bauer, the Unteroffizier said, "You just couldn't shut up, could you?"

The two men went to a corner of the barn where Meunch's face grew hard. "I expect my NCOs to set an example for the men, Felix. What you did there was uncalled for and dangerous."

"But, sir—"

"I'm not finished," Meunch hissed. "The next time I witness something like that I will bust you back to Grenadier and have you shoveling shit for the rest of the war. Is that understood?"

Glass stiffened. "Yes, Herr Lieutenant."

"Cut that crap out, Felix. Take it like a professional. You are one of my best NCOs. Before this war is over, I'll need the best to get this company through it."

"Sir."

"Right, see to your men."

Glass walked back to his men and Meunch looked around at his. Bauer was right, if they didn't get warm clothes soon, then many of them would die when the snow started to fall.

———

Moscow, November 1941

Heavy snow fell outside as Zhukov entered Stalin's office. He'd been summoned before the despotic leader who looked out the window at the gray skies. He turned and stared at Georgy and stroked his mustache. "Good, you are here."

"I came as soon as I heard you wanted to see me, Comrade."

"How goes the defense of our great city?"

For a moment Zhukov thought about lying and hesitated. Stalin must have sensed this and asked, "Can we hold Moscow?"

"I need more men and tanks."

"How many?"

"Two armies and a few hundred tanks," Zhukov replied.

"And if I give them to you?" Stalin asked.

Zhukov stared at him, unsure of what he wanted him to say. "Comrade?"

"What do you propose to do with them if I give them to you?"

"Try to hold Moscow."

Stalin shook his head. "I will give you men, Georgy, but you must give me something in return."

"What is that, sir?"

"An attack. I want you to hit the Nazis while they least expect it."

Zhukov almost had heart failure. The fool wanted him to attack when he'd be lucky to hold. "Comrade Stalin, I—"

"I hope you're not about to tell me that an attack would fail, Georgy?"

"No, Comrade."

"Good, I will release the reserves that we have, and you shall use them to your own advantage. But they must attack."

———

The Moscow Front, November 1941

Why one would order an attack in such conditions was sheer lunacy. The temperature had dropped below minus thirty and snow fell in a steady stream. The punishment battalion had been reinforced once more with prisoners and had been one of the first thrown against the German lines.

On their left was one of the green battalions which had arrived on the front in the past few days. As was the one on the right. When the forces had smashed against the German line the two new battalions had dissolved like sands being washed away by the tide. However, the punishment battalion had punched through the German defenses and caused a breach some half a mile wide and the same deep.

The ground was frozen and too hard to dig in so the battalion was forced to use craters, snowbanks, destroyed vehicles, and anything else they could use for cover.

The one thing that the Red army had that the Germans didn't at that stage of the war was great coats. And against the cold as severe as it was, they were a necessity.

Anatoly ducked as a shell exploded close to the

crater where he and some of his men had taken shelter. Beside him, Sobol shivered as the cold found a way in. From reports they were receiving from the other companies, the Germans were now pushing in on their flanks because the two newer battalions had capitulated.

From beside the sergeant a soldier cursed. Sobol turned and stared at him. "What is the problem, Dimitri?"

"My frigging hand it stuck to my gun barrel."

Sobol's eyes flared as he looked at the hand. It was that cold. Anything metal touched by bare flesh stuck immediately. "Where are your gloves?"

"I'm not sure."

"Get it unstuck before the Germans come. Useless Govnosos," Sobol said using the Russian expletive for shit sucker.

Dimitri turned to the man next to him. "Hey, piss on my hand."

"What?"

"Piss on my hand. Get me unstuck."

"You're crazy."

"Just do it."

The soldier undid his fly and pulled his dick out. He then grunted and a deep yellow stream came out and spurted on the hand and barrel of the rifle which was in it. Steam rose from the urine and within moments the hand was free of the rifle. Dimitri looked up and said, "Thanks. I—"

WHACK!

The soldier's head snapped back as a bullet punched into the man's skull. Dimitri cursed and threw himself back against the crater wall.

"Germans to our front!" Sobol shouted as he opened fire.

Bullets cracked as they passed low overhead while others smacked into the frozen earth. One soldier cried out and fell face down near Dimitri. The gloveless soldier looked tentatively at the dead man whose gloves gave off a siren's call, and he lurched forward to remove them from the lifeless hands.

A scramble of movement and Zorkin slid into the crater. He looked at Anatoly and said, "Tanks are pushing in on the right flank. I need a couple of dogs."

Anatoly looked at Sobol. "Where are the dogs?"

"No idea,"

"Shit," Anatoly swore. "Go back to your men, Ilya. I'll be there soon."

Zorkin disappeared and Anatoly scooted over beside Sobol. "Take over here. I'll be back."

Holding onto his PPD, he crawled over the lip of the shell crater and ran towards the rear of their position. Bullets whipped past him and a shell caused him to fall flat onto the frozen ground. The explosion washed over Anatoly and dirt and muddy snow rained down atop of him.

"Zhopa!" he hissed vehemently before climbing back to his feet and continuing.

Twenty yards further on, Anatoly found what he was looking for. Three men in another crater holding onto five dogs each. Every one of them wearing a special vest. He pointed at one of the handlers. "You, come with me."

"Yes, sir."

Anatoly climbed out of the crater and started a mad dash towards Zorkin's position, the dog handler with five dogs hot on his heels. They reached the location where Zorkin had his men set up behind a snowbank. There were dead soldiers laying on the frozen ground while another wounded man cried out while writhing in pain.

To their front, Anatoly could see three tanks waddling towards the position like fat ducks. Turning towards the dog handler he said, "Let them loose."

Freeing them, the man said, "Idti, idti. Go, go."

The five canines ran forward out onto the hard white ground splattered with red of blood and the black scars where shells had landed. Once clear of the Russian position the dogs separated, then started towards the tanks.

Anatoly watched on as one of the Panzer IV machine gunners changed his aim to concentrate on a fast-approaching cur.

The weapon chattered and bullets struck all around the racing animal. The dog lurched to one side and disappeared in a fireball as the explosives on its back detonated.

The four remaining dogs ran on, the first reached its target and immediately slipped under the Panzer IV. The trigger on its back was tripped and the pack the animal carried exploded, engulfing the tank.

Out of the three remaining dogs, two found their targets while the third was killed by enemy fire.

Soon black smoke billowed skyward from the burning tanks. At one point, some of the crew emerged from the armored vehicles, two were on fire. Gunfire from the Russian soldiers mowed them down almost immediately.

"There's more coming in," Zorkin said, pointing beyond the burning hulks.

The dogs had done damage to the German attack but there were more tanks pushing hard. Anatoly said, "Hold for as long as you can. Await my orders."

"Don't leave us hanging out here, Captain."

"Don't worry, I won't."

Taking the PPD, keeping low, Anatoly ran back to where Sobol was still urging his men to keep fighting. Two were down with ghastly wounds. One look and Anatoly knew they were gone. "Nicolai, get your men falling back. We cannot hold. The attack is doomed."

"But what of our orders?"

"Screw the shitting orders. What will they do, send us to a punishment battalion?"

"Maybe," he replied.

"Get them moving."

"Sir."

Anatoly grabbed a private closest to him. "Run and tell Lieutenant Zorkin we're pulling back. Then tell the dog handlers to let them loose. Understand?"

"Sir."

"Go."

The private took off across the frozen ground. Anatoly looked around him and then held a hand up to his mouth. *"Fall Back! Fall Back!"*

The German army was once again pushing closer to Moscow.

————

"HERR LIEUTENANT, ORDERS."

Glass held out a message which had been passed onto him by a messenger from another company. Meunch took the piece of paper and read it.

"We're stopping the counterattack."

"But why?"

"Weather. The tanks are freezing up and can't be brought forward to reinforce the ones which have been lost."

"We have them on the back foot."

"Get Hans for me."

"Yes."

Glass disappeared and Meunch called another gefreiter over to him. "Carry a message to the other platoon commanders. "Have them hold where they are."

The tired-looking man nodded. "Lieutenant."

A few minutes later, Bauer appeared. "Did Felix tell you what was happening?"

"He did."

"What I want you to do, is anyone who still doesn't have appropriate clothing to deal with the cold, have them strip the dead of what they need."

"But, Lieutenant—"

"Do it, Hans. If they don't, they'll end up lying in the snow beside them. All throughout the Second Panzer Army men are being taken out of the line because of frostbite and other things related to the cold. Officers are telling me that their men are freezing to death overnight. I want our men to have the best chance of surviving the winter. There's enough troubles with the Ivans. Understood?"

"I will see to it."

"Thank you."

———

Leningrad, November 1941

It was cold—no, freezing. The temperature had dropped to below -20F and inside the homes most people had no real form of heating. Anya and Olga had joined the que at the food station for their ration supply. Up at the head of the line a woman was arguing with one of the political officers overseeing the distribution.

"What's she arguing about?" Anya asked Olga.

"Something about not getting enough food and that she's got three children to feed."

"Don't tell me they've cut the rations again."

Olga nodded. "I guess we'll find out soon enough."

Since the beginning of the siege, the Leningrad landscape had changed dramatically. Anti-aircraft guns had appeared in parks and on the streets. More were stationed around St. Isaac's Cathedral. Bodies of the dead were being left frozen in the streets, and people were lining up to get drinking water.

The arguing woman was pushed away from the food station. As she stumbled crying past Anya and Olga she slipped on the frozen street and fell. The distraught woman lost her grip on her rations, and they spilled to the ground. Immediately a starving woman in front of Anya leaped from the line and pounced onto the food.

The woman who'd fallen desperately scrambled to retrieve what she'd dropped but she was too slow. The other woman was already pushing a large part of it into her mouth.

"No!" the first woman screamed. "My children. The food is for my children, you bitch."

She lunged at the thief who pushed her away. Once again, she slipped and fell, this time into an unmoving heap.

Anya looked at the woman ahead of her who was still chewing the food. She said, "Why did you do that?"

The woman turned and glared at Anya. "Mind your own business, you cow," she managed around the mouthful of food.

"What about her children?"

The woman had dark hair, gray eyes, and a solid build. She stepped towards Anya and stared at her. She chewed slowly and then swallowed. "I don't care about her children."

Anya was suddenly aware that three other women who had been standing in line had become interested in what was happening and had taken up threatening stances. Olga moved beside Anya. "The line has moved."

The women turned away and moved across the gap. Anya said, "Who is she?"

"Galina Sharapova. I've heard stories about her and the women with her. They have been stealing rations from others. Forcing them to give up their share."

"What is wrong with them?"

"It's the war."

Anya stepped out of line and went to help the distraught woman to her feet. "Thank you," the woman said meekly.

"Wait here," said Anya. "Will you do that?"

"Yes."

The line moved forward and one-by-one each person collected their rations from the food station. When it was Anya's turn, she looked down at the meagre five-ounce morsel of bread which fitted into the palm of her hand. She looked at the soldier in front of her. "What is this?"

"Bread."

She stared at it knowing full well that it was nothing like the bread which she'd once been used to. The soldier looked around her and said, "Next."

Olga pushed past her and took her own ration. She screwed her nose up at it and moved out of the way, taking Anya with her.

"What is in this thing?" she asked.

Olga broke her bread open and held it closer to her eyes. She picked something out of it and said, "They're using sawdust."

"Good lord."

The woman was still where Anya had asked her to wait. She looked a forlorn figure. Anya held out her hand. "Take this home for your children."

"Thank you, thank you, thank you," the woman repeated.

"I just hope it's edible," Anya replied.

Olga stepped forward and gave the woman her bread as well. "Take it. I'm sure you need it more than I do."

"I don't know what to say," the woman said.

"Where do you live?"

"On the other side of the square," she said motioning over her shoulder. We are in the basement of a building over there. Our house was destroyed two weeks ago when a bomb hit it."

"Do you have enough clothes?" Anya asked.

"We get—"

Suddenly a freight train ripped across the gray sky and exploded fifty yards from the food station. Frozen street and earth heaved upward and rained down in large chunks. Screams sounded from the lined-up women as they started to scatter.

Another shell followed hard on the heels of the first. This one slammed into a brick building further along the street, blowing a large hole in its façade. "Get down," Anya called out to the woman who'd begun to run away. But, like a good portion of the others, fear had gripped her, and she would not be stopped.

Two more shells came in and the earth trembled beneath Anya's prone body. The first landed a hundred yards further along the street, the second was closer and she watched on in horror as the woman was engulfed by the explosion.

"No!" Anya gasped and put her head down, hands over it for cover.

Another handful of shells rained down on Leningrad, killing and maiming more citizens. Or maybe they were being put out of their misery for the hell that was about to come. Then as suddenly as it had started, the shelling stopped.

"That was close," Olga said.

Anya raised her head and stared along the street to where she'd last seen the woman. "She's gone."

"What? Who's gone?"

"The woman we gave the food to. She was hit by a shell."

"Oh my," Olga groaned.

"Olga, the children."

"Anya, we can't—"

"They will die on their own."

Olga helped her to her feet. "We must help them, Olga."

"You're right. Let's go and find them. But when we do, you're telling them about their mother."

CHAPTER NINE

2nd Panzer Army HQ, November 1941

GUDERIAN LOOKED UP FROM WHERE HE SAT AT THE TABLE when his adjutant, Lieutenant Willi Schultz walked into the farmhouse kitchen from the other room. The 2nd Panzer Army commander and his staff had set up his HQ in the only building left standing for miles. Such had his advance slowed, he expected to be there for the next few days until the reinforcements he'd asked for arrived.

"What is it, Willi?"

"Message from command, sir. There will be no reinforcements."

Guderian felt his anger start to simmer beneath his calm façade. "Do they not understand the situation which we face here?"

"The message was very specific, General. As you wished. They also want you to keep attacking."

The general snatched the piece of paper from his adjutant's hand and read it.

"Attack? Do the fools not realize what I'm facing? The Russians are moving more reinforcements into the line in front of me. I have five tanks left after the attack two days ago and my men are worn down. I'm not going anywhere."

"There are reports that the weather is worsening as well, Herr General."

"Get my car, I will see Bock myself."

Schultz looked troubled. "Ah—"

Guderian realized that most of the roads were impassable. "Fine, get me a damned halftrack, anything you can find that will get me there."

"Jawohl, Herr Genaral."

———

General Von Bock's Headquarters

"Where is he?" Guderian asked as he stormed past Von Bock's adjutant.

Alarmed, the officer lurched to his feet. "Sir, the general is very busy. You can't go in there."

Guderian ignored him, forcing open the door that led into the sitting room where a raging fire burned to stave off the cold. The thin-faced commander was seated on a long lounge. Beside him was a woman, perhaps twenty years younger than the aging general. Both were in a not too advanced stage of undress. His head whipped around. "What is the meaning of this?"

Guderian's lip curled. "While your men freeze to death in the snow, you sit in the warm with some whore."

"Get out, Heinz," Von Bock snarled.

"I will not. You call yourself a commander? Then damn well command. Stop this ill-conceived attack before you lose the Second Panzer Army altogether."

Von Bock looked at the woman beside him. "Leave us for a moment, my dear, while I deal with this."

The red-headed woman grabbed her clothes and left the room. The Army Group Center commander came to his feet. His braces attached to his pants hung loosely at his side, his undershirt partially opened. "All right, Heinz, you have three minutes before I have you removed. Make the best of it."

"The attack must be stopped, Fedor. I have very few tanks, my men are freezing to death in the snow, we've not received warm clothing nor reinforcements, and the Ivans are moving fresh troops into the line in front of us. Then there is the damned weather which is worsening by the minute."

"Out of the question."

"For heaven's sake, why?" Guderian demanded.

"Because Moscow is within our grasp, Heinz. Hermann Hoth has his Panzers at the edge of the Volga-Moscow Canal. The Fourth is virtually there as well. The Fuhrer is most pleased. So you see, Heinz, even if I wanted to stop the attack, I couldn't. You must advance. Moscow is ours."

The general's eyes blazed wildly and Guderian's eyes found the bottle of vodka on the small table beside the lounge. He shook his head and said, "Moscow belongs to those who occupy it, Fedor. And right now, that is Stalin."

———

GUDERIAN'S FEARS were realized by the end of November when the Red Army threw their reserves into the line and stopped the Second Panzer Army in its tracks. Then on the 5th of December Soviet artillery opened fire on the German line at what they considered to be their weakest points.

With manpower stretched thin, troops exhausted, no aircover because of the blizzard-like conditions, the Third and Fourth Panzer Armies were driven back. Over the coming days Zhukov's reinforcements had penetrated the furthest of all the Russian divisions.

It was a thrust the German Army would never recover from and they would never be within sight of Moscow again.

CHAPTER TEN

Over the Volga River, February 1942

THE THRUM OF THE YAK-1'S MOTOR RANG IN KATYA'S ears despite her flying helmet. Below her, stretched out like a serpent splitting the stark white landscape was the Volga River. Katya's flight had been directed to patrol the region north of Stalingrad because of the main bridge at Saratov. Leading them was their commanding officer, Yevgeniya Prokhorova.

"Keep an eye out for German bombers," Prokhorova reminded them for the fourth time since they'd arrived on station.

Five planes, the same number as the day before when they'd been attacked by German fighters. The flight banked for its next leg, and through her canopy Katya could see the two black stains on the pristine snow cover from where two Yaks had crashed after being shot down.

"Kozlova, close up," Prokhorova snapped into her radio. "Keep your eyes open."

"Yes, Comrade."

Although finding it hard at first, Katya had finally passed flight training in the top echelon of the group. But that counted for nothing when the shooting started. The German pilots were battle hardened while the women of the 586th were as green as the spring grasses.

The pitch of her motor changed, and Katya adjusted her fuel. She closed with the rest of the formation and breathed a little easier.

"Bandits, Comrade Senior Lieutenant," a voice said over the radio. Katya made it out to be Elena Guseva's voice. "Ten o'clock, high."

"I see them, Guseva. You have good eyes. You might make a pilot yet."

"Thank you, Comrade."

"Everyone, follow me," Prokhorova said into her radio. "Watch out for fighters."

—————

EDMUND WAGNER WASN'T EXPECTING TOO much in the way of resistance, not after the stories he'd heard from the fighter pilots about the air battle the day before. Besides, they hadn't even dispatched an escort with them.

They were eight minutes from their target and the He III gave a jolt from some invisible air turbulence. He yawned, complacently. This was his fiftieth mission since the German army had rolled across the frontier, and he, along with all the Reich's pilots were feeling it.

There were ten bombers in the formation. All that the wing could put up that day. The others were grounded with the cold.

The sky was clear and in the distance to the south and east dark plumes of smoke rose against the white and pale blue background.

"Five minutes to target," Jurgens the navigator said over the radio.

"Achtung! Fighters Kameraden!" The call came from a plane to their port.

"Where?" Wagner demanded.

"Coming up from below?"

"Where damn it?"

The rattle of rounds from the attacking Yaks hammered into the Heinkel's fuselage, punching through and admitting daylight into the dark recesses of the aircraft. The planes blew through the bomber formation, causing them to scatter.

"Get the guns working!" Wagner ordered.

He looked out the side of the cockpit and saw a Heinkel starting to fall away, its starboard engine aflame.

Wagner turned his plane away from the burning aircraft.

"What about the bomb run?" the navigator, who was also the bombardier and nose gunner bleated into the radio.

"Just get the damn gun operating," Wagner snarled. "Shit!"

Catching the blur of another Yak coming towards them, Wagner put the Heinkel into a dive. Throughout the bomber the sound of machine guns coming to life didn't do much to reassure Wagner. He looked around to see where the fighters were. When he couldn't determine their location, he said, "Where are those shitting fighters?"

"They're coming around behind us."

Wagner turned to the right and then back to the left. He then put the Heinkel into a turn and dive at the same time. More bullets peppered the bomber and Wagner heard one of his crew cry out. Ignoring it he concentrated on flying.

However, he soon realized that for them to survive this situation, he needed to get low where the fighters had less room to maneuver. So, he put the nose down and headed for the deck.

———

"ONE OF THE Nazi scum is headed for the basement," Elena said over her radio in an excited voice.

"Let him go," Prokhorova replied. "There are still more up here we can get.

Katya put her Yak into a tight turn and brought it around onto the tail of an already smoking Heinkel. She pressed the firing button on her yoke and felt the plane give a satisfying shudder. She watched as the rounds impacted the Heinkel's fuselage and then saw bits fly from it. Then the already smoking bomber started an inescapable dive towards the frozen ground below.

Katya pulled her plane upward and put it into a banking turn as she looked for another target. Her head whipped around as though on a swivel. Then she spotted another bomber. It was below her and flying away to the northwest. Leveling out, she put the nose of the Yak down and pushed the throttle all the way forward.

The engine of the fighter roared as it gave chase to the fleeing Heinkel.

The rear of the bomber grew large in the front of the canopy. Katya unintentionally held her fire, staring at the plane before her as though in a trance. She was snapped out of it violently as a gunner from the bomber opened fire and rounds pierced her plane.

"*Der'mo!* Shit!," she exclaimed and worked savagely to get the Yak out of harm's way. "Stupid bitch."

Katya felt the pressure of the G-forces at work on her slim frame as she put the plane into as tight a turn as possible.

"What the hell was that, Kozlova?" Prokhorova demanded over the radio. "Asleep, were we?"

Katya winced. She would see it. The woman had eyes like a hawk. "No, Comrade Prokhorova."

"Have another go and do it right this time."

Katya brought her fighter back around and once more bore in on the bomber's tail. This time she opened fire. Three short bursts. The engine on the German's right wing burst into flames before the wing itself fell away.

The Heinkel started to spiral out of control, pinning those who were still alive within the stricken aircraft. Katya watched until it disappeared from her line of sight and then turned her Yak to look for another target.

But there weren't any. Those bombers which had evaded being shot down were gone. Managed to escape. Prokhorova's voice came over the radio. "That's it, ladies, head back to base."

———

586th Fighter Aviation Regiment Airfield

"Kozlova, a word."

Katya rolled her eyes. She was tired and had only just climbed from her Yak. She took off her flying helmet and let her hair fall. "Yes, comrade?"

"What happened up there?" Prokhorova asked.

"I don't know."

"Well, whatever it was, get it worked out. Before you die up there. You're too good of a pilot to get yourself killed because you don't know. Get the ground crew to refuel and rearm your plane. We're back up in an hour."

"Yes, Senior Lieutenant."

"How many planes did you get?"

"Ah, two."

"Good work. You'll be an ace in no time. Get your hair cut. Dismissed."

Katya watched her walk away and became aware of a presence at her elbow. "I thought you shot down three."

She turned to look at Elena. "I did."

"Why didn't you tell her that?"

"I think she already knew," Katya said. Then, "You know we're back up in an hour, right?"

"So I heard."

"I'd kill for a sleep," Katya told her.

"I'd kill for a man," Elena responded. "I don't care what man; any man will do."

Katya looked around the airfield. "Take your pick. Just remember you've only got an hour."

Elena chuckled. "I won't need an hour."

Leaving her to her needs, Katya made sure that her Yak was to be refueled and rearmed before walking slowly over to the pilot's quarters. She looked at her watch before laying down. She still had forty minutes before they were up again. She only needed thirty.

Just as she was about asleep, the door crashed open, and Elena appeared dragging one of the ground crew behind her. "Don't worry about us," she said to Katya. "We won't be long."

"Go away," Katya moaned. "I'm trying to sleep. The last thing I need is to hear you and Casanova grunting like pigs."

"Then block your ears."

With another moan, Katya pulled her blanket over her head and tried to block out the noise.

———

"GET UP! ALARM!"

The screech was high-pitched and brought Katya from her deep, albeit brief, slumber. She threw the blanket aside and staggered to her feet. From the cot beside her, two naked figures rolled out onto the floor.

"I'm going to kill that bitch," Elena growled as she started to pull her clothes on.

Katya said, "She probably saved you from getting frostbite on your ass. And let's face it, there's a lot there to bite."

"Shut up."

Katya ran outside and looked around. Already some of the Yaks were taxiing to take off. "What is happening?" Katya called out to a passing pilot.

"An air raid."

"Why aren't the sirens sounding?"

"They're frozen and can't be turned."

"Shit. Frigging winter."

Suddenly she heard a sound which they had come to dread. The howl of the siren placed under the JU 87 which instilled fear in the hearts of everyone on the ground. It was air operated and howled loudly as the bombers plummeted towards their targets.

Katya looked up and saw four of them. The first one was already in an almost vertical dive. Beyond it came the others.

Without another glance upward, she ran to the nearest air raid trench and dove in just as the first Stuka released its bomb.

The earth trembled from the impact of the explosion, frozen clumps of dirt and snow were thrown high into the air. The plane had already pulled up and screamed loudly as it passed above Katya. The sound was deafening and blocked out the screams of some of the wounded.

The other planes made their runs and dropped their bombs amongst the grounded Yaks, the ground crew, and the scrambling pilots.

And then it was over.

Katya climbed from the air raid trench and looked around her. Two planes were burning where they'd been parked. She felt lucky that one of them wasn't hers.

Cries of the wounded sounded from different directions, medical officers scrambling to attend them. She looked around for Elena but couldn't see her anywhere.

"Kozlova!"

She turned to see Prokhorova waving at her. Katya ran over and stopped in front of her. "Get in your plane and get it up," her commanding officer snapped. "Take

Raskova, Guseva, and Davydova with you. You will be in command."

"What about you, Comrade Prokhorova?"

"My plane has been destroyed."

"All—All right."

"You will patrol the bridge again. Understood?"

"Yes, Senior Lieutenant."

"Good, now go."

———————

Over the Volga River

"Comrade Kozlova, I can see planes below us. Three o'clock."

The call had come over the radio from Nika Roskova. Katya looked out and saw the black specks in the distance. There were five of them. One more than them.

"What will we do, Katya?" Elena asked.

She thought for a moment before she said into the radio, "We attack."

Katya rolled the Yak into a dive and pushed the throttle on the fighter all the way forward. The engine howled in pain as the plane streaked towards the Germans' aircraft. As they grew bigger Katya could see that they weren't bombers. They were Messerschmitts. Fighters.

"They're Nazi fighters," she said over the radio. "Fly through their formation so you can put some distance between them and us before they react. Watch each other's backs. Elena, with me."

The German pilots must have been asleep for the

Yaks were upon them before they even looked like reacting. The Russian planes flew straight through the formation as they sprayed it with bursts of fire.

One of the German fighters fell away towards the white landscape below. The other planes scattered, one trailing smoke.

Katya pulled back on the yoke of her fighter and felt herself pushed into the seat as G-forces claimed her. She worked the pedals and stick, and the plane rolled, did a sharp turn and came back around until it was pointed at an Me 109 which was flying straight at her.

The closing speed was immense and in the blink of an eye the German fighter blew past the tip of her port wing with inches to spare.

"Wow, Katya, did you see that?" Elena cried out over the radio.

"If I didn't, I just shit my pants for no reason," she replied. "Where did he go?"

There was a moment of silence before Elena said, "He's trying to get around onto my tail."

"Keep flying straight," Katya told her.

"But—"

"Trust me," Katya said.

The one rule they were taught in training was that in a combat situation, never fly straight for any length of time. It courted disaster. There was no quicker way to be shot down. And this was what Katya had asked her friend to do.

Once again, she put the Yak over into a roll and then made it double back on itself. When the maneuver was complete, she was a thousand feet below the two aircraft above her. Katya looked up through the canopy at the German fighter and pulled up, putting the Russian fighter into a steep climb.

Once she was within a good range, she pressed the firing button and the weapons on the Yak spewed their deadly payload at the Me 109.

Katya saw the strikes on the thin-skinned fighter and smoke billowed from the cowling. Flames appeared and within a heartbeat the plane exploded in mid-air, forcing Katya to change course.

"Katya, help me! I can't get this plane off my tail."

She recognized the voice straight away. It was Raskova. She looked around the sky and saw the Yak streaming smoke against the blue sky above. "I'm coming, Nika, hang on."

Katya pulled back on the yoke and pushed the throttle forward once more. The fighter climbed higher towards the desperately maneuvered plane above.

"Elena, where are you?"

"I'm busy." The sound of weapons firing in the background reached out through the radio as she spoke.

A quick look around and she could see Elena's Yak on the tail of another Me 109.

"Katya!"

"I'm coming, Nika. Keep moving."

"He's all over me. He—"

The transmission stopped and Katya watched on as Roskova's plane lazily slid over onto one wing and started its terminal dive towards the ground.

"Nika, answer me. Nika!"

There was no reply.

"Bastard," Katya hissed and kept her plane on course to intercept the German fighter.

Just as she came within range the pilot turned his

plane away. With a frustrated yelp, Katya planted her thumb on the firing button and let out a long burst of fire, only stopping when her ammunition ran out.

"Der'mo!" Katya hissed as she watched the plane fly away. "Elena, are you still with me?"

"Only just," came the reply as she slid her plane in beside Katya's.

"What about Aksinia?"

"She's gone. She was shot down. I didn't see a parachute."

"The same thing with Nika," Katya informed her. "Come on, it's time to go back. I'm out of ammunition and from what I can see, you need to land before that thing falls from the sky."

CHAPTER ELEVEN

Leningrad, March 1942

THE SOUND OF ARTILLERY ALWAYS SEEMED LOUDER AT night, Anya thought to herself. The Russian army was trying to breakout once more and punch through the German defenses. However, the Germans were giving as good as they got and rained as many shells down upon the Russian lines as crashed through their own.

Her stomach growled. It had been two days since her last meal, and what little food her and Olga had they'd shared with the children. All ten of them.

What had started out with looking after three children had grown exponentially after taking in orphans from the neighborhood. Six boys and four girls. Their ages ranged from thirteen to four.

Olga moved over to sit beside Anya on the sofa. "We need to find some more food."

"I know," Anya sighed. "I went to the distribution point today and they had nothing."

"Galina and her whores have more than enough," Olga told her.

"I know. Food that they've stolen from others as well as what they've slept with soldiers for."

"Maybe we should try that," Olga said.

"No."

"Then how will we get food to feed the children and ourselves?" Olga demanded, her voice containing a brittle edge.

"I don't know. I will find something. I'll go out tomorrow and see if there is anything."

"Good luck," Olga replied abruptly.

She moved off the sofa and sat closer to the fire. She put the leg of what had once been a table onto it. It had come from a shelled house further along the street. The occupants had been killed by the blast, but the torn apart building had supplied them, and others as well with vital wood to keep them warm.

Anya looked up as movement from the doorway into the living room caught her eye. One of the children, a girl, had woken. She looked at Anya and said, "I can't sleep. I'm cold."

Anya held out her hand. "Come, Fekla, sit with me."

The girl was no more than nine and had long dark hair and dark eyes. She sat next to Anya who wrapped her arms around her.

Fekla's parents had been killed, like so many, by German shelling. Also killed was her brother. Fekla herself had been outside playing in the snow with her friends when the shell came bursting in, the only reason she had survived.

Each child had their own story.

Is that better?" Anya asked.

"A little."

They sat that way for a few minutes before Fekla looked up at her and said, "I'm hungry."

Anya kissed her forehead. "I know, baby. I know." She then looked across at Olga who was staring at her. Then she continued. "I'll get us some food tomorrow. I promise."

Olga shook her head and turned back to the fire.

———

THE GUNS HAD FALLEN silent sometime during the night. The following morning presented an eerie silence as Anya stepped outside into the cold. She walked along the street through the snow, past several shelled houses as well as bomb craters.

She walked past an older couple who were scavenging through the wreckage of a house looking for wood and other stuff to burn. The old woman looked up. "You wouldn't have any food to spare, would you?"

Anya gave her a wan smile. "I'm sorry old one. I'm in the same situation you are."

"Are you sure? I'm not too proud to beg."

"I'm sorry."

She kept walking, passing others who were also looking for things to burn. Two more women asked her if she had any food to spare and it made her feel even more somber to tell them no.

For the next hour Anya walked Leningrad trying to find something for herself and the others to eat. But all that she found was more death and destruction. Bodies of the dead piled in the streets because the ground was too frozen to bury them. Apartment blocks leveled from either shell or bomb; homeless people frozen where they lay. And for a moment of fleeting hope, the carcass of a dead horse, stripped of everything edible.

Then as she rounded a corner she was greeted by a cacophony of noise. Before her was a snow-covered park littered with Soviet troops. Hundreds of them. Wounded and dead. Medical orderlies carried stretchers with soldiers upon them, some missing limbs from horrific wounds.

"You! You there!" a voice shouted at her.

Anya turned and saw a bald man waving at her. "Me?"

"Yes. Come over here and help."

Anya walked over to him and as she came closer, she saw that he was perhaps in his middle forties and was covered in blood. His hands were black, a dried crust covering them. "What happened?" she asked.

"The attack last night failed. A waste of good young men and women. Now we have to deal with the fallout."

Anya looked around at the devastating scene. "How many?"

"Use your eyes. Can't you see?"

"Shouldn't we try to get them warm?"

He shook his head. "The cold is their friend. It makes their vessels retract, their blood flow slows, and it stops them from bleeding out. The ones who are too far gone it helps them by being merciful. They go to sleep and don't wake up."

Anya was shocked at the matter-of-fact way he explained it. He could see her uncertainty. There were two ways he could deal with her. He chose the second. "What is your name?"

"Anya."

He pointed at a wounded soldier. "Good. Now, get over here and help me with this man."

Anya walked over and looked down at the man on the stretcher. She immediately looked away, not wanting to see the two bloody, mangled stumps where his legs used to be.

"Look at me," the doctor said. "We cannot save this man. He will be dead before too long. I want you to go through the wounded and any wounded you think will die, are to be taken and put over there."

The doctor pointed at the only cleared spot on the edge of the park. "I will give you four men. Have them take the hopeless cases over there."

Shock appeared on Anya's face. "I—I can't. How would I know if they are to die or not?"

The doctor stared at her. "Listen to me. Most of these men will die anyway. Be brave, make the decision."

"I don't know if I can. Being responsible for sending them to their death."

"You have to. Or even more will die if we have to keep doing it ourselves. Now, start with him."

Anya nodded stiffly.

The doctor started to walk away. "Wait, I don't know your name."

"It's Leonid," the doctor called over his shoulder.

Anya saw him call two men over. They took their orders from him and then hurried towards Anya. They stopped in front of her and the taller of the two said, "We are here to help you."

"What are your names?"

"I am Jasha and this is Grigor."

"I am Anya." She pointed to the legless young man. "Take him over there where it is clear."

Jasha nodded and they bent and picked up the stretcher. Instead of watching them go, she moved onto the next. By that time, two more young men had arrived. She looked at them. Tell me your names."

"Kostya and Melor."

"Anya. Take this soldier and put him over there with the other one."

The young man she'd picked had a stomach wound. It was packed full of rags to hold everything in, and Anya knew there was no hope for him.

And so it went on for the next hour and soon Anya had the once cleared area filled with hopeless stretcher cases. She looked around and felt the weight of the world suddenly bear down upon her, for there were still hundreds more for her to get through. Her eyes filled with tears as she wiped at her forehead feeling the dampness there even though it was still freezing.

"Are you alright?"

She looked around and saw Leonid standing a few feet away from her. He was even bloodier than before. She nodded, her eyes red-rimmed. "No."

"Keep going."

Suddenly air raid sirens sounded. Anya looked up in alarm. Leonid said, "Do not worry. Keep going. If a bomb falls on you there's not much you can do."

She was shocked at his calm resignation, thinking that he'd already accepted death as a forgone conclusion to the part he played in the war.

Bombs began falling like rain on Leningrad and Anya did her best to try and block out the thud of the explosions. Occasionally, one would land close, and she could feel the vibrations through the ground shuddering beneath her feet.

By the time she had finished, the German bombers were long gone. Anya looked over at where the orderlies were continuing to lay the dying. It was then that she saw them. Two women who seemed to be leaning over them, as though they were caring for them. Anya frowned, not sure she had seen it at first. Then she saw it happen again. They were checking the pockets of the doomed soldiers.

"No," Anya gasped. "No, no, no."

She rushed over to where the two women were working. They saw her coming and stood erect. Recognizing them, Anya snarled, "Get away! Go on, clear off."

The two women remained unmoved. The taller of the two said, "If you know what's good for you, you'll walk away."

"No, I will not."

The woman opened her coat just wide enough for Anya to see the pistol she was keeping in her belt. "Yes, you will."

Anya took an involuntary backward step, her mouth agape. The tall woman said, "Go, and maybe I won't tell Galina about you."

The two women stared at her, daring her to try something. Instead, Anya, shoulders slumped, turned and walked away.

As she passed a wounded soldier, she saw another bent over him, talking. The young man had a PPD-34 submachine gun in his grasp.

Anya stopped for a moment before saying, "Excuse me."

The young soldier stood erect. "Yes?"

She stared at him for a moment trying to think of something to say. Then, "You shouldn't have your weapon here amongst the wounded. What if one of them goes crazy and takes it?"

He looked at her as though she were stupid. "Are you—"

"Look, I can get one of the doctors or I can take it, and you can get it from me when you leave."

"But—"

Anya held out her hand.

The young soldier shook his head and passed it over. "Where will you be?"

"I'll be easy to find."

The young man crouched back down, and Anya looked at the unfamiliar weapon in her grasp. She looked over at the two women who were still going through pockets and back to the gun. Suddenly her jaw set firm, she took her first step towards the two thieves.

Both women were far too busy at their looting to take notice of Anya as she approached. Even when she stopped not far from them, they still never looked up from their efforts.

Knowing she needed to show some semblance of authority, Anya took a deep breath and said in a confident voice, "Right, you bitches, it's time for you to leave."

They straightened up, the taller woman's lip curled in a snarl which never passed her lips because her gaze fell upon the PPD. "What do you think you're doing?"

"Empty out your pockets," Anya snapped.

"You're making a mistake. Galina won't like this."

"Empty them."

The shorter of the two women firmed her jaw and said, "She's not game to do anything with that gun."

Anya pointed the PPD at the clear sky, closed her eyes. And squeezed the trigger.

The rattle of the weapon echoed across the park as it burned through the magazine of ammunition. The empty shell casings rained down at Anya's feet while the two women before her ducked low in case a stray round might hit one of them.

When the shooting stopped the two thieves stood erect. Anya pointed the empty weapon at them. "Empty your pockets."

"What's going on here," Leonid demanded hurrying up behind Anya.

"They are stealing from these wounded men."

"Are they?" the doctor asked, a grim expression on his face.

"I told them to empty their pockets, but they refused."

The young soldier whose weapon Anya had borrowed, arrived on the scene and gently took it from her. "Wait," Anya said. "I'm not done."

"It's empty," the young soldier told her.

"Oh."

Leonid stared at the two women as the young soldier reloaded. "You will come with me."

The taller of the two women shook her head. "No. We're not going anywhere."

The doctor nodded. "Soldier, shoot them. I have the authority."

"Yes, sir."

"No, wait," the women exclaimed. "We'll come with you."

"I thought you might. Anya, wait here, I'll be right back."

The two women glared at Anya as they were led away. She waited for Leonid to return and when he did, he could see that he wasn't happy. "What happened?"

"The political officer told them to go away."

"That's it?" Anya asked in disbelief.

"Yes. He said he had more important things to deal with."

"That's not right."

"No, it's not. But there's nothing I can do about it."

Anya nodded. "I must be getting home. I came out today to try and find food for my friend and the ten children we look after—"

"Ten?" Leonid blurted out.

"Yes, they're orphans."

"Good Lord."

"We ran out of food two days ago and..."

"Maybe I can help you with that," Leonid said.

He hurried away and was gone for five minutes. Anya was beginning to think he wasn't coming back when he appeared with two orderlies carrying two crates. "Here is some food. These men will help you get it home."

Anya shook her head in disbelief. "I can't—"

"Yes, you can. Now go."

Anya threw her arms around him. "Thank you, Leonid. Thank you."

He eased her back and smiled at her. "You're most welcome. Now, go, feed those children."

———

THE ORDERLIES PERSEVERED with the weight of the two crates all the way back to where Anya and the others lived. They made no complaint even though they were obviously tired.

"Not far to go," Anya told them as they rounded the corner of the street where she lived. But something was wrong. The street had more debris on it than usual. Anya stopped and looked at the building further along across the street. Or rather what was left of it. It had been completely destroyed. As had another further along.

The bombing from earlier in the day. Her heart skipped a beat as she hurried along the icy pavement. Two more houses were gone as though someone had walked along the street and earmarked them for demolition, leaving out the others.

Then she arrived at where her home had been, a blackened pile of rubble was all there was to be found. A searing pain shot through her chest as she looked around for the children, for Olga.

She sighted a lone man across the street walking along the pavement. Anya hurried across the street. "Excuse me. Excuse me."

The man stopped and looked up. She knew him. Vadimir from further along the street. "Vadimir. What happened? Have you seen Olga and the children?"

He gave her a sorrowful look. "Any. Dear, dear, Anya. We thought you were in there too."

"What do you mean? Where is Olga, the children?"

"Gone. They're all gone."

Anya felt as though she'd been punched in the stomach. She slowly sank to her knees on the frozen sidewalk and wrapped her arms around herself. Then after a few moments she threw back her head and screamed in sorrowful anger.

CHAPTER TWELVE

Vitebsk, March 1942

EVA KOZLOVA SAT OUTSIDE ENJOYING THE WARMTH THE autumn sun was affording her. Beside her sat the old man who'd saved her life and nursed her back to health under the noses of the Nazi occupiers. Doctor Luka Chernoff. "Tell, me," he said, "how is it you are feeling this morning?"

"I'm ready," Eva replied.

The doctor nodded. "I thought you might be. I have someone coming this morning to see you. He will get you where you need to go."

Eva was instantly cautious as her mind started to work anxiously. "Who is he?"

Chernoff reached out and placed his hand on Eva's. She twitched under his touch, a result of her time with the SS. "It's all right, Eva. He is a good man."

"If you say so."

———

The Banks of the Don River

Gerhard Meunch was still getting used to being given command of the 3rd Battalion, 194th Infantry Regiment, 71st Division as he stared out across the Don River at the two three-hundred-foot pontoon bridges. The engineers had built them and secured a foothold on the other side, knocking out any of the scattered Russian resistance. Paulus had then ordered his divisions to cross the expanse and hold on the other side while they reorganized.

Tomorrow, Meunch's regiment would cross.

"Sir?"

Meunch turned to see Unteroffizier Bauer. "What is it?"

"The lieutenant was looking for you. Orders, sir."

Meunch nodded. The heat of the day was starting to become intense, and he could feel the dampness beneath his uniform. "Where is he?"

"Back this way, sir."

"Take me to him."

Bauer led him back to where he found the stick-thin, Lieutenant Gregor Eklund with a worried expression on his face. "You were looking for me, Lieutenant?"

"Jawohl, Hauptmann. New orders. You are to take the battalion across this afternoon."

"Really? Why is that?"

"I have heard that General Paulus wants an attack tomorrow. A final drive to Stalingrad."

"There goes the leave we thought we were getting," Bauer groaned.

Meunch stared at him. "The only leave we'll get is one the Ivans give us. Find Glass, will you?"

"Jawohl."

Upon his promotion to battalion commander, Meunch had made two decisions. One was to promote Glass to unteroffizier, and the other was to keep both Glass and Bauer alongside him at all times with them only answerable to him. "Lieutenant, have your company ready. You will lead us across the river this afternoon."

"It would be an honor, sir."

"Not if the Ivan planes catch you in the middle, it won't be. Dismissed."

———

Stalingrad, August 1942

Yeryomenko looked up as Gordov entered his office. "What is it, Vasily?"

"Intelligence reports that the Germans are preparing another attack, sir."

"What is it saying?"

"Paulus' Sixth Army and Hoth's Fourth Panzers are shaping for one of their pincer movements. Classic German assault."

"Then pull our men back. We will need them all for the coming battles."

"Are you sure—"

"Of course, I am bloody sure," Yeryomenko snarled at Gordov for questioning his order.

"I will see to it."

"Thank you."

Gordov disappeared back out the door leaving Yeryomenko to study his map again. "Damn it."

He picked up the crumpled piece of paper which sat on the middle of the map. He unscrewed it and read the message once more.

Can't send reinforcements at this time. Do what you can. Will send men as soon as possible.

Suddenly Yeryomenko felt as though his head was well and truly on the chopping block and he was waiting for the ax to fall.

———

East of the Don River, August 1942

SS-Untersturmfuhrer Karl Egger stood in the turret of his Panzer and looked at the scene before him. The horizon was dotted with black smoke plumes rising into the air. "The Ivans are burning more of their things again," he said over the intercom.

"Maybe they heard we were coming for their women," Lehman replied.

"I wouldn't touch them with your shriveled dick," Blumenberg retorted.

"That's enough," Egger reprimanded them. "Keep going."

He turned around and looked back at the line of tanks following him. Beside them marched lines of Wehrmacht soldiers.

The sun above him beat down. It was hot, made even more so by the steel monsters in which they traveled. On either side of the rutted road were burnt out and destroyed vehicles. Blackened corpses lay charred on scorched earth. The tank tracks rattled and screeched as they followed the rest of the 6ᵗʰ Army towards their destination.

"All tanks stop," Egger ordered as an officer approached his tank. It was a Wehrmacht Oberst. "What is it?"

"The Ivans have fallen back. Some were left behind to cover the retreat, but the rest have gone."

"Why are you telling me this?"

The Oberst wrinkled his nose in distaste of Egger's attitude. "No reason."

"Then we shall continue. Driver advance."

The Oberst stepped aside and muttered something under his breath. But Egger didn't care. He had a war to fight and Russians to kill.

———

Northeast of Stalingrad, 23rd August 1942

Anatoly marched at the head of his men under a burning sun. The battalion was pushing hard towards Stalingrad where they would reinforce the city's garrison. The punishment battalion had itself been reinforced and all of the companies were brought up to strength with officers and NCOs who were made scapegoats for the failings of the high command.

Anatoly had recently been promoted to captain by Serov who was currently at the head of the column riding in an old farm truck which he'd requisitioned along the way. Sobol moved in beside Anatoly and said in a low voice, "I hope that fat bastard is enjoying his ride."

"Maybe it will break down and he'll be walking like the rest of us."

"He'd never walk anywhere. With the Germans behind us he'd run faster than the rest of us."

Anatoly smiled. "You shouldn't talk about your commanding officer like that, Sergeant."

"You're my commanding officer, sir. Not him."

Anatoly grunted.

"Do you know why they pulled us out before we had a chance to fight?"

"Not really. All I've heard is something about reinforcing Stalingrad."

"Fighting to save our fearless leader's great city. Let it burn, I say."

"It will be if the Germans come," Zorkin said as he fell in beside them.

Anatoly looked at him. "What have you heard?"

"Word is we hold the city, or we die. With the river at our back, it's a good possibility."

Sobol hissed. "We're marching into Hell."

Anatoly nodded his agreement. "Then the three-sixtieth can find the Devil and kick him in the ass."

Hour after grueling hour the troops kept marching southwest. The sun grew higher and hotter still then come mid-afternoon someone from in front of them cried out, "There!"

The three men craned their necks to look to see what the fuss was about, and then Anatoly saw it. The first outlines of the city through the heat haze. Smoke rose from burning buildings hit by an earlier air raid, acting as a beacon to bring the Russian troops in. In a quiet voice he said to Sobol, "There's your Hell."

They had finally reached Stalingrad.

———

*6th Army Headquarters, Northwest of Stalingrad,
23rd August 1942*

General Friedrich Wilhelm Ernst Paulus was in a good mood. He studied the map laid out before him and looked over the 6th Army's advances for the day. His divisions had pushed hard that day. The 16th Panzers had led the way and were closing on Stalingrad from the northeast. Behind them reports were that the 3rd Motorized Division followed close behind. Then came the 60th Motorized Division.

Soon reports started coming in that the advanced armored columns had sighted Stalingrad's buildings in the distance, the most notable being the smokestacks. Then the lead elements came under fire from the defenders whom they dispatched quickly.

The tanks rolled on until they could go no further, for they sat atop a steep cliff to the north of Stalingrad, which overlooked the Volga itself.

From there they turned south and entered the village of Rynok. The Stalingrad front had been cut in two and the railway between Stalingrad and Moscow was severed.

Paulus looked at his watch. It was almost six in the evening.

The dark-haired general with a receding hairline looked up when a figure loomed in front of him. "What is it?" Paulus asked his adjutant. "Do you have news?"

The thin-faced man nodded. "Yes, sir. The lead elements have been joined by others and we now have a foothold along the Volga. It will be a place where we can launch our attack against the city."

"Good," replied Paulus. "Everything is coming together."

———

Yeryomenko's Headquarters, Stalingrad, 23rd August 1942

While the Germans advanced throughout the day, Yeryomenko was run off his feet trying to keep on top of things. Reports filtered through about a German thrust from the northwest and that it couldn't be held. When Yeryomenko asked if the attack was on a broad front, he learned that the thrust was a narrow one designed to punch through the defensive line and sever it.

Two columns, he was told. Two columns of tanks numbering no more than one hundred in each. Behind them came trucks and infantry.

Yeryomenko's phone rang. He reached for it. "Hello?"

"What is happening, Andrei?" Commissar Nikita Khrushchev asked.

Yeryomenko told him.

"I'll be right there."

Khrushchev arrived within the half hour. He walked into Yeryomenko's office and said, "Tell me about it, Andrei."

The general explained it again.

"What are we doing about it? Can we keep them from Stalingrad?"

"It's a matter of reinforcements," Yeryomenko said. "Ones that I don't damn well have."

The phone rang. Yeryomenko answered and then listened. And as he listened, for the first time he was starting to let his anger take over. "Damn it, do your job."

He slammed the phone down and stared at Khrushchev. "The Nazis just burned a large supply depot."

Before the commissar could answer, two more officers appeared in the office doorway. "General," said the taller of the two. "We've finished building the pontoon bridge, sir."

"Thank you, gentlemen, now go back out there and destroy it."

"Sir?"

"You heard me, destroy it. Deny the enemy the crossing."

"But we've just—"

"I know. Just do it."

After the generals left, Yeryomenko stared at Khrushchev. "You don't agree, Comrade?"

"I can see why you would do it, but the pontoon bridge would be useful."

"To us or the Germans?"

The commissar nodded. "Like I said, I can see why you would do it."

The phone rang again. "I'm sick of this damned thing already." He picked it up. "Yes?"

Yeryomenko listened for a while and then hung up. "The Germans have another air raid coming in."

"Nothing new," Khrushchev said.

"This one is bigger. A lot bigger."

—————

Stalingrad, 23rd August 1942

"Get everyone under cover, now!" Anatoly shouted as he stared at the incoming waves of bombers. He turned. *"Move!"*

Sobol and Zorkin started barking orders and the company began to scatter. Anatoly ran towards an air raid trench which had been constructed in the park across the street. As he went, he continued to shout at some of the civilians who were present.

He dived into the trench with a grunt. Sobol landed beside him. "This is it, huh? Sitting in a ditch waiting for the Nazis to drop bombs on us from a great height."

"We've been bombed before."

Sobol looked up. Already the bombers were surrounded by flak. "Yes, but not by that frigging many."

He'd no sooner spoken the words when the lead planes started dropping their bombs. There was no specific target, only the city itself.

The deep throated booms started in the distance as bombs landed. The noise gradually grew louder, the earth trembling. The bombs seemed to walk forward like a giant carpet unfurling until it started to roll over them in a violent display of force which lasted for ten minutes.

Once it was finished, Anatoly peered out from the trench. He could feel himself shaking. They'd been shelled before by artillery, but this had been different again. He looked around at the devastation that greeted him. Beside him, Sobol said, "That's how you level a couple of city blocks in no time."

"Go and check on the men."

Zorkin found him. Anatoly said, "I've got Sobol checking on the men."

"I'd dare say our fearless leader has shit himself and run off somewhere?"

With a shrug, Anatoly said, "Or found himself a nice deep hole to crawl into. If he could find one wide enough."

"Speak of the devil," Zorkin said.

Anatoly tracked his gaze and saw Serov walking towards them. His uniform was covered in dust, and he'd lost his helmet.

"Kozlov." There was a tremor in his voice. "Where have you been?"

"Trying not to get killed, Comrade. The same as you."

"Gather your company and take them to the northern part of the city."

Anatoly waited for him to continue but when he never he asked, "And do what, exactly?"

"Wait for the Germans to arrive. What else?"

"I see. Do we know how far away they are?"

"Like you," Serov sneered. "I am not supposed to ask questions. Just carry out orders."

"Fine," said Anatoly. "I will leave immediately. Are we to be going alone?"

Serov's eyes narrowed. "Just go, Captain."

"Sir. Lieutenant, have the men fall in. It's time to go to war once more."

———

Stalingrad, 23rd August 1942

Yeryomenko stood outside the blast doors of his head-quarters and looked up. It was almost midnight and the whole of the gorge was ringed with an orange glow from the fires above. Reports were coming in of the casualties from the hours of bombing. As one flight had left off, another would come in soon after to take its place. The figures were somewhere north of twenty thousand killed.

The general was bone tired. He sighed and turned to walk back inside. There was still one person left to speak with to about the day's events and he would be expecting a call. Stalin.

Once in his office, Yeryomenko picked up the telephone handset. Within moments it was answered. "What have you to report, Andrei?"

"Mostly bad news, sir."

"Bad news?"

"I'm afraid so. The advance part of the German forces has reached the northern parts of the city. We've sustained heavy bombing for most of the day and Stalingrad is on fire. I have been asked by some to blow up the factories and evacuate their contents across the river. To save them. A move which both I and Commissar Khrushchev oppose."

"Such a move is out of the question," Stalin growled. "I will not even consider it."

"Yes, sir."

"You will hold the city, Andrei. Hold it until the last man. There will be no retreat, understood?"

"Yes, Comrade."

The call disconnected and Yeryomenko stared at the

handset in his fist. It had been decided. With those words, Stalin had condemned thousands to death.

———

East of the Volga, 23rd August 1942

"Come on, you lot, keep moving," the big sergeant ordered as soldiers walked past him. "By the time we get there the war will be over."

Eva stumbled over a rock before straightening herself. She hissed loudly and limped for a few steps as the pain from her rolled ankle shot up her leg.

"Can shoot the eye out of a needle at eight-hundred yards, Kozlova, but can't walk without falling over something," the sergeant growled. "Just as well you're a sniper and not a normal bitching soldier."

"Stick it in your ass," Eva muttered.

"What was that? I don't think I heard it properly."

"I said, yes Comrade. You're right."

"I know I am. Now, keep marching."

As she walked further the pain lessened until it was gone. The column had left their bivouac early that morning and had been fast approaching Stalingrad when they were ordered to divert to approach from the east.

Most were green troops. Reinforcements who had been trained and brought to fill the vacancies in decimated regiments. It had been a long journey for Eva. At first, she thought the guide who had gotten her out of Vitebsk was taking her to Stalingrad, however he'd taken her through the German lines to Moscow. Once there he'd abandoned her. With nothing else to do, and a burning, deep-seated passion to kill Germans, she joined the Red Army.

Her prowess with a rifle had been noticed right off, and immediately she'd been taken from her company and trained as a sniper.

Suddenly the column stopped. Ahead of Eva men and women, soldiers all, spread left and right. Eva moved to the right to try and see what they were looking at. Once she had a clear view, a slight gasp escaped her lips. The horizon before them was lit by an orange glow and for the first time she could hear the crump of explosions.

Beside her the sergeant said in a low voice, "That, young Kozlova, is Stalingrad. The Nazis made it before we did. It's a good thing we're on this side of the river."

"How do we get across?" Eva asked.

"How about we worry about that when we get there. Fall back in, there's a good girl."

Eva gripped her Mosin-Nagant Sniper Rifle tightly in her right hand and rejoined the ranks of the regiment as it started forward once more. All the while the booms in the distance grew louder.

———

Over Stalingrad, 23/24 August 1942

The plane lurched as flak was fired up at it from the burning city below. Edmund Wagner gripped the yoke tighter and adjusted his course. Another burst of flak rocked the plane and a voice over the radio said, "Two minutes to target."

This was their second mission for the day. The first

having been earlier that afternoon. Below them the whole city looked to be on fire but this last time, before they'd taken off, the flight had been warned to stay away from Stalingrad's northern outskirts.

Another flak burst and this time the Heinkel He111 felt as though it had been belted by a giant fist. A scream could be heard over the intercom and Wagner said, "Call in."

Everyone did so except for the side gunner. "Schwarz, check in."

Nothing.

"Schwarz check in."

Still nothing.

"Klein, go back and check Schwarz."

"Jawohl," the navigator replied.

Wagner suddenly felt the plane shudder. Something wasn't right. He changed direction and everything functioned fine which meant it had to be engine related.

"Damn it. Someone check the engines. I want to know if you can see them."

"What are we looking for?" a voice came back.

"How about you see if it's still there. Stupid frigging question."

"Schwartz is dead, Hauptmann."

"Leave him where he is until we get back."

"Hauptmann, the port engine is on fire."

"What?" Wagner leaned over, looking back as best he could, seeing the flames flaring from the engine. "Shit, let's get these bombs out of the damn plane."

Within moments the bombs were released, and the plane was lighter. Immediately Wagner turned the engine off and feathered the prop before turning it away from its current course and put it on a heading away from the city.

"How's that engine looking?"

"It's going out."

"Keep an eye on it."

Slowly the flak from over the target dissipated and fell behind them. Wagner checked his instruments and saw that he was slowly losing altitude. He adjusted accordingly and tried to keep the air speed up.

"The fire is out, Hauptmann."

"Good. Now all we have to do is get home."

————

Stalingrad, 24th August 1942

Dawn brought with it the true picture of total devastation to Stalingrad. The center was all but destroyed and up to one-hundred blocks still burned from the furious blazes caused by the bombing. Without flowing water, the firemen were helpless and could only watch on as their city burned.

The river Volga was a scene of utter chaos. Thousands of civilians were trying to get across it to escape. Boats were overloaded and some with severe lists sank, disgorging their human burden into the dark depths. And while civilians were going one way, the boats on the return trip brought in more reinforcements by the brigade.

"I cannot believe what I'm seeing," Eva Kozlova whispered.

Her sergeant cleared his throat as words caught

there before he could get them out. He tried again. "This is concerning."

The sky above the city was dark, the sun unable to peek through the thick smoke. From somewhere near the bow of their vessel a political officer shouted encouragement to the soldiers.

"I wish he'd shut the hell up," the sergeant growled.

"I could shoot him for you," Eva said drily.

He looked at her with blue eyes. "Don't tempt me, girl."

"Where do you think they will all go?" Eva asked, indicating the civilian-filled boats.

The sergeant's lined face creased thoughtfully. "I do not know."

"Are you scared?" Eva asked him.

He frowned. "Are you?"

Eva shook her head. "No. I've been afraid before but not now. I've died and been brought back to life so dying does not worry me. Living is hard."

Her words confused him. For someone so young to have spoken words like this was unusual. "When we get ashore, girl, stick with me."

Eva nodded. "I will, Sergeant."

She looked at him. Sergeant Karik Lagutov was a big man with dark hair. In his fists he held a PPD submachine gun which almost seemed like a toy. For some reason, the thirty-four-year-old Russian had gravitated towards Eva despite his gruffness. And after a time, she was feeling somewhat relaxed around him.

The snipers would be split into teams of two and it appeared as though Lagutov had chosen Eva for himself.

The gray Volga flowed past them, littered with

bodies and other debris. On the far bank as they approached a sea of wretched humanity waited their arrival. With all the shouting and crying, it was a discordant symphony that assailed the senses, along with the smell; raw sewage, dead people, burnt buildings.

The boat slid in beside the dock and a surge of civilians washed towards it like a wave on the sand. Soldiers and political officers battered them back so that the newly arrived regiment could disembark from their vessels.

Once she had feet on solid wood, Eva felt Lagutov's presence behind her. He guided her thin frame through the crush, and he felt her tense as the civilians crowded close. "Keep moving," he told her. "You'll be fine."

They forced their way through the swarming hordes while political officers bawled orders at anyone who would listen. At one point, a man tried to push past one and the officer casually drew his sidearm and shot him.

Eva stopped and stared at the sight. How could this happen? Lagutov's hand pressed on her back. "Keep moving, girl."

And then they were out of it, moving up the riverbank towards the city itself, past a more organized line of waiting civilians. They crested the rise to be greeted by a scene of devastation. With a sudden shout, the organized line disintegrated as everyone in it sought cover.

Eva looked up and saw what the drama was. At first, they were black specks but there was no doubt; they were German bombers. Looking on, she could see that the planes were already dropping their bombs. Dark shapes fell in clusters from the bellies of the aircraft. Once the explosions started, they seemed to walk forward to where Eva and Lagutov watched on.

The big sergeant pushed Eva towards a pile of rubble. "Get down behind there," he shouted urgently.

They both took cover behind the concrete and block refuse, the ground shaking as the carpet of explosions grew closer. Then it was on top of them. Blasts rocked the air all around them. Eva covered her head to protect herself from falling debris. She cried out as she felt a rock, or brick, or whatever it was hit her back. The shout however was swept away in the wave of the next explosion.

Then the blanket of bombing passed over them and continued making its way across the city.

Lagutov rolled onto his side and stared at Eva. "Are you alright?"

She winced and said, "I think so."

They climbed to their feet and looked around. Cries of wounded sounded eerie in the sudden silence, and Stalingrad had lost more of itself to the Nazi invaders.

Eva looked at Lagutov. "This place is—"

He nodded knowing what she was trying to get out. "Yes, it is. Come on, let's go and find the rest. There's a war to fight."

CHAPTER THIRTEEN

Moscow, August 1942

ONCE MORE ZHUKOV HAD BEEN SUMMONED BY STALIN who informed him that the matter was most urgent. His driver sped almost recklessly through the streets towards the Kremlin. In the rear of the vehicle, Zhukov could only guess at the subject of such importance that he'd been flown directly to the capital for a meeting with the supreme leader. However, if he had to guess, there was only one major area of concern along the front which would trouble Stalin enough to demand his presence.

The car stopped outside, and the driver opened the door before stiffening to attention and his passenger climbed out.

Zhukov climbed the steps and went inside. In Stalin's office were other members of the STAVKA, or high command. Stalin greeted him with a welcoming smile and a shake of his hand. Zhukov said, "I got here as soon as I could, Comrade."

"You did well, Georgy. Thank you for coming."

"What seems to be the problem?"

"One word. Stalingrad."

Zhukov nodded. He'd been hearing nothing but troublesome reports coming out of the city. "What can I do to help, sir?"

"I need you to take over full control of the strategy, Georgy. What you did for Moscow and for Leningrad was a military miracle."

"Leningrad holds, sir, although I'm not sure I would class it as a miracle."

"I would," Stalin reiterated. "The fact that they still hold is nothing but. A new offensive is being organized as we speak to release the shackles."

Thousands dying every week was hardly something to celebrate, Zhukov thought to himself.

Stalin continued. "I have directed three more armies to the south to try and break the German blockade."

"Might I ask which ones, Comrade?"

The other officers present looked at each other cautiously waiting for Stalin to erupt with anger. Instead, he smiled at Zhukov and replied, "The First guards, the Twenty-Fourth, and the Sixty-Sixth."

Zhukov considered what he'd just been told. He knew of the armies the supreme leader spoke of and that all three were well below optimum strength.

Stalin noticed the concern on his face. "I know what you're thinking, Georgy. And I agree, they are under-manned. However, the Nazis are stretched thin where they shall be attacking. Besides, once you arrive, I'm sure you will strengthen the attack and rid the city of these bastards."

"Yes, Comrade Stalin."

Once more Stalin smiled. "Good. Now I have one more thing to inform you of before we adjourn for dinner. I am pleased to inform you that I am promoting you to Deputy Supreme Commander of the Red army."

Zhukov was stunned. Such a promotion would put him second in command to Stalin himself. "I—"

"Think nothing of it, Georgy," Stalin said jovially. "Everyone in this room overwhelmingly agreed that you should be the one chosen."

Zhukov looked at them and saw the pained smiles on their faces. "Thank you," he said to them.

Stalin slapped him on the back. "Come now, Georgy. Let's eat, and drink Vodka. Tomorrow you will leave for Stalingrad. And for victory."

Zhukov forced his own smile. His mind thought back to the reports he'd seen coming out of Stalingrad. Morale was so bad that desertions were climbing at an alarming rate. There were even stories of whole tank crews deserting with their tanks. Other stories had been told of officers from reinforcing divisions shooting their men for cowardice and spreading disinformation, before they'd even gone into battle.

Stalin looked back at Zhukov. "Are you coming, Comrade?"

"Yes, sir. I'm right behind you."

———

Leningrad, Early September 1942

It was getting dark, and Anya needed to find a place to shelter before it closed in. The streets of Leningrad at night were a dangerous place for a person to be alone.

Dangerous at the best of times, now made worse by the emergence of the Vixens.

A chill ran down her spine as she thought of them. The Vixens were responsible for the deaths of many as they took whatever they wanted or needed to survive. Even with the soldiers in the city, they still did as they pleased due to the soldiers caring only about the enemy not the civilian population.

The band was led by an old enemy, Galina Sharapova. Their den, as it was referred to, was in the east of the city, but they roamed far and wide in their search for what they needed. So far, Anya had managed to avoid them, but figured it was only a matter of time.

There was a damaged building across the street in which she figured to stay the night. Not ideal if it rained but at least she would be off the street.

Since the day that she'd arrived home to find everything gone, her life had consisted of living—no surviving, day to day. Like so many others who were left in the battered city, she had nothing except for the clothes in which she stood up in. Even those weren't hers. Anya had found them in a bombed out home when she'd been searching for food.

She stepped tentatively inside the building. The interior was trashed. Anything of wood construction had been stripped, burnt for warmth the past winter. The top part of the building's interior was scorched by the explosion. The second floor had a huge hole in it which revealed the sky above.

With every step Anya took, her shoes crunched on the debris beneath them. There were stairs to her left which had once led up to the second floor but now they had been bastardized and the handrail and most of the timber stairs themselves were gone.

She walked through what used to be the foyer and into another room towards the back. It had been the kitchen. She looked at the cupboards. All the doors were gone. As with the stairs, anything made of wood had been burned the last winter. Her eyes stopped when she saw a flap of fabric covering one of them.

With a frown, Anya walked forward and pulled the flap back. Her eyes widened when she saw the contents. Food. Tins of food. She gasped and hurriedly looked around. Seeing no one she took out a tin and examined it. Pears. The tin she held contained pears. All she had to do was get them out.

Anya looked around the kitchen. All the drawers were empty. Like the cupboard doors, they too had been burned. Her eyes went to the floor and found all the cutlery scattered across it. She walked across and stared down, trying to locate anything that might open the cans. Spoons, forks, knives, Anya bent low and picked up a knife with a sharp point. She walked across to the bench and placed the tin of peaches upright on the countertop.

With the knife in her right hand, Anya raised it. She thought about it for a moment and brought it down.

The knife hit at an angle and skidded across the lid. It hit the raised lip and flipped onto its side. The knife ricocheted dangerously off to the side and if Anya hadn't been quick with her reflexes the knife would have opened a wicked wound in her left hand.

A hiss of alarm escaped her lips and the tin rolled onto the floor.

Anya paused, more than a little shaken for she knew

what could happen if she cut herself. There would be more than a small chance of infection. And infection could well mean death.

She bent down and picked up the tin. Placing it back on the counter she thought seriously about trying to stab it with the knife once again. Instead, she had an idea. Anya went back outside and picked up a broken brick off the pavement, returning quickly.

By now her stomach was growling at the thought of eating. She'd put nothing in it for the better part of two days. But that was about to change.

Anya placed the point of the knife in the center of the tin and held it there with her left hand. With her right she raised the broken piece of brick and brought it down.

The knifepoint pierced the tin and a thin spurt of juice erupted from it. The liquid landed on Anya's hand, and she greedily licked the liquid up. She worked the knife back and forth slowly increasing the size of the hole. Before long it was big enough to extract the fruit from within. Anya tasted it hesitantly at first. But the sweetness of the pears overcame her caution and soon she was hungrily digging the contents out. Once finished, she drank the juice as well, not willing to waste a drop.

Anya looked back at the cupboard where the rest of the food was and then started walking towards it.

———

Someone was there. It was why she came awake. Anya lay there and listened. At first it was faint, almost indiscernible. But it was there. A quiet murmur of voices.

Anya climbed from where she was sleeping and moved towards the room's exit, careful of where she stepped.

She stood beside the doorway and held her breath for a moment as she tried to keep calm. Then she heard, "Someone has been into it."

"How do you know?"

Both were women's voices.

"Are you dumb or something? Just look at it."

"I suppose you're right."

"Galina isn't going to like it."

Good grief, she'd stumbled across a stash of the Vixens.

"We should look around," one of the women said.

Anya took a step back.

"No," replied the other. "We'll tell Galina and she'll probably want us to shift it."

"One of us should stay here and watch."

"Are you volunteering?"

"Not me."

"All right then, let's get out of here."

Anya breathed easy as she heard them leave. Then she got to thinking. There was no way she could leave this food to the Vixens. Not with so many people out there still starving. She sighed. It was going to be a long night.

———

Stalingrad, 14th September 1942

It was mostly a scene of destruction. Some buildings were down, others still stood. Three, four floors high. Others used to be that tall but now were missing a floor or two. Debris littered the streets and alleyways along with bodies bloating under the sun until they could expand no more and gasses released in a stinking hiss.

This was downtown Stalingrad on the 14th of September as the Germans pushed in on a broad front.

Hauptmann Gerhard Meunch waved men on his right forward as they tried to infiltrate the center of the city. Lieutenant Edgar Baum led his company forward along the north side of the street towards an intersecting one up ahead. As they traversed the sidewalk they'd stop and use alcoves for cover.

"What is that idiot doing?" Glass growled from beside Meunch. "There's no cover there, the horse's ass."

"Take your men forward on the left. If the Ivans hit now he'll get pinned down."

"Sir."

Meunch looked around and found his runner. "Fritz. Go to Lieutenant Faust and tell him to push his company up on the right behind Baum. Then go to Baum and tell him to keep pushing forward and not to stop until he secures the cross streets."

"Jawohl, Herr Hauptman."

The battalion commander gripped his MP40 as he watched Baum continue his leapfrog action along the street. Stabsfeldwebel Hans Bauer appeared at his side. When Meunch had been promoted to commander of the battalion, he'd promoted Bauer to sergeant major.

"Sir, Lieutenant Gold says they are moving up on the street over to the left. No resistance yet."

Meunch frowned. His gaze went high as he checked the buildings. "Something isn't right."

The words had only just escaped his lips when

gunfire erupted from the building on either side of the street. "Shit!"

Ahead of him men dropped to the street. Some wounded, others dead. He saw Baum waving to his men to get down. "No, no, no. *Keep moving!*"

"I'll go, sir," Bauer said.

"Tell him to get off the street and start clearing the buildings."

On the left of the street Glass had used his initiative and his men all retreated into the buildings. Meunch knew he'd start clearing them as soon as he got inside.

"Hauptmann Meunch."

The battalion commander turned to see Gold beside him. "Lieutenant, I want you to take half of your men to support Baum. Start clearing the buildings. Send the others to support Glass. He's up there on the left with his platoon."

Gold nodded. "Sir."

An explosion erupted from the middle of the street as a Russian grenade exploded. Two German soldiers fell to the ground and never moved. Meunch watched as Gold's company filed past him at the run and then split into two.

"Hauptmann Meunch, what is the hold up?"

Meunch looked up to see the regiment's commanding officer, a hawk-faced man by the name of Helmut Kalb standing beside him as if there was no danger. "I'd not stand there like that if I—"

WHACK!

The bullet punched into Kalb's chest and the Oberst sank to his knees before falling onto his side.

"Snipers!" Meunch called out and ran to his left,

keeping low until he reached the semi-cover of a shopfront.

He looked along the street and saw Bauer running back to him. "The lieutenant has started to clear the buildings, sir."

"Good." He looked back to where his other companies were. "Come with me, Hans."

Meunch ran back along the street until he reached his second in command, Hauptmann Isaak Lenz. "Isaak, bring the two remaining companies and come with me."

"Where are we going?" the squat officer asked.

"To secure the cross streets."

"But, sir—"

"Move, Hauptmann."

"Jawohl, Herr Hauptmann."

They pressed forward on either side of the street. The two companies with Meunch at their head. The fire from the windows was intense but then enemy soldiers appeared at the cross streets ahead of them.

Meunch stopped and opened fire with his MP40. The weapon rattled furiously, and a Russian soldier fell as bullets stitched a line across his chest. Beside the battalion commander, Bauer took out a grenade, primed it, and then threw it towards a machine gun which a pair of enemy soldiers were setting up behind a mound of rubble to use for cover.

The explosion ripped through the two Russian soldiers and killed them instantly. The two companies pushed harder, moving as they fired. The enemy soldiers were gradually pushed back as the Germans closed in on the cross streets.

Bauer threw a second grenade and more Russian

soldiers died. Meunch looked at his man and snapped, "We are to clear these buildings. Take a team and—"

There was a faint whistle and then a whack as a bullet from seemingly nowhere smashed into Bauer's head. He crumpled to the ground, his helmet rolling away. Meunch took cover behind a mound of rubble and looked across at his dead man. "Shit!"

———

THE MOSIN-NAGANT RIFLE slammed back into Eva's shoulder once more and another German soldier fell. This time it was the big Nazi who'd been throwing the grenades. She worked the bolt and searched for another target. Beside her, Lagutov said, "You need to relocate, Eva."

"In a minute," she replied as she fired once more.

"Now," the big man said firmly. "You know the rules."

She turned to look at him, her expression angry. "Rules, Karik? What rules would that be?"

"Don't give me that, Eva. Now move."

Eva grunted as another explosion from down on the street shook the building. She moved to another room where there was a hole in the wall. Ducking through it, she entered the next building which gave her a better view of the cross streets.

Eva took up her position and went to work, ignoring Lagutov's urges to change position once more. It was as though she had gone into a killing trance, and no one could break through it, while down below on the street the bodies piled up.

Lagutov was suddenly aware of the shouts on the floors below. Not Russian, German. "Eva, we must go."

She ignored him and fired again.

"Eva!"

Another shot, this one caused a soft cackle to escape her lips. The sergeant grabbed her shoulder and slapped her hard.

Stung, Eva grabbed at her reddening cheek. Her eyes wide. "What did you do that for?"

"The Germans are in the building. We need to leave."

But it was too late. The boots on the stairs told him that.

Lagutov turned just as the first German soldier appeared in the doorway. He opened fire with his PPD and sprayed the soldier with bullets. The German crumpled to the ground with a shout of pain. Behind his prone form another appeared. The Russian killed him too.

Now, wise to the fact, the following Wehrmacht soldiers stopped out of sight.

One of them poked his MP40 around the doorjamb and opened fire.

Lagutov threw himself to the floor as bullets cut through the air above him. Eva did the same, jarring her left shoulder when she landed heavily.

The sergeant used the remaining rounds in his PPD on the paper-thin wall where he figured the enemy soldier to be standing. The wall seemed to explode, and a cry of pain sounded. Lagutov changed out the magazine in his PPD and moved swiftly towards Eva. "Move!"

Before she knew it, she was being propelled along by a giant hand in the middle of her slender back. The sergeant pushed her from one building to the next through the rabbit warren of holes prepared earlier for the coming fight for downtown Stalingrad. A thud came from behind them and Lagutov knew exactly what it was. "Down!" he shouted and gave Eva a hard shove.

The grenade exploded just as they hit the floor. The roar was almost deafening, and Eva's ears rang. She felt the blast wave wash over her and the room they were in filled with dust and debris like a thick fog.

She felt a tug on her tunic and her body being lifted by the thick material. "Come on, girl, get up," Lagutov coughed.

With her rifle still in her hand, Eva was once more propelled forward. For a moment, the pressure of Lagutov's hand ceased and she heard his PPD open fire behind her. German voices shouted out and their weapons spoke in response to the Russian one.

Eva felt the tug of a bullet which sliced through the coarse fabric of her uniform. She turned to fire her rifle through the dust fog but never got the chance because Lagutov crashed into her just as a pair of MP40s spewed a hail of bullets towards them.

The air was forced from Eva's lungs as the two hit the floor once again. Another explosion rocked the building. Eva heard Lagutov curse and then say, "These bastards are pissing me off."

They were about to climb to their feet when a third explosion crashed and the floor beneath them gave out.

———

WITH THE CROSS streets secure Meunch knew they had to keep pushing towards their objectives. The main train station and the ferry.

"Sir," Glass said, stopping beside his commanding officer, "the streets are secure and the buildings have been cleared."

"Thank you, Felix. Get your men and push forward towards the train station. The rest of the battalion will follow you."

"Sir." He looked around. "Where is Hans?"

"He's dead. You're promoted to Feldwebel."

And just like that, the war went on.

Meunch looked for Lenz and found him talking to an unteroffizier. "Lenz, I've just ordered Glass to take his men forward to push towards the railway station. I want you to take your company and see if you can reach the ferry. If you can't, send word and I'll get you some more reinforcements. But I want to use the three other companies to take the station if I can."

Lenz nodded. "My unteroffizier was just telling me that the Ivans are using runners. Their communications are shot. It could work in our favor."

"Let's hope so. Now, go. Get it done."

"Jawohl."

———

PAIN.

It coursed through Eva's body as she slowly came around, becoming aware of her surroundings. She stifled a moan while rolling onto her side and more pain shot through her body. Slowly she opened her eyes and saw Lagutov lying beside her.

"Sergeant?" she whispered tentatively.

There was no response.

"Sergeant Lagutov?"

"Humph."

"Are you alright?"

Without opening his eyes, he said, "Do I look alright?"

"I—I don't know."

"I feel like shit. Have the Germans gone?"

Eva listened for a few moments and could only hear the distant gunfire and the dull crump of explosions. "I think so."

They struggled to their feet. Debris crunched under their boots and jolts of lightning shot through their bodies. Eva looked up at the hole where the ceiling used to be. Two floors higher. "Shit, we fell that far."

Lagutov craned his neck to let his gaze join hers. "It would seem that way."

He looked around his feet until he found his PPD. He picked it up and then did the same to Eva's rifle. "Come on, let's get out of here."

"Where are we going to go?"

"Somewhere the Nazis aren't."

"Moscow?"

"Funny. Now, move your ass."

CHAPTER FOURTEEN

Stalingrad, 14th September 1942

GENERAL VASILY IVANOVICH CHUIKOV STUDIED THE MAP before him in his headquarters. Reports had been coming in that the Germans had punched through their line and were about to overrun the train station as well as the ferry. Commanders were crying out for reinforcements and all the dark-haired man from Tula who was in charge of the 62nd Army could tell them was that they were on their way. First, they had to get across the Volga.

One such division was the 13th Guards which had already crossed under constant artillery fire. Their commander General Alexander Rodimtsev had come ashore and hurried to a position near Mamaev Hill. What he found troubled him immensely. Red army soldiers were frantically trying to dig in on the slope while the 295th German Division had already taken the top and had a clear view of the city as well as a clear field of fire.

Unhappy with the situation, Rodimtsev moved

quickly to find his commanding officer at Tsaritsa Gorge which was where he was now.

"I do not like it, Comrade General," he said to Chuikov. "The Nazis are above us and can see everything we do."

"Then you need to push them off, Comrade."

The thirty-six-year-old division commander gave Chuikov a pained look. "Most of my men are across, General, but to take that hill I will need more."

"How many more, Alex?"

"Two-thousand."

"That is a lot of men," Chuikov said grimly.

"There are a lot of Germans."

The Army commander nodded. "I will see what I can do."

"Thank you."

"One more thing, Comrade..."

———

SEROV SWALLOWED HARD. "Could you repeat that order please, sir?"

Rodimtsev sighed. "Take one of your companies and hold the railway station. The order is simple."

"Yes, sir."

"General Chuikov says that it must be held. Is that understood?"

"Yes, sir."

"Well, what are you waiting for, get going. Have them in position before daylight."

Serov snapped a salute and hurried away. Ten minutes later, after negotiating rubble and narrow pathways through it, he found the man he was looking for. "Anatoly, I have a job for you and your bastards."

A flare sparked in the night sky and started to float towards the ground, illuminating the surrounding blocks. "What is it, sir?"

"Take your company to the train station and hold it."

"Just like that?" Anatoly asked.

"Just like that."

"What fool gave that order?" Anatoly asked. "It'll take more than a company to hold the station."

"It comes from General Chuikov himself."

"Then maybe he should come here and participate in the idiotic lunacy."

"Just carry out the order, Captain."

Anatoly stiffened. "Yes, sir."

Serov left and Anatoly turned to Sobol. "Get the men together and tell Ilya I want to see him. If we're going to do this at least it's dark."

Anatoly found a creased map to try and work out the best approach to the rail station. Not that any way was a good way because of all the destruction to the intervening area. He was still scratching his head over it when Zorkin arrived. "You wanted to see me?"

"You sound tired."

"Aren't we all?"

"Serov has just been given an order from Chuikov. The train station is to be held. We leave now."

"Frigging hell."

"That's not the good part. Pick some men and go ahead of the company. I don't want to be walking into an ambush."

He could sense Zorkin's apprehension. "Do not

worry, Ilya, the rest of the company will be right behind you."

"Yes, sir."

Zorkin moved out through the ruins five minutes later with Anatoly leading the rest of his men behind them. Anatoly hadn't been surprised when Zorkin had chosen Sobol to go with him. After all, the sergeant was the best man in the battalion.

———

THE DARKNESS all around them was suddenly lit with tracer fire. The Russian soldiers under Anatoly's command hid amongst the rubble while the Germans kept up the fire from the large concrete train terminal to their front.

"So much for getting here first," Anatoly growled to Zorkin. "Push left. No one fires. I don't want the Nazis to know what we're up to. We'll have a base of fire here. Deploy the two machine guns and a squad to help them out. Once we're in position, we'll attack from the flank. I'll leave Nicolai here with the machine guns."

"I'll get the men ready to move."

Anatoly found Sobol and informed him of the plan. "I need you to stay with the machine guns. The more fire they can put out will make it likely that the plan will succeed."

"I'll have the men melt the barrels, sir."

"Good man."

The plan worked perfectly. Once in position the machine guns opened fire while Anatoly and Zorkin led the attack on the flank. After ten minutes of heavy weapons fire, grenade blasts, and tracers streaking through the air, the enemy abandoned the train station.

Anatoly sent word to Serov that the station was now in Russian hands and that casualties had been light.

Now all Anatoly had to do was dig in and wait for the inevitable counterattack.

———

Stalingrad, 17th September 1942

Anatoly's left arm hurt, and dried blood was stuck to the right side of his face along with the dirt and grime from what was left of the station. They'd been there for the best part of three days and repelled countless attacks from the Germans.

Then there was the bombing. The aerial raids had reduced the train station to a mound of rubble and twisted steel. Buried beneath it were most of Anatoly's men, including Zorkin who had been interred, along with three of his men, beneath one of the walls that had come down.

Now those who were left, were surrounded on nearly every side.

"Nicolai," Anatoly called out.

"Over here," the sergeant called out from behind a mass of twisted steel.

Anatoly acknowledged his presence and started to leapfrog from cover to cover until he reached his sergeant. Sobol said, "You should have let me come to you."

"It doesn't matter. I'm here now."

"How is your arm?"

"It hurts but it'll be fine," Anatoly allowed. Then he said, "We need to move position across the street to the building there."

"Are you, sure, sir? We've got good cover here."

"Over there offers us a better field of fire for the cross street which leads down to the Volga."

"Yes, sir."

After a moment of silence, Anatoly said, "How many?"

Sobol gave him a questioning look. "You already know how many, sir."

He nodded. "I thought for a moment I might have been dreaming when you originally told me."

"We're all tired, sir. But no, you weren't dreaming. We're down to about thirty men."

Thirty out of around two hundred who'd come to Stalingrad. A miniscule figure compared to what the city would eventually claim.

"I'll give the order, sir," Sobol said.

————

HAVING FINALLY BEEN FORCED from his headquarters in Tsaritsa Gorge, Chuikov now found himself further north of his previous HQ. His current one was nothing but a trench with tin over the top of it.

When his adjutant entered, he stared at the man with red-rimmed eyes. "This had better be good news, Grisha."

"I'm afraid not, sir."

"Well, out with it then, man."

"The grain elevator has fallen to the enemy, sir."

A guttural growl came from Chuikov's throat. "There is more. There always is."

"The company at the train station has been cut off and the 13th Guards has been decimated. Without reinforcements they cannot hold. The punishment battalion has also been hit hard. Their commanding officer was killed this morning."

"Who is in command now?"

"A captain. Anatoly Kozlov. But I doubt he knows it; his company was the one that led the defense of the station. He's probably dead too. They call them Anatoly's Bastards."

Chuikov nodded thoughtfully. Even if they were cowards, thieves, and murderers, the punishment battalion was the only one of his units who actually showed some spine on the front line. "Send a messenger to Kozlov. If he's alive have him told he's now in command of the battalion. Tell him his country needs him."

"Yes, sir."

———

Stalingrad, 21st September 1942

"Sir, we have tanks!"

Shit a frigging brick, didn't it ever stop? Anatoly looked at the corporal who was in command of one of the decimated companies. "Pull back into the rubble. The tanks can't get in there. Do it now."

"Sir."

"Nicolai?"

"Here, sir," Sobol answered and came over to Anatoly.

"There are tanks coming in. Pull everyone back into the rubble. Do it now."

"First bombers, now tanks. Fantastic."

"Now, Sergeant."

"Yes, Comrade."

He hurried away, leaping through the detritus of the demolished buildings. Anatoly turned and looked through the thin veil of smoke to the only route the tanks could take to reach them.

The battalion had been regrouped for the past couple of days. Since then, they had taken even more of a pounding. He wasn't sad that Serov was gone. The battalion was better off without him. He'd never asked for command, however, here he was. And here they were. Out of food and water and almost out of ammunition.

What was left of the battalion did as they were ordered. They pulled back into the rubble of the destroyed buildings, and all the tanks could do was fire into it. Even then it proved to be quite effective.

One of the platoon sergeants found Anatoly deep in the rubble. "Sir, the Germans are starting to close in behind us. If we don't move now, we're going to be trapped."

Anatoly could see in his mind what that would mean. "Alright. Find me sergeant Sobol and then start pulling your men out. Do you see that building back there?"

He pointed to the damaged building further along the street.

"Yes, sir."

"Take them there. The rest of us will follow you."

"Yes, Comrade."

The sergeant left just as another shell from a Panzer IV came in. Debris shot up into the air before raining down over the defenders. Sobol appeared at Anatoly's side and the battalion commander said, "We're moving."

For the next few hours, the Russian defenders were forced to move from building to building; but only after the attacking Germans set fire to them.

Eventually Anatoly found a position he could defend. Then, with less than fifty men from the whole battalion, they dug in and waited for the onslaught to come.

———

Stalingrad, 25th September 1942

Eva picked the maggot out of her bowl and flicked it away before continuing to eat. The ground beneath where she sat trembled from the artillery fire landing five decimated blocks to the north. Beside her, Lagutov cleaned his weapon as he leaned against the sandbag wall. Suddenly a stray round shook them to their core and dirt and dust covered them from the makeshift roof.

Eva picked some of it out of her food as she'd done with the maggot and continued to eat once more.

"Shitting bastards," Lagutov growled and started to blow dirt from his weapon.

One of the younger men in the shelter cringed under the sound of the explosion. He'd been there one day, and his reaction was the same each time. Eva said to him, "You need to relax. You won't hear the one that kills you."

The young man looked horrified and Lagutov smirked at her words of wisdom. "She's right, you know."

"Great. That makes me feel even better."

"You need to beat your meat and get rid of the tension," Eva said matter-of-factly.

The young man gave her a look of confusion. She gave a heavy sigh. "Must I spell it out. Masturbation. Just pleasure yourself and the tension will be gone."

"And this works?" the young man asked skeptically.

"Yes, I do it all the time."

"Really?"

Eva nodded.

He looked around himself at the others in the shelter who were now taking an interest in the turn the conversation had taken. "I—I don't think I could do something like that. With all these people in here."

With a grunt Eva came to her feet and changed her position. She sat beside the young man and asked, "What's your name?"

"Maksim."

There was a time that the young man's closeness would have given Eva cause for anxiety but now, after what she'd witnessed in her short time in Stalingrad, it had given way to a coldness and an acceptance that she was already dead. The doctor had wasted his time.

"I can help if you wish, Maksim."

"Y—you can?"

She smiled at him. "Sure."

Her hand touched his thigh and he lurched. Lagutov had also noticed the change in Eva recently and said, "Leave him alone, Eva. He's not ready for you yet."

"Are you, Sergeant Lagutov?"

He shook his head and went back to cleaning his weapon.

Eva turned her attention back to Maksim. Her hand traveled up his thigh to his crotch. She started to massage him and felt him respond. Maksim struggled to swallow, and Eva leaned in close to whisper in his ear.

Suddenly another shell landed close to the shelter with a shattering sound. With a choked yelp, Maksim launched himself to his feet and ran out of the shelter. Everyone within burst out in laughter, except for Lagutov.

Another shell explosion followed hot on the heels of the previous one and again the shelter was rocked. Ignoring it they all went about their business. Not long after that, Maksim appeared at the entrance, a stunned expression on his face. Few eyes stared at him to start with but then someone realized what was wrong with him.

A murmur brought Eva's attention to the young man she not long before had teased. His arm was missing above the elbow. "Oh shit."

They stabilized Maksim and got him out of there. For a while Lagutov didn't speak to her and Eva knew he blamed her for what happened. "I'm sorry," she said to the sergeant.

"Tell the kid that, not me," he replied abruptly.

Eva withdrew into herself as she contemplated Lagutov's harsh words. For the next hour she sat in silence before an officer entered the dugout. He looked around the interior and said, "I was told there was a sniper in here."

Eva stared at him. "I'm a sniper."

He gave her a doubtful look. "Are you sure, girl?"

"She is what she says," Lagutov interjected. "Probably better than most."

The captain nodded. "All right, if you say so. I have a job for you."

Eva waited quietly to hear.

"The Germans have set up a command post over near the Red October Plant. One of the officers is a general. Kill him."

With a nod, Eva said, "I can do that."

"Good."

———

AT THE SAME time that Eva and Lagutov were receiving their orders to assassinate a German general, seven men emerged from the ruins around Red Square. Seven men; all that remained of the 360th Punishment Battalion.

Anatoly, Sobol, a big man called Bear, and four others. The rest lay dead in the rubble of the city.

They were confronted by a colonel from the 451st Rifle Division who thought them to be deserters. "Who are you?" he asked them.

"Captain Anatoly Kozlov, commanding officer of the 360th Punishment Battalion. Appointed by Comrade Chuikov himself."

The officer looked at him skeptically. "Really? Where is your battalion, Captain?"

"You're looking at them, sir. All seven of us."

"Just seven?"

"Yes, sir."

"Out of how many?"

"Six-hundred. Give or take a few."

"I see."

Anatoly didn't think he did see. Anatoly didn't see. He didn't even know who to report to.

———

CHUIKOV STUDIED the two bedraggled men in front of him. "You are all that's left?"

"Yes, sir," Anatoly replied. "There are seven of us. We did the best that we could, sir."

The general nodded stoically. "So I heard. The question is now, what to do with you?"

"Yes, sir."

"Why were you with the punishment battalion, Captain?"

Anatoly told him.

"Yes, well...I'm promoting you to major."

Anatoly was stunned. "But, sir—"

"I'll have no argument. Tonight, you will cross the Volga and find men to rebuild the battalion. Once you have enough, you will cross back and report to me for further orders. Is that understood?"

"Yes, Comrade. But what men shall I get?"

"Trust me, Major, there are plenty of men on the other side of the river for you to choose from. I will have an order written immediately. Wait outside. Dismissed."

The two men left the office and waited. Sobol couldn't help but notice the stunned expression on Anatoly's face. "Quite something, huh?"

"Quite."

"Congratulations, Major."

Anatoly's head snapped around. "Are you laughing, Sergeant?"

"Not me, sir," Sobol smirked.

"The hell you're not. You think it's funny, then laugh at this—Captain."

"What?"

"Laugh about that, Nicolai."

Five minutes later, they were called back to see Chuikov. He passed Anatoly the written orders and said, "This will help you. Watch out for the political officers. They like to shoot people they think are deserters."

"Yes, sir."

"Good luck, Major."

"Thank you, sir."

CHAPTER FIFTEEN

Stalingrad, 25th/26th September 1942

Eva and Lagutov crawled through the open drain which crossed the street just south of the Red October plant. It was night and flares constantly illuminated the new Stalingrad landscape. The flickering light made it appear to be an image from another world.

A slight breeze carried dust and the stench of the dead. Summer was cruel on bodies, both the living and not.

The pair froze in the middle of no man's land as another flare lit the sky. A flurry of movement to their right made Eva hold her breath. A handful of German soldiers trying to take up a new position were caught out by the sudden illumination.

The rattle of a PM1910, Maxima machine gun opened fire and bullets cut through the air. The five Wehrmacht soldiers in the open were cut down.

Eva tried to press herself lower into the drain while

the enemy soldiers died. Behind her, Lagutov touched her leg, reassuringly.

The flare dimmed and went out, darkness enveloping them once more. Eva started forward again with the sergeant behind her. Once across the street they came out of the drain and moved into the rubble of a destroyed building.

For the next three hours, the pair were constantly stopping and starting as they continued to traverse the detritus of no man's land. Then four hours before daylight, Lagutov pointed at a skeletal structure reaching up from the moonscape. "There," he whispered. "We go there."

It took them a further hour to reach it. But once there, they found a perfect hide amongst the steel and rubble. Then all they had to do was wait.

———

THE BOAT ROCKED as the current tried to drag it down stream. Flares reached up into the sky over the city followed by the sound of sporadic gunfire. The deep, throaty booms of explosions rocked the night, and somewhere on the other side of Stalingrad the orange glow of a fire could be seen.

The traffic on the river was constant. Back and forth. Wounded out, reinforcements and supplies in.

The captain of the small ferry was kept busy dodging and weaving. At one point, Anatoly heard him mutter a curse then he saw the small motorboat loom out of the darkness. The captain adjusted his course and then muttered some more profanities.

And if that wasn't enough, the Germans chose that time to start shelling.

It sounded like God was having a tantrum and throwing freight trains at the insignificant figures on the river. Screams of incoming shells were followed by explosions and eruptions of dark water.

One landed close to Anatoly's ride, showering everyone in it with water.

Eventually the brief bombardment ceased, allowing them to make the far bank. Once out of the boat, they were accosted by an NKVD officer. "Deserters?"

"No, we're here under orders from Comrade Chuikov."

"Do you have them?"

"I do, but there's no way you'll be able to read them in this light."

"Why are you here?"

"Looking for men to rebuild the punishment battalion? The general said I would find them over here."

"You will. A mile or so out on the steppe. There is a holding ground for all political prisoners, deserters, and murderers. Make it fast, they're being shot come daybreak."

Anatoly and Sobol found them an hour later. There were perhaps six hundred in all. Officers ranging from colonels to lieutenants. Then there were the NCOs and enlisted men. When Anatoly and Sodol were led to them, the new battalion commander shouted, "I want four good officers."

Ten stepped forward.

The sun was starting to rise in the east and he could see their faces. Anatoly studied them for a moment. He pointed at one man, a tall, proud-looking candidate who'd, like the rest, had been stripped of his insignia. "Name and rank?"

"Mirsky, Major, Four-Hundred and First Rifle Division, commander of the Third Regiment."

Anatoly nodded. The 401st had been wiped out near the Barrikady Gun Factory the day before Anatoly had been ordered to the station. "You're now a company commander, Captain Mirsky. That's if you don't want to be shot this morning."

"What, regiment?"

"No regiment. You'll be part of the Three-Sixtieth Punishment Battalion. All I can promise is a quick death and a fighting chance to live."

The former major nodded. "I'll take it."

Anatoly picked out three more men and got them to step forward. "Will you join us?"

They all nodded.

"Good. You're all now company commanders. Find yourself some men and report back here when you're finished. You've got one hour."

By the time they were finished there was not one man left to be shot that morning. The company commanders had them lined up as though on parade when Anatoly and Sobol joined them again.

"My name is Major Anatoly Kuzlov. I will be your commanding officer. The man beside me is Captain Nicolai Sobol. He answers only to me. If you are given orders by this man, you will obey them. If you do not, or you try to desert, I will shoot you myself. Do you understand?"

"Yes, sir!"

The reply was clear and precise.

"Sir?" Mirsky stepped forward.

"What is it?"

"We need weapons."

"You shall have them. Get ready to move out."

———

THE SUN HAD BEEN UP for over an hour and Eva had lain statue-still since several hours before daybreak. Despite the discomfort of a full bladder, she'd remained still, pissing herself in situ, the strong smell of urine now filtering into her nostrils.

Beside her, camouflaged in the debris, Lagutov regulated his breathing. "I can see movement," he whispered. "To the left of the destroyed elevator."

Eva moved her rifle to sweep left with her sights. She scanned the mass of twisted metal until taking in what the sergeant did. A German soldier. He looked to be doing something, then Eva recognized what it was. He was pissing.

She watched him until he finished then he disappeared inside what looked to be a hastily constructed shelter. "That is it. The headquarters."

Somewhere close came the sound of artillery fire. The deep crump of the impacting rounds made it impossible to discern whether it was theirs or the enemy's. It grew closer and closer until a round landed close in no man's land not far from where they'd set up their hide.

A second and then a third round followed quickly and before they knew it, Eva and Lagutov had a full-scale artillery barrage raining down around them.

They hugged the dirt beneath their cover and prayed that they would be lucky. A feeling of terror and helplessness almost overwhelmed Eva who tensed to flee. A reassuring hand in the middle of her back from the sergeant beside her helped keep her in situ.

When the artillery stopped, the ground ceased to tremble beneath them. "Are you alright?" Lagutov asked.

"That—that was bad," Eva replied hoarsely. "If not for your hand, I would have run."

"I almost did," he informed her.

She turned her head to look at him and saw the sweat on his brow. She reached out and affectionately wiped some of it away as a mother would a child. "It's a good thing we didn't, wasn't it?"

He nodded. "A good thing."

Eva smiled. "I think I pissed myself again."

Lagutov snorted. "I don't know about pissing but I shit myself."

They chuckled silently and then settled down to wait once more. The sound of small arms fire playing like a distant orchestra.

Another hour had passed before Eva said, "I have something."

Lagutov brought up his own rifle, having traded the PPD for a cloth covered, scoped Mosin-Nagant. The same as Eva's. He peered through the scope and saw the officer. "This must be the target we were told about. Take the shot."

Eva pulled the butt of the rifle into her shoulder and took a deep breath. The crosshairs of the rifle settled onto the German officer, and she let out a long slow breath before squeezing the trigger.

The rifle slammed back into her shoulder, sending the missile streaking across the open ground and slamming into the officer's head, knocking his peaked cap from his head.

Eva worked the bolt and waited, looking through her scope. More Germans appeared, the shot bringing them running. Two were officers while a third and fourth were enlisted men. She relaxed her body as she sighted on the next officer. Before she could fire, Lagutov touched her arm. "No, Eva. You have your kill. All you will do now is give our position away."

"But—"

His stare grew hard. "No. We go."

She pouted at him with her dirty face and then watched as he turned and slithered from their hide. Then with one last glance towards the German dugout, she started to follow him.

Stalingrad, 26th September 1942

Chuikov slammed the palm of his hand down on the map and swore vehemently. The officers standing before him in their bedraggled uniforms were half expecting one of them to be shot for delivering the bad news. But after several moments, the general started to calm down and assess the situation.

"We've lost the main ferry crossing?"

"Yes, Comrade."

"That means the only part of Stalingrad that we hold is the factory district."

"Yes, Comrade. But all is not lost. The tugs are pulling the barges across the Volga to the factory district as we speak."

"How many reserves do we have on the east bank waiting to come across?" Chuikov asked.

"Maybe ten-thousand with more coming every day."

"Then get them across. I don't care how you do it, just do it. We need to shore up our position before the Nazis overwhelm our forces."

"We will do it immediately, Comrade General."

"Dismissed."

———

The Don River, 26th September 1942

General Friedrich Paulus looked at the information before him and was shocked by it. It had taken the 6th Army six weeks to advance from the Don River to where they were now on the banks of the Volga. Six long, bloody weeks. An advance which had cost the lives of almost 8,000 men. More troubling was the figure of the thirty thousand wounded. Ten percent of the 6th Army had been lost and the worst was yet to come.

Men and ammunition were low which would be a problem for the major battle to come, the one in which he knew that were they to take Stalingrad, the factory district was a must.

Pain ripped through his guts. His dysentery was getting worse. Just like it was in his men at the front.

Paulus' adjutant knocked and entered. "What is it?" Paulus asked.

"You sent for me, sir."

The general nodded. "Yes, sorry. I need to send a cable to Army Group B."

"Yes sir."

"Tell them I need reinforcements most immediate. If I don't get them, we'll still be bogged down in this city when winter arrives."

"In those words, Herr General?"

"Yes."

"I will see to it."

The adjutant left and Paulus sat down in a chair. He let out a long sigh. He knew what the answer would be and for the first time felt as though he was standing on the edge of a cliff staring into the abyss. An operation that began so strongly was now bogged down in the ruins of Stalingrad. "So close," he muttered. "So damned close."

Stalingrad, 26th September 1942

Meunch and his men had gained no further ground than they'd reached on the 14th. He'd sent countless forays forward to reach the Volga, and while other battalions had succeeded, his had still fallen short. Now only fifty men remained from his whole battalion, and below them in the basement of the building they'd forted up in, were Russian soldiers who'd broken in through smashed windows.

Outside, where the surrounding buildings once stood were mounds of steel and rubble, craters, and blackened ruins from fires which had burned out. But most of all there were bodies. Bloated. Fly-blown corpses which were now putrid from being under the Stalingrad sun for so long.

"I don't think I'll ever get used to that smell," Glass said from beside his commanding officer.

"Me either," Meunch replied. "How are we off for ammunition?"

"It won't be long, Hauptmann, and we'll be throwing bricks at the Ivans if we aren't relieved."

"I take your point."

"Sir, shouldn't we just pull out? Leave our friends below to have the place." Glass was about to continue when shouting erupted from the stairwell leading to the basement.

An explosion rocked the ruins of the building, quickly followed by the rattle of gunfire. More shouts and another explosion. This time it was deeper indicating that the grenade had gone off on the floor below.

Silence followed then Glass returned. "We need to do something about those bastards in the basement."

"How many grenades do we have left?" Meunch asked.

"Five. Six, maybe."

"Get some men together. We'll get rid of them once and for all."

"Jawohl, Herr Hauptman."

Glass gathered six men together. All were armed with MP40s. He distributed the remaining grenades amongst them and said, "We toss three grenades down there and then we go down after them. If we need to do more, we will."

Meunch looked on as Glass took over the assault. "Feldwebel?" he said.

Glass turned to Meunch. "Hauptmann?"

"The last I looked I was in command of the battalion, yes?"

"Sir."

"Then I will lead the assault."

"No, Hauptmann."

"What do you mean, no?"

"You are our commander. You do not need to be taking any unacceptable risks. That's what we are here for. Now, if I have your permission, I will lead the attack."

"All right, Felix. The assault is yours."

Glass straightened and saluted. Meunch returned it. "I'll see you when you're done, Feldwebel Glass."

"For us who are about to die, we—"

"Piss off, Felix."

Glass smiled. "Good luck, sir."

Meunch stood back and watched them start. They threw down three grenades and with the cessation of the explosions, the soldiers followed Glass down the stairs. Shouts and gunfire commenced almost immediately. Another explosion and the battalion commander took a hesitant step forward before stopping himself.

More gunfire, then silence.

Meunch waited patiently for his men to return. When they did, there were only three. Glass led them out.

"Report, Felix."

"The issue has been fixed, Hauptmann. I'm sorry to report, we have sustained many casualties."

"Thank you, Feldwebel. I'm glad to see that you are all right."

"I guess now we go back to doing what we were before," Glass said. "We wait."

Meunch nodded. "That's right. We wait."

Moscow, 28th September 1942

Two men were with Stalin that day as they discussed the plans for an operation called Uranus. Georgy Zhukov and Alexander Vasilevsky. Stalin grunted. "You'd better tell me what I'm looking at, gentlemen."

"First, Comrade, if I might suggest a change?" Zhukov said before starting.

"What is it?"

"The Don Front, Comrade. I'd like to put Konstantin Rokossovsky in overall command."

Stalin stared at his deputy. He knew the name. The man had been imprisoned with all the other traitors when he was ridding the Motherland of them. However, it had been judged that the man was innocent and let go. "Good officer. Go with it."

"Thank you, sir. Now, what we're suggesting is that with Nikolai Vatutin in command of the Southwestern Front to the north of Stalingrad and Andrei Yeryomenko in command of the Stalingrad Front to the south of the city, we think that if Rokossovsky could attack Stalingrad from his Don Front it would force Paulus to drag in more of his reserves from the other two fronts. Then Vatutin and Yeryomenko could attack from the weakened northern and southern fronts. If they can break through, then they can encircle the whole of the Sixth Army in Stalingrad and they will be trapped."

Stalin liked what he was hearing. "How many men will you need?"

Vasilevsky cleared his throat. "Georgy and I have

talked about it at length, Comrade, and we estimate that we can find enough soldiers to bring the strength for the attack to one million."

Stalin's eyes widened in astonishment. "One million? You can find one million to reinforce the depleted armies? Where are these soldiers? How come I have never heard of them?"

Zhukov said, "It will be tricky, but it can be done, Comrade."

"How long will it take?"

"We think it can happen by November."

Stalin was skeptical. "November? That is still over a month away. Stalingrad could fall by then."

"I will bolster the defenses at Stalingrad, sir," Zhukov told his premier.

"Well then, Georgy, if I'm going to approve this plan of yours, you'd better go back to Stalingrad and see that the damned city holds."

"Don't worry, sir, Stalingrad will not fall."

———

Stalingrad, 29th September 1942

"With all of the fanfare around him you would think he was bigger," Eva said insolently to the dirty-faced young man before her.

"And I thought you would be older," Vasily Zaitsev replied.

Zaitsev had arrived in Stalingrad on the 20th of September and had already made a name for himself as a sniper.

"They make you out to be some kind of hero," Eva shot back at him. "How many men have you killed?"

"Forty-five."

"Come and see me when you get to sixty," Eva said dismissively.

Zaitsev smiled at her. "I like you. Why don't you come with me today and we'll work together?"

Eva glanced at Lagutov. He shrugged. "Sure, why not? I'm looking to have a rest today anyway."

She turned to Zaitsev. "Where are you going?"

"The Barrikady Gun Factory."

"Fine. I will come with you, Vasily Zaitsev. Then we'll see how good you really are."

———

THE PROGRESS WAS slow and tedious as they made their way to the gun factory. Through sewer pipes, piles of debris and twisted metal, past the swollen, rat-infested corpses of the dead. Past what might possibly be one of the only dogs left in the destroyed city, one which had evaded capture and being eaten, and now feasted on one of those corpses, until they reached a good position for a hide in the middle of no man's land.

A large, partially standing building, of which they could use the one remaining staircase to climb to the second floor and look over the remains of the Barrikady Gun Factory, one side and the remains of the workers' settlement on the other.

"How many times have you been here?" Eva asked.

"Not for a few days."

She moved to a gaping hole and looked out across the

devastation of the workers' settlement. Eva raised her fabric wrapped rifle and swept the area. It all looked quiet, but she knew the Nazi soldiers were out there somewhere.

"Why are we here, Vasily?" she asked.

"There is only one reason. To kill Germans."

He stared at her then continued. "Look out there, towards the Panzer."

Eva peered around the corner of the pile of charred bricks where she stood and took in the tank. It was a Panzer IV, or what remained of it: a blackened, twisted hulk. "I see it."

"There is a wire near it."

Eva brought up her rifle and stared through the telescopic sights. She found it no problem. "I see it."

"Shoot it."

"The wire?"

"Yes, the wire."

"I have better things to waste ammunition on than a pissing bit of wire," Eva growled.

"Just do it," Vasili instructed. "Unless you can't." The challenge had been set and it was taken up immediately.

Eva took a couple of heartbeats to sight on the wire then squeezed the trigger. The rifle recoiled as it sent the 7.62 round streaking across the two-hundred yards to the wire's location.

The wire parted under the impact of the bullet and Eva turned to give Vasily a self-satisfied look before saying, "There. Now we should move."

"Not yet," Zaitsev replied. "Let's see what happens."

They didn't have to wait long. An hour later a German appeared as he started to lay a new cable. Eva said, "Is it him you wait for?"

"Yes."

"Then I will kill him."

"No, wait," Zaitsev snapped.

"What for?"

He moved over beside her and raised his rifle. He started to sweep the bleak landscape as she watched him. "What are you looking for?" Eva asked.

"Shh."

Anger flared in her eyes, but she remained quiet, watching him. It wasn't long before he stopped. "Beside the burned-out halftrack."

Eva frowned and put her rifle back up to her shoulder. She looked through her scope and it took a moment to see it. She ducked back, gasping.

Zaitsev looked at her. "Don't worry. He won't fire and give away his position until we do."

"A Nazi sniper. He knows we're here."

"Yes, he knows we're here, but he doesn't know where we are. The soldier is bait. We shoot, then he shoots. We kill the soldier, then he kills one of us."

"They do that?"

"Yes. I found out the hard way," Zaitsev said and poked his finger through a hole in his tunic.

The penny dropped. Eva said in an accusatory tone, "You knew this would happen and that is why you asked me to come along."

He shrugged.

"Frigging asshole," she spat.

"Think of it as me saving your life. Now you know to look for it."

"Shit."

"Do you want the sniper or the wire man?" Zaitsev asked.

"Screw you," she shot back at him and settled her sights on the scope where the German sniper was hidden.

Zaitsev nodded. "I'll take the wire man."

He settled his sights on the target and said, "Three, two, one, now."

Both rifles rocked the ruins. The wireman's helmet flew from his head as the bullet from Zaitsev's weapon punched through it. Eva's round was fired with great accuracy, and she saw the Nazi's rifle lurch and slide forward. She drew back and leaned against the wall. "Happy now?"

"Not until we get out of—"

Zaitsev's words were cut off as the first round from an artillery shell came in. It was quickly followed by another, and another.

The world suddenly erupted around them. Bricks, steel, metal splinters from the artillery rounds. The air seemed to be filled with it all. Eva felt the world tremble as the incoming fire increased.

"We have to get out of here!" Eva shouted.

"No, stay where you are."

"No."

"Damn it. Don't—"

Eva didn't wait for him to finish. Another shell landed closer than the last and she was up and moving. "Damn it," Zaitsev growled and sprang to his feet.

He followed Eva to the ground level and was closing the gap when a shell landed close. The explosion knocked him from his feet, blacking him out for several moments. Metal rain kept falling and there was nothing the helpless sniper could do except wait for it to stop.

Five minutes later, it did just that.

Zaitsev climbed to his feet and glanced around. The air was thick with dust and he peered through it looking for Eva but couldn't see her. He took a few steps in the direction he'd last seen her running. Then he heard the low groan.

With hurried steps, Zaitsev walked toward the source of the noise. He found Eva laying under a wall of debris. He leaned over her.

"Eva?" he said as he started moving rubble. Then he gasped as he saw the wound in her side and the sliver of metal sticking out of it. "Hang on, I'll get you back."

Her eyes fluttered open. "Leave me."

"No," he said with a shake of his head. "Who else will I annoy if you're not around? Besides, I think that big sergeant of yours would strangle me if I came back without you."

Eva gave him a weak smile. "Maybe feed you your balls."

"And I'm not that hungry," he replied. Then, "Hang on, this is going to hurt."

Zaitsev put his rifle over his shoulder and bent down to pick Eva up.

"No, no. Leave me, Vasili."

Shaking his head, he said, "I'm sorry."

He straightened and Eva screamed.

CHAPTER SIXTEEN

North of Stalingrad, 8th October 1942

KATYA CHECKED TO SEE THAT HER FLIGHT WAS STILL IN formation. "Kesha, close up."

"Yes, Comrade Kozlova."

She watched the Yak slide back into position. "What do you ladies think this is? Some of you are going into battle for the first time. Keep an eye on each other."

For Katya this was the hardest part of being in command. It was a given that some of her flight wouldn't be coming back. That was war. The German pilots were far more experienced than and the only way to get that experience was to fight and survive.

Two flights of the 586th had been transferred to the Stalingrad sector to bolster the hard-hit air groups already there.

The day was clear, and already the Germans had sent two bombing raids over the devastated city. To the south, Katya could see the plumes of smoke rising above the city. She'd heard stories about what was happening there. Men and women were being slaughtered in their thousands. The fighters from the glorious Red Army were still hanging on by their fingernails, and columns of reinforcements were coming in across the Volga every day.

Two days ago, she had taken her flight over the city for a look. What she saw had been horrifying and she wondered how anyone could survive what was happening there.

"Katya, it looks like we are too late," Elena said over the radio.

Looking ahead, Katya could see the flak above Stalingrad. Another raid was in progress. "Everyone, follow me, we'll hit them on the way out. Keep an eye out for fighters."

Katya turned southwest and pushed the throttle of her Yak further forward. She felt the vibration sing through the airframe as the power picked up.

And now, she could see the Ju 88s as they were turning for their home leg. One of them was on fire and sinking towards the ground. Another was trailing smoke and falling behind the main flight.

"Bronya and Elena, take the straggler then join us. The rest of you, follow me."

Before they reached the main flight the bombers were already starting to break up. Some dove low while others tried to climb. Katya picked out a Ju 88 and flew her machine towards it. When within range, she pressed the firing button. Rounds spewed forth and she saw them hit.

A gunner from the bomber opened fire at her and she felt the Yak shudder under a couple of strikes. Katya let the bomber have another burst and put her plane into a shallow dive so that it flew under her target.

Behind her another Yak followed. This one was flown by a new pilot. Kesha Ivanova. She heard her exclaim over the radio. "I've got it. I've got it."

"Shut up and keep an eye out for fighters," Katya snapped.

She looked up through her canopy and saw a second Ju 88. Katya pulled back on the yoke and pointed her aircraft at it. Closed within a few hundred yards and opened fire.

———

EDMUND WAGNER FELT the bullets tear through his aircraft and knew vital damage had been done to the machine. Once again, they'd been screwed over by the staff who had sent them to Stalingrad without an escort. It was pure luck that the first two raids of the day had managed to get through without one; a third was pushing it, and there was no guarantee they wouldn't encounter trouble. Now they were under heavy attack by Yak fighters and going to pay a heavy price for command's ineptitude.

"All station call in," he growled as he fought the new idiosyncratic nuance the Junkers had just developed.

No one answered and Wagner new instantly the plane's communications were out. One of his crew appeared behind him. "The intercom is out."

"I know."

"That last pass hit us hard."

"I know."

"It feels like—"

"I know, damn it. Get back to your station."

Another Yak howled past the stricken bomber and inflicted more damage upon the Ju 88. The port engine started to smoke, and Wagner killed it. Then he looked at the starboard one and saw the huge hole in it. "Shit."

He shouted at the top of his voice to get some attention. The same crewman he'd snapped at before appeared again. "Get everyone ready, we're going down."

The plane sank lower and lower until skimming just above the level ground.

"Damn I hate crashing," Wagner muttered. "It hurts too much."

Then the plane hit.

As luck and good flying would have it, every man aboard survived the crash. Even if they were a little worse for wear. Scrambling from the wreckage, they lumbered from the plane just as it exploded.

————

KATYA SAW the enemy aircrew get out of the plane before she rolled the Yak to port and put it into a climb. Above her the other pilots from her flight were still engaged with the bombers. Their excited voices could be heard over the radio.

"I'm hit! I can't control my plane."

The voice was panicked and straight away Katya could tell it was one of the new pilots. She looked around and saw the smoking Yak starting to go down. "Get out. Do you hear me? Get out."

A few moments and then, "I can't, the canopy is jammed."

"Use your pistol. Shoot it."

"It didn't work. I'm stuck. Help me. Someone, help me."

With the pleas for help ringing in her ears, Katya watched as the stricken Yak plummeted into the ground below with an enormous explosion.

"Damn it," she muttered and slammed her head backward in anger.

Katya looked around for another target to take her frustration out on and saw one in the distance. Then before she could go after it, Elena came over the radio, "I'm low on fuel, Katya."

The curtain of red lifted when Katya looked at her own fuel and saw the same. She said into the radio, "I am too. We'll return to base. Everyone, form up."

———

Leningrad, Mid-October 1942

Anya knew they had to be fast. She was all but certain that Galina had her Vixens watching the stashes where the stolen food supplies were stored. But getting starving, emaciated people to move at any more than a shuffle was hard. "Quickly now," she urged the two men with her. "We have to be quick."

They stumbled through the partially destroyed building towards the rear where she knew there to be a trapdoor in the floor. Beneath that trapdoor were bags of non-perishable food which could be taken back to the commune as they called it.

The commune was a group of homeless citizens who lived and worked together to help each other out.

They scavenged the city for things they needed to survive. Unlike the Vixens, they only took what wasn't already claimed.

Except when they raided the Vixen's stash. They used it to distribute amongst those who needed it. It was no more than they deserved.

The building had once been a theatre and they had to traverse the aisles and rows of seats to reach the rear. They made it to the stage area and climbed up to go backstage to the dressing rooms.

"So, this is who is stealing my property!" The voice came from the back rows of the theatre.

Anya froze and then turned. The two men with her did the same. She could see Galina with her two hench-women standing either side. All three were armed.

"Nothing to say, bitch?" Galina growled. "Not going to plead for your life?"

"People are starving, and you have all of this food," Anya called back.

"It's mine. Let them get their own."

"How can you be so heartless?" Anya demanded.

"It's called surviving," Galina shot back at her.

"It's called cruel."

The woman shrugged. "It doesn't matter though, does it. You won't see the end of the war."

The two women either side of Galina raised their weapons and opened fire. Bullets ripped across the void between the two groups and found flesh.

The man to Anya's right cried out and collapsed to the stage. She started running to the left but the wood from the stage seemed to explode in front of her as the bullets from the two PPD submachine guns smashed into it.

Anya cried out and changed direction towards the rear of the stage. Behind her the second man she'd brought to help cried out and she heard the faint thud of him falling.

More bullets chased Anya as she made the doorway from the stage and passed through it. Bullets chewed splinters from the walls either side, but she managed to get through unharmed.

Anya had no idea where she was going. Just run, she told herself. Just run or die.

She negotiated two more doorways and then as she came through another, realization of her error dawned on her. She had crossed from stage left to stage right through backstage and was almost back where she'd started. As she looked out across the damaged wooden front of stage, she could see Galina and her two friends crossing the bullet riddled timbers. One turned and saw her.

"There!" she shouted bringing the PPD around. "The bitch is there."

Anya gave a yelp and threw herself back through the doorway. The gun spat bullets at her, and they passed close overhead while others burned into the walls. She scrambled out of the firing line and then found her feet. Anya began running once more.

This time she took a different doorway, one she assumed would lead her further into the back of the building. Except there was no back of the building. Not anymore. What was once a series of dressing rooms and store rooms had been demolished by a bomb, leaving nothing but a large opening into the rubble beyond.

Staring at it, Anya felt her heart lurch. Somehow,

she had to negotiate it to get away. How on earth was she going to do that?

———

"Do you see her?" Galina snarled. "The bitch. Steal my food. Find her and kill her."

The two women with Galina started to sift through the debris at an almost painful rate. Their commander was already losing patience with them even though they'd only just started. "Come on, you stupid blind cows. How hard can it be?"

"Maybe if you'd help—" one of the women started but was cut off by the withering stare she received.

They continued the search until Galina had finally had enough. "She's not here. Let's go. We will find her eventually. Leningrad may be big, but it is small."

The women disappeared and after what seemed to be a long time, a piece of debris moved to reveal Anya's hiding place. She tentatively emerged into the open. Tears streaked her cheeks. But they were not tears of sadness, they were tears of frustration, anger. In that moment, Anya changed. "You will not get away with this, Galina Sharapova. You will pay."

———

Don River, One-Hundred Miles Northwest of Stalingrad, 17th November 1942

The T-34 came to a grinding halt beside another parked in a line to the left. The heat from its exhaust rose behind it like a thick fog as it mixed with the frigid air on the steppe. The tank fell silent and soon after, the crew and commander disembarked. They removed their helmets to reveal tight-cropped hair beneath. All except the driver who had locks with waves through it.

The commander turned to the driver and said, "Kozlova, make sure that miss is fixed before it gets dark."

Marya Kozlova stiffened and said, "I'll see to it right away, Comrade."

The commander turned away from the rest of his tankers and strode off. Marya looked at the hustle and bustle around the bivouac. Tanks, soldiers, trucks, supplies. Something big was being organized and there was no doubt they were about to be part of it.

"I will give you a hand, Marya," Lenya Klimov the tank's gunner told her. Just tell me what I need to do."

Marya was a good tank mechanic. She had learned quickly while working in a production factory in the Urals after the Nazi invasion. Many of the tank factories had been shut down at that time and all production transferred.

Now, after many tries, she had been accepted as a driver on a T-34 tank crew. At first, the others had treated her with contempt, after all, what right did a woman have being a driver in an all-male tank crew? But so far, she hadn't put a foot wrong, and they were gradually accepting her presence. Almost. Her commander, Gennady Berezin, was holding his judgement. He still has reservations about her capabilities under fire; if she screwed up, they could all die.

Klimov could tell what she was thinking about. "Do not worry, Kozlova, he will come around."

Marya shook her head. "No. Not until after our first battle together. I just hope I don't prove him right."

The bow gunner chuckled. "If you do, don't worry about it. He won't be able to punish you, we will all be dead."

To add emphasis to his joke, the twenty-four-year-old slapped her on the back. Marya rolled her eyes. "Now I am certain that you have two dicks, Lenya."

"What?" he asked confused. "Two dicks?"

She nodded. "Comrade, you cannot get that stupid pulling one."

Arman Grafov, a thin built young man from Moscow laughed loudly at the retort. "She knows you too well, Lenya."

Klimov glared at him. "Shut up, you frigging goat humper."

Marya returned the favor of slapping him on the back. "Do not be sad, Lenya, when you return home, the ladies will love you."

"What about you, Marya?" he shot back at her.

She raised both her hands in mock surrender. "No, you are way too much man for me."

His ego seemingly stroked, Lenya said, "Let's look at this tank."

"While you do that, I'll see if I can find out what is happening?" Grafov the loader said. "It is too cold to be standing around doing nothing."

"Ask Marya to keep you warm."

Suddenly Marya's foot shot out as she kicked Klimov in the shin.

"Ouch! What was that?" he cried out.

"Sorry, Lenya, my leg had a spasm, and it just did it."

He grinned. "I'm sorry, Marya. I shall watch my words next time."

"Yes, right."

They all laughed together which for a moment seemed to keep the awful cold at bay. Then, while Grafov went in search of answers, Marya and Klimov went to work on the tank.

After about twenty minutes, Marya held up a fuel filter. "That is the problem, Lenya. Shit in the filter."

She passed it to him so he could see for himself. Marya had made a point of showing him everything when he helped so he could learn. Who knew, maybe when the war was over, it might help him get work somewhere.

Marya cleaned the fuel filter and replaced it. Once everything was put back together, she climbed in and fired the T-34 up. It roared to life, and she revved it a couple of times before killing the motor. Standing in the driver's hatch, she said, "That's better."

A gust of icy wind came off the steppe and chilled her to the bone. A shiver ran through her. "Damn cold," she muttered.

"Hey! I found out what's going on," Grafov called out as he approached.

They looked up, eyeing him with curious anticipation.

"There's a big attack coming. We're going to hit the Romanians."

"What Romanians?" Klimov asked.

The loader smiled. "The ones in front of us."

CHAPTER SEVENTEEN

Don River, One-Hundred Miles Northwest of Stalingrad, 19th November 1942

JUST BEFORE DAWN, 3,500 SOVIET ARTILLERY PIECES opened fire with the first shots of Operation Uranus. For the Romanian army opposite it was like hell rained down upon them as hundreds died in their trenches.

Not long after the furious barrage stopped, another sound sent shivers down the spines of the Romanians. After a warning of the buildup opposite them was mostly ignored, the distant roar of tank motors rolled across the steppe from the Russian Fifth and Twenty-first tank Armies as they headed towards the devastated front.

A line of T-34s pushed forward through the snow. Already the Romanian line was starting to crack, and the shattered soldiers were running away.

Marya had her tank racing forward. Explosions began erupting along the tank line and then came the sound of bullets ricocheting off the armor. Over the intercom she heard Berezin snap, "Firing!"

The tank rocked violently as the main gun belched flame. Then came the next order. "Reload. High explosive."

Ahead of her, Marya could see great gouts of earth rise from the steppe. Beside her, Klimov opened fire with the bow machine gun. Romanian soldiers started to fall under the constant fusillade.

"Trench ahead," Berezin warned but Marya had already seen it.

She slowed and the tank dipped marginally as it crossed the former Romanian position.

"Traversing right." Pause. "Firing."

Once more the tank rocked.

"Bow gunner. Get that machine gun."

"What bloody machine gun?" Klimov growled. "I can't see shit except for straight ahead."

"Driver, come right to two o'clock."

Marya turned the T-34 to what she figured two o'clock to be.

"Now do you see it?"

The machine gun rattled again. "Got the bastard."

For the next thirty minutes the Soviet tanks forced their way forward. Opening the breach in the Romanian line wider so more could pour through. Some of the Romanian soldiers tried to regroup and stem the oncoming tide but their plight was futile. The Soviet tanks roared onward.

———

Paulus' Headquarters, 19th November 1942

"A message from Hauptmann Behr at Golubinka, Herr General."

Paulus turned to look at his adjutant. "What is it?"

The Soviets have broken through, Herr General. The Romanians are in full retreat."

Paulus' eyes widened. "What? Send Behr an order to hold. He must hold."

"He says to hold, he needs reinforcements, sir."

The general moved to his map and looked down. After careful thought he looked at his adjutant and said, "We can hold them. Have orders made up for the Forty-Eighth Panzer Corps. They are to move north immediately."

"Jawohl, Herr General."

The officer hurried away while Paulus studied his map closely. He traced a finger along a path to two small towns. Both would be key to crossing the Don River. One troubled him more than the other.

Kalach.

———

South of Stalingrad, 20th November 1942

Andrei Yeryomenko was worried. The fog was thick and mixed with the snowfall it made seeing any distance all but impossible. The weather had closed in upon his armies and he'd made the decision to hold off on the order to attack. What worried him more, however, was the fact that he didn't know where the German reserves were or if they'd all been called north.

When his commanders had demanded that he explain why the delayed attack, the answer was simple. "My men cannot see in front of themselves. Tanks have run into each other because the fog is so thick, and my air support cannot fly."

Their response, "You will attack."

He managed to hold them off until around ten in the morning before ordering his artillery to open fire.

Almost immediately the soldiers of the 4th Romanian Army started to flee like their northern brothers. Yeryomenko radioed his commanders as reports came in, that he was having great success. The reports, however, were not as good as he thought. Over one-hundred miles to the north, the lead element of the advancing column of T-34s had run into the 22nd Panzer Division and after a furious fight, the Red tanks were forced to retreat.

Meanwhile other elements of the Romanian divisions took up defensive positions on the steppe and were annihilated.

———

The Northern Front, 20th November 1942

The ground before them appeared flat. But looks can be deceiving, especially with the snow covering the steppe. Scattered around was the detritus of a retreating army. Burned out vehicles, bodies, discarded packs and weapons.

The line of T-34s marched forward in a steady line. Each tank carried with it a handful of soldiers. Others ran along behind them.

Marya swore as her tank coughed and then surged. "Damn it,"

"I thought I told you to fix the problem," Berezin growled over the tank's intercom.

"I did," Marya shot back at him. "The useless pricks gave us fuel with shit in it. It blocks up the filter. The only way to fix it is to drain the tank and clean it out."

"Why didn't you do that?"

"Because I didn't think I needed to."

"And now?"

Marya felt like a child being scolded by her mother.

Suddenly Berezin's radio lit up. "Tanks! I see tanks to the southwest."

The T-34 commander peered out of a port in the tank's cupola. He saw them coming out of the snow. Five, no six Panzers. The looked to be MK IVs. "Damn it. Load with armor-piercing. Get off the road."

Marya turned the tank to the left while furious action began behind her. An AP round was placed into the breech and then the turret started to shift.

WHAM!

The tank behind them was hit and exploded violently.

"They've opened fire!" Berezin snarled into the intercom. "Move, Marya, move!"

The tank lurched forward as she gave it more throttle. Berezin fired and the tank rocked.

"Miss! Reload!" he shouted. "Marya, keep us moving!"

Marya worked the levers with all her skill. The T-34 skidded to the right and then shot forward. A loud clang echoed almost deafeningly through the tank's hull.

They'd been hit but the shell had ricocheted off the armor.

Meanwhile, outside the armored deathtrap, more Soviet tanks were being hit. Three were already burning, black smoke rising like beacons against the stark white of the snow-covered landscape. While another two had the tracks blown off them.

However, the German Panzers hadn't escaped totally unscathed. Three were smoking wrecks and another was disabled.

"Marya, come back left. Drive towards the tree line on the horizon. Klimov, get that damned machine gun working."

The T-34 moved across the steppe toward the distant trees. A stream appeared ahead of them, the banks steep down to the frozen water below. Marya turned the T-34 to the left, the violent motion bringing the wrath of the tank commander upon her.

"What in Stalin's ass are you doing?"

"Creek, Comrade commander."

With a grunt, Berezin used his ports in the cupola to find another target. "Load with armor piercing."

The round went in and the commander started to traverse the turret to the right. It seemed like it almost went one-hundred and eighty degrees before it ceased moving. "Marya, stop."

The tank came to a halt. The crew looked at each other wondering what their commander was up to when he fired. "Well done. Keep moving, Marya. There is some dead ground to the right. Put the tank in there."

Marya worked the levers and saw what Berezin referred to. It was a bowl-shaped depression in the middle of the plain. Upon reaching it, she noticed its depth. When the tank was parked at the bottom, the only part of the T-34 visible was the turret.

"Halt here," the commander said and then started moving his head around the cupola something akin to an owl.

"Load with HE, one round."

Grafov loaded a round into the breech. "Ready."

The turret traversed maybe thirty degrees. "Firing."

With a mighty roar, the 76mm main gun sent its projectile on its journey. Out on the plain, an eruption of earth near some Panzer grenadiers had them collapsing to the ground, blown off their feet by the blast wave, while others fell with metal splinters buried deep in their flesh.

Berezin looked around the ports once more and stopped suddenly, his eyes widening. "Shit. Load with armor piercing, now. Hurry."

Grafov slid an AP round into the breech. "Ready."

Muttering to himself, Berezin started to traverse the turret to cover the quickly closing Panzer IV. "Come on, come on."

For what seemed like an age the turret kept turning until it stopped and Berezin fired.

Too quick. The shell ricocheted off the Panzer IV's turret and screamed off across the steppe.

"No, no. Reverse, Marya, reverse!"

Marya slammed the tank into gear and stomped on the gas. The T-34 shot backward as the Panzer came towards it. The Soviet tank roared backwards out of the depression in a cloud of black smoke from its exhaust.

"Load with armor piercing!"

"Ready!"

"Marya, come left."

She worked the steering levers and the T-34 swung. Berezin moved the turret the rest of the way until his sights came on. Then he fired.

The shell struck the Panzer IV where the turret met the body of the tank. There was a bright flash and the turret lifted clear of its mount and landed beside the now burning hull. Black smoke rose skyward staining the gray sky.

Another transmission came over the radio. *"All tanks break contact. I say again, all tanks break contact."*

"Marya, get us out of here."

"Yes, Comrade."

The tank lurched as Marya brought it around and the force of T-34s disengaged from the German attackers.

Later statistics would show that even though the German force had lost ten tanks, the Soviets had been hit harder, losing over twenty in the brief battle.

———

Paulus' Headquarters

Uranus was the beginning of the end for the German 6th Army. With reports coming in about the breakthrough getting worse, Paulus sent word to Army group B to ask permission to withdraw from Stalingrad while he still could.

The commander of the army group kicked it further up the chain. He too pleaded Paulus' case. To the south the Romanians had caved under the onslaught and the fourth Tank Army had been split in two. The weather was closing in, regiments were surrounded and being wiped out by Soviet armor. There was no way of stopping them.

As he looked at his map, Paulus could see where the Russian Armies were headed. Kalach and its bridge across the Don River. The escape route that the 6th would need to get more than 250,000 men out of Stalingrad.

The request went all the way to the top and landed before Hitler who looked at it and said, "No. There will be no retreat. Paulus must hold where he is. Even if he is encircled, he can be supplied by air."

When word filtered back down the chain many agreed that supplying an army by air would be madness.

Paulus looked at the message in his hand and then lifted his gaze to General Arthur Schmidt. "Hold and we will be supplied by air? What does the man think is going on out here?"

Schmidt shook his head. "Impossible. The weather will keep the planes grounded. I urge you to take your destiny into your own hands, General. Pull your men back now before it is too late."

Paulus shook his head. "No, we wait."

"Then Stalingrad will be the death of you, Friedrich. And of the glorious Sixth Army."

Two days later, the bridge over the Don at Kalach was captured.

———

Moscow, 28th November 1942

Word was coming through from the front about the encirclement of the enemy forces at Stalingrad. Stalin looked at the map and then at Zhukov. "Your plan was a success, Georgy. I am pleased."

"Thank you, Comrade."

"How many of the enemy are trapped inside the perimeter?"

"We estimate twenty divisions, sir."

Stalin raised his eyebrows. "Wonderful."

"Yes, Comrade."

"The question is, what do we do now that we have them there?"

Zhukov said, "We have seven armies encircling them, sir. It is important that we don't rush our next move."

"We must wipe them out, Georgy. Crush them into the steppe."

"We will do what we can, Comrade Stalin."

Stalingrad, 29th November 1942

Anatoly moved through the rubble with Sobol as they reconnoitered the ground ahead. Word had come down from headquarters that the punishment battalion were to send out a patrol in their sector to see what the Germans were up to since the breakthrough and encirclement had occurred. So far, they had found nothing; it was as though the German army had disappeared beneath the earth.

"Signal the men forward, Captain."

Sobol turned and waved the rest of the patrol to follow them. Anatoly gripped his PPD and kept moving through the debris.

A gust of wind came off the steppe, carrying with it the thousand needles of bitter cold. Smoke from many fires hung over the city to the south. Sobol said, "Something isn't right."

Anatoly nodded. "I feel it too. Let's push a little farther forward to the ruins ahead. If we can get to the second floor it will give us a better view of the area."

"With a little luck the Nazis have all frozen to death?"

"I wish."

The patrol consisted of eight men. Not many if the Germans discovered them and threw a platoon at them. Then there were the snipers. The city was riddled with them. Theirs and the Germans.

They walked past a couple of bodies. Both were stiff from the cold and covered in a light dusting of snow. The exposed skin was blue. As he walked past them, Anatoly could see that one was German and the other a Russian. The latter had a bayonet still embedded in his chest while the enemy soldier had been shot by the looks of him, and by the grimace permanently frozen on his face, had lain there in agony until he died.

Just another day in Stalingrad.

Something snapped under Anatoly's boot and for a moment he thought he might have stepped on a mine. When he looked down, he saw a hand barely sticking out of the snow which was now missing two fingers.

Anatoly swore and kept moving.

A noise caused him to drop to his knee. His men

silently followed his lead. For a moment there was nothing. Then a German soldier appeared before disappearing again into a ruined building, most of its first floor all that remained standing.

Anatoly waited patiently before moving further towards their target. They had only gone a few more steps when a shot shattered the silence. The men from the punishment battalion went to ground almost immediately. Anatoly was looking around trying to see where the shot had originated. Suddenly no man's land came alive with enemy soldiers and savage gunfire.

The Germans seemed to come out of the ground like weeds after a good rain. Anatoly opened fire with his PPD and mowed down a charging enemy soldier with a rifle. The bullets stitched the soldier across his chest, and he dropped his weapon at his feet as he fell.

Sobol opened fire with his own weapon at an enemy soldier who was about to throw a grenade. The soldier cried out and dropped the grenade. It exploded with a roar and the dying German disappeared.

A shout near Anatoly drew his attention and he saw one of his men fall, his face a mask of blood. Another German soldier appeared, a wild beard upon his face. His eyes were wide, and a snarl escaped his lips as he blazed away with an MP40.

Bullets whipped around Anatoly as the German's weapon chewed through the magazine. Suddenly it ran dry. Anatoly recovered and made to fire his PPD at the big enemy soldier. His finger depressed the trigger, but nothing happened.

Anatoly froze and stared at the man in front of him. The German had already reloaded and was cocking the MP40. There was no way Anatoly could beat him.

A bullet snapped past his head and the German stiffened, a cloud of red spray exiting the back of the man's head from where it had been blown away by a bullet.

Anatoly dropped down behind some debris and reloaded. All around him gunfire and explosions sounded and rocked the Stalingrad rubble. With the PPD reloaded Anatoly rose to shoot. He fired at a retreating soldier and saw him fall, moving his aim towards another one running away and he fired a burst at him.

Then they were gone. They left as they had come, melting into the devastated landscape.

Anatoly looked at Sobol. "Check on the men."

While the captain did as ordered, his commanding officer looked back behind him. Somewhere back there was a sniper. He was certain of it because whoever it was had saved his life.

"You looking for someone?" a voice asked.

Anatoly shifted his gaze and saw two figures standing fifty feet from where he was. He frowned. One of them was a woman. Both held rifles. They started to walk closer. The woman said, "I wouldn't hang around here too long, the Germans will be back soon."

"I wasn't planning on staying. Who are you?"

"Eva Kozlova, Twenty-First—"

"Eva?"

"That is what I said, Comrade. Are you deaf?"

"You'll have to excuse her, Comrade Major, the girl can be irritating at times."

"I've no doubt about that," Anatoly replied. "Even as a little one she annoyed me no end."

"Anatoly? Is that you?" Eva asked excitedly.

"Who else, little one? What are you doing here?"

Eva thrust her rifle into Lagutov's hand and ran forward. She wrapped her arms around her brother and buried her face into his chest. "Anatoly, I can't believe that it is you."

He returned her hug. "It is good to see you too, Eva. You have no idea how good."

She stepped back and looked him over. "You look tired."

He nodded. "Maybe we should get out of here before we start catching up."

"You're right."

"Major, we lost two men in the attack."

Anatoly nodded. "Gather the men, we're leaving."

"Yes, sir."

———

"A PUNISHMENT BATTALION?" Eva asked incredulously. "You command a punishment battalion? How did that happen?"

"I will tell you one day. How is it you are here and not in Leningrad?"

"Mother made me leave. Things happened and here I am."

She moved and winced.

"Are you alright?"

"I was wounded. Still getting over it."

"Have you heard from mother? The others?"

"No, I've heard nothing. All I know is that Leningrad is still besieged." Eva stared at her brother. "Tell me about you, Comrade Major?"

Anatoly gave her a wry smile before going into his

story. When he was finished Eva was stunned by what she'd heard. "That is bullshit."

Her brother shrugged. "It is what it is. All I can do is try to change their minds of me. Besides, I now command a battalion."

"I will transfer to you. You will now be my commanding officer."

Lagutov cleared his throat. "It's not that easy, Eva."

"Why not?"

"He's right," Anatoly said. "This is a punishment battalion, Eva. Not a normal front-line unit."

"So, to get here I need to be accused of something? Do something wrong?"

"That's about it."

Eva came to her feet and headed outside. "Where are you going, Eva?" Lagutov called after her. Then to Anatoly, "Where is she going?"

Anatoly jumped up and started to follow her. "If I know Eva, it won't be good, Sergeant."

Even though they hurried they couldn't catch up to her. And when they did, they could only watch on in horror as she fronted a junior lieutenant and punched him in the mouth.

Anatoly groaned. "Christ on a crutch."

"I wasn't expecting that," Lagutov commented.

"Neither was I."

The big man said rolling up his sleeves, "Do you need another sergeant?"

CHAPTER EIGHTEEN

Paulus' Headquarters, December 1942

IT WAS COLD. BITTERLY SO AND IT WAS ALL PAULUS COULD do to stay his hand from shaking as he wrote a letter to his wife.

> *My dear Coca,*
>   *I hope this letter finds you in good health. Each day here grows colder than the previous one but at least this winter we have better clothing than the last.*
>   *I will keep this brief just to let you know I am well even though the enemy has been a little more aggressive of late. They are a formidable opponent and stretch my mind to almost beyond its limits. However, I hope to fix the issues they pose and...*

He looked up. Could he really believe that things were about to get better? Would Manstein come through for him? So far, he'd been let down on all fronts.

The morale and discipline of his men and their officers was still good but that wouldn't last. Couldn't last. Not with promised supplies failing to reach them in the promised proportions. The planes were taking off, but they were failing to reach the Kessel. Bad weather, enemy fighters, and heavy anti-aircraft fire all took its toll.

They were still able to evacuate the wounded as required and medical equipment was still in good supply. However, word had reached him of some soldiers starving to death. This troubled him greatly.

Paulus had been promised that he would get all he needed. In the days since the air lift had begun, he was getting only eighty-four tons per day. Well short of what he needed. If it kept up, more of his men would die.

Hitler had promised relief but kept sabotaging his own promise. Manstein was waiting on reinforcements to push through but the units which were meant to arrive were diverted elsewhere.

The 17th Panzer Division was directed to the west of Stalingrad because Hitler expected an attack there, and the 16th Motorized Division remained in place because Hitler feared an attack on their front.

Paulus snorted, his anger rising to the surface. "To hell with the fool. If no one will come, I will save them myself."

———

West of Stalingrad, December 1942

The Panzers of the 6th Panzer Division pushed hard towards Stalingrad. With it was an element of the 41st SS Panzer Regiment. The tanks of the SS were the tip of the spear and at the tip, was Untersturmfuhrer Karl Egger.

His Panzer IV lurched as it left the road and drove through a ditch. Egger's gaze was concentrated forward through the port in the cupola at the oncoming T-34s. Hundreds of them.

"Open fire!" he yelled over his radio and no sooner had the words left his lips when the tank's main gun roared to life.

As he watched, the target tank exploded and burst into flames. "Another round of armor piercing!"

While Lehman reloaded, Egger called to the rest of his tanks over the radio, "Pick your targets and make every shot count. Good luck."

"Gun ready."

Egger shot back, "Tank at one o'clock."

The layer turned the turret until his sights came on and then fired. The shot missed.

"Reload," Egger snarled. "What do you call that, Heinrich? You can't afford to waste ammunition like that. Do I need to replace you?"

Another round went into the breech and Heinrich made adjustments. An explosion close to the Panzer buffeted the steel monster but never concerned those within. Heinrich fired again and this time the T-34 lost its turret.

With his head in the cupola, Egger looked around. T-34s were starting to burn everywhere but the mighty Soviet tanks were also striking back. Already he had lost three tanks. He ground his teeth together and looked for another target. "Tank at three o'clock. Driver, turn right away from the ridge ahead."

The tank came around while Heinrich fired once more. His shot caught the tank in the tracks, disabling it. Men tumbled from the vehicle into the snow and as they did, a bow gunner from a Panzer nearby opened fire with his machine gun and cut them down.

For the next thirty minutes, armor met armor on the snow-covered plain. Columns of black smoke rose skyward and when it was finished, all the Soviet tanks had been knocked out of the fight.

"Driver halt," Egger said over the radio. He then opened the hatch on the cupola and climbed up. He stood and looked around, taking a mental count of his losses. Five tanks. Not too bad considering they had destroyed upwards of thirty Soviet ones. In the distance he could see their target. A village the Russians had set up as a stronghold before the point the German advance had to cross the river to continue. Egger sat back in his turret again and closed the lid. He said into his radio once more just as the first anti-tank shell exploded close to the Panzer, "All tanks advance."

———

"Sir, we are almost out of ammunition," Lehman called to Eggers.

The tank commander growled deep in his throat as he saw once more the assault troops falling back from the village. "Why can't they hold the damned thing?"

Twice already the Soviets had relinquished the village only to retake it with heavy counter attacks. On the plain outside the perimeter were countless bodies stiffening in the cold. German and Russian. Before each new assault occurred, Stukas attacked to soften the defenses and then the artillery chipped in to do their part.

And once more, with tank support, the soldiers of the Wehrmacht would go back in to throw the defenders out.

"Sir, the ammunition?"

"What about it?"

"We have two armor piercing and three high explosive rounds left."

"Shit, shit, shit. All tanks report ammunition status."

The remaining tanks called in and Egger realized that he wasn't the only one in the position of being almost out. He muttered a curse under his breath. "All tanks pull back to rearm and refuel. Heinz, turn us around."

For the next few days, the German and Russian armies clashed heavily as the former tried to break into the Kessel to help their comrades. Manstein assured Paulus they were still coming. He just didn't know when.

One more thing was set to seal the fate of the 6th Army. Headquarters all the way back safely in Berlin redeployed two bomber squadrons away from the Stalingrad front. It seemed that little by little the 6th Army was being abandoned.

Then on the 23rd of December, after an exchange of communications between Paulus and Manstein, the force which had tried so hard to break through into the Kessel, turned around and started back the way they had come. The collapse of the Italians on the left flank had left Manstein exposed. It needed to be stabilized before anything else could be done.

The 6th Army, some 250,000 men, were doomed.

————

Stalingrad, 21st January 1942

"Sir, you're wanted at headquarters," the Obergefreiter told Muench as he sheltered with some of his starving men in the basement of a partially demolished house near a bread factory.

"What is it about?"

The man shrugged weary shoulders. "I have no idea, sir."

"Find Felix for me."

"Yes, Hauptmann."

A few minutes later, Glass appeared. "I've been summoned to headquarters. Come with me, Felix."

"Jawohl, Hauptmann."

They climbed out of the basement and started making their way through the snow-covered rubble. Headquarters for the 51st corps was another basement not much larger than the one the two Wehrmacht soldiers had just come from. Inside they found Oberst Clausius waiting for them.

"I was expecting just you, Meunch."

"The sergeant is my second in command, sir. What you have to say to me, you can say in front of him. I trust Felix with my life."

The officer nodded grimly. "You are to be flown out of the Kessel immediately."

The battalion commander was stunned. "Flown out, sir?"

"Yes, while the airfield is still operational."

"I cannot abandon my men sir. I—"

"Orders are orders, Hauptmann. You have been chosen for your knowledge of military tactics."

"But there are others better—"

Clausius cut him off again. "You are the one who has been chosen, Meunch. And you will go. Good God, man, don't you understand? The Sixth Army is doomed. Help will never reach us, we're about out of food and ammunition, and men are starving if they aren't freezing to death. Get on the plane and get out of here. Now, go."

"Permission to take Feldwebel Glass with me, sir?"

"Hauptmann—" Glass protested.

"Granted."

Meunch snapped a salute. "Thank you, sir."

The two men were put into a car and rushed to the airfield. They were met by an officer who stopped them from approaching an already wound-up Ju 52. "You can't go any further, Hauptmann. That one is loaded. There's not another until tomorrow."

Meunch showed him his orders. The officer shook his head. "I'm sorry."

Glass tapped his commanding officer on the shoulder. "What about that?"

They turned and looked at a Heinkel He III. "Well?" Meunch asked.

"It can fly, I guess."

"Get the pilot."

A few minutes later, the pilot was before them. "Is that plane of yours flyable?"

"Yes, Hauptmann. For a while?"

"What do you mean?"

"It is almost out of fuel."

"Does it have enough to get outside of the Kessel?" Meunch asked.

The pilot shrugged. "Maybe."

"Then we'll find out. Get it started, we're leaving now."

"I'll have to thaw everything out first, Hauptmann."

"Then hurry up. Before the Ivans arrive."

Thirty minutes later, the Heinkel was bumping along the runway as it left the slaughter of Stalingrad behind.

Ten days later, on the 31st of January 1943, Paulus officially surrendered the southern sector. Followed by the rest on February 2nd. Since November, 90,000 soldiers had died of starvation and exposure. In the last month alone, 100,000 died in battle. Finally, it was over.

CHAPTER NINETEEN

Leningrad, February 1943

THE CITY SHOOK FROM THE VIOLENT EXPLOSIONS OF THE incoming artillery. Anya sheltered in a trench as the explosions of the heavy German guns seemed to walk across Leningrad.

A hundred yards along the street what was left of an already destroyed three-floor building became even less. Civilians scattered as they sought shelter from the onslaught. Closer still the street exploded upward taking with it the torso of a man or a woman, it was hard to tell.

Already the month of January had seen an increase in the artillery barrages from the Germans, and Anya hoped it wasn't a sign of things to come.

News had reached the north of the German surrender at Stalingrad. People rejoiced at hearing it as there was plenty to be happy about: in January the Red Army had been able to open a corridor which allowed supplies to pass through. And although the siege had not ended, the food was beginning to flow.

The incoming rounds stopped, and Anya climbed out onto the street. Sudden shouts reached her and she saw a young man running along the street. "It's here! It's here!"

"What is?" someone else called out.

"The first train. The first train is here."

"Wait," said Anya. "Did you say a train was here?"

"Yes. There are more on the way with a lot more supplies."

He ran off before Anya could ask any more questions. Instead, she decided to go and have a look for herself.

———

THE RAILYARD WAS BUSY. Soldiers, civilians, supplies being unloaded. For the fourth time since she'd arrived the train's whistle had been sounded, its high-pitched shriek a beacon to attract more people.

A colonel barked orders as did a political officer as they tried to keep things in order. Slowly the train was emptied, freight car by freight car.

Anya smiled. It was good to see that there was hope again amongst the people and soldiers alike. Then something caught her eye. Amongst the confusion of the freight yard someone was taking advantage.

And she knew just who that someone was.

Hurrying across to a large stack of crates, she checked around the corner and saw the culprit disappearing beyond the rear of the train. There was, however, another woman coming towards her. This one she recognized from the theatre where she'd tried to kill Anya.

Coming closer, the woman waited until she thought she wasn't being observed. Then she picked up a crate and started towards the rear of the train.

Anya stepped out and began to follow her, keeping her distance just in case. When the woman disappeared, she quickened her pace.

"What are you doing here?"

Anya froze and turned to see a soldier staring at her. He was armed with a PPD. "Ah—I was—"

"You should not be here," he said gruffly. "Get back to the others."

"But—"

"Now!"

"But someone was stealing crates."

He looked surprised. "What? Where?"

"They went that way," Anya said pointing toward the end of the train.

"Who?"

"I'm not sure," she lied.

"Show me."

The soldier followed Anya towards the end of the train. She peered around it and saw the two women loading the stolen crates into some kind of hand cart. With them were two others. One she recognized straight away. Galina Sharapova.

"Hey! What are you women doing?" the soldier demanded.

The four women turned to look at them. Galina recognized Anya immediately and her lips curled up into a snarl. "It's that damn bitch again."

"I asked what you are doing?" the soldier said again.

"We are doing nothing, Comrade," Galina said confidently.

"It doesn't look like nothing," he shot back at her.

The fourth woman of the group stepped forward. She was younger than the others. She said, "Comrade, maybe we can help each other, yes? How long have you been without a woman?"

"What?"

She took another step forward. She reached up and grasped her right breast through her heavy clothing. "You would like me to keep you warm?"

Anya said out of the corner of her mouth, "They are trying to trick you. Do not trust them."

"Shut up," the young soldier snapped.

"They will kill you," Anya warned him urgently.

He turned his head and glared at her. "I told you—"

There was a single shot and the side of the soldier's head exploded. He fell to the ground, dropping the PPD.

Anya gasped. She glanced at the dead soldier and then at Galina who held a revolver in her hand. "Now it's your turn," she sneered.

Anya dived behind a couple of large wooden boxes just as Galina fired. The bullet flew harmlessly above her, but the witch wasn't done yet. Two more shots cracked. This time they plowed into the boxes, ripping splinters from them. Anya flinched with fear. Was this going to be the end?

Every fiber of her being was screaming at her to run. But if she ran, she would be forever running, and Galina would hunt her now more than ever. She glanced at the dead soldier and saw the PPD. With a deep breath, Anya lurched out from her cover, grabbed it, and with a yelp when a bullet cracked past her head, dove back behind the boxes.

Now Anya looked at the weapon in her hands. She'd fired one before. All she had to do was aim and shoot.

Anya rose from behind the scant cover the boxes afforded her and squeezed the trigger.

Nothing happened.

Horrified, she threw herself back down just as all the women began firing at her. Anya looked at the weapon. She was starting to panic. Why wouldn't it fire? She looked at it, turning it over. Then she saw the thing like a lever on the side. Anya pulled at it and the lever slid back and then a spring brought it forward.

After a shrug she pointed it away from herself and squeezed the trigger again. The PPD jumped in her hands as a burst of fire came from its muzzle. Now, with a determined expression on her face, Anya rose once more and this time, fired.

The weapon bucked again in her hands as bullets lanced across the gap towards the women. They seemed to be hitting everything except for the Vixens and their leader. Then suddenly one of them cried out and fell to the ground. Galina screamed at Anya before she started to run away, her friends following close behind.

The PPD fell silent as the magazine ran dry. Shouts from behind Anya told her that her actions had attracted more than a little attention.

"Put the gun down, woman," a voice from behind her snarled.

Anya dropped the PPD and slowly turned around. Standing there was the officer she'd seen in charge of the unloading. He was soon joined by more men and the political officer.

"What happened here?" the political officer snapped.

"They were stealing supplies," Anya said.

"The Vixens."

There was a flicker in the man's eyes. He'd heard of them. She continued, "They shot the young soldier when he tried to stop them. Then they tried to kill me. I picked up his weapon and fired it."

The political officer grunted with respect. "It looks like you got one of them."

"I—yes."

"Wait here," the political officer said.

He and the colonel walked over to where the woman lay beside the boxes of food they had tried to steal. They talked and then walked back to Anya. "Do you know where these women are?"

"They get around from time to time."

"Could you find them?"

"Maybe."

"Wait in the yard until I return."

Anya nodded. "Yes, Comrade."

So Anya waited in the yard for most of the day until the political officer returned. This time he was with a woman in uniform. "I don't even know your name. What is it?"

"Anya Kozlova."

"Well Anya Kozlova. I am Political Officer Dasha Travkin and this is Captain Sabina Morova. She is the officer in command of the Leningrad Women's Security Battalion."

Anya nodded at the young woman. She figured her to be about Marya's age, with light colored hair and a dimple in her cheek when she smiled. "I am pleased to meet you, Anya."

"And I you."

"I will leave you with her," Travkin said.

He walked away and Morova turned to Anya. "Comrade Travkin said you could help us find the Vixens."

"I might be able too."

"You know Leningrad well?"

"I think so. But there are a million places in which they could hide. They will soon know that you are after them and that will make it harder still."

"That is where you come in. I'm sure with your help we will find them. Even if it takes a while."

"I'll do what I can."

Morova studied her for a moment. "Are you hungry?"

Anya nodded. "Come with me. I'll get you something to eat. Where do you live?"

"Wherever I sleep. Some of us congregate together. It's safer that way."

"How would you like a place to sleep every night and clean clothes and regular—semiregular meals?"

"How?"

"Join us."

Anya chuckled. "I am too old."

"You are never too old. Think about it."

———

Kharkov, 11th March 1943

Sobol got off the radio and looked at Anatoly. "They have split up coming along the tracks. Two heads of the snake. Tanks and infantry. They should be here soon."

Anatoly looked around the rail yard. It was a good defensive position. "Make sure everyone had enough ammunition, Nicolai."

"Yes, Comrade."

Anatoly hurried across to where the anti-tank guns sat, their field of fire good. If tanks wanted to get into the yard there were only two possible access points, and each was covered by a 45mm 20-K anti-tank gun.

"Garald, they're coming. Be ready."

"Yes, Comrade Major."

Anatoly kept moving around the positions. He stopped where one of his two heavy machine guns was set up. "Lev, make sure that you don't waste ammunition. Not like last time. Understood."

"Understood, sir," the young man smiled showing blackened teeth.

"Anatoly!"

He turned to see his sister coming towards him with Lagutov. He sighed. "Eva, how many times do I have to tell you to call me major in front of the men?"

She shrugged. "Has it done any good so far?"

"No, it hasn't."

"Then give up."

"The Nazis are coming. Soldiers and tanks." He nodded towards a water tower. "Up there."

"It is too exposed," Lagutov said.

"It is the only decent highpoint here."

"I will go. Eva can find a good place somewhere

else."

Eva looked unhappy. "Are you trying to protect me, Sergeant?"

"No, I'm just saying that you could do better somewhere else." He stared hard at Anatoly.

"Fine. Both of you find somewhere else."

Lagutov was relieved. Sure, it was the best highpoint in the rail yard, but it was also exposed and a death trap.

The pair of snipers disappeared. Once again, Anatoly looked around the yard. His men were ready for the German thrust; he just hoped his understrength battalion could hold them.

———

The Road to Belgorod, Kharkov, 11th March 1943

While the German 2nd Panzergrenadier Regiment attacked along the rail line into Kharkov, the 1st SS Panzergrenadier Regiment along with its armor element, attacked along the Belgorod road towards the northern suburbs. First, however, they had to take the Kharkov airport and it was there they would meet their first stiff resistance.

The T-34s were hidden behind the large hangars on the left flank of the advancing German column. As backup to the tanks, a battalion of troops was also there. As they waited, Marya waited for the order to advance listening to the hum of her tank's motor.

"Is the gun loaded with AP, Comrade?" Berezin asked.

"Ready to fire, sir."

"Marya, I'm glad to see you finally fixed the miss in the motor."

"Purrs like baby kitten, Comrade."

"Maybe you will make a good driver after all," he retorted.

"I have got you this far, have I not?"

"Then get us a bit further."

Suddenly the radio lit up. There were incoming tanks and troops along the road. "Driver advance," Berezin ordered.

The revs on the T-34 came up and the steel monster lurched forward. From behind the other hangars more tanks emerged. Soon the concrete apron saw twenty tanks lined up along it. "Tank halt."

As he looked through the port in the cupola the tank commander could already see the tanks and trucks of the enemy starting to react. Berezin moved the turret and main gun to center on a Panzer IV. As soon as the sights came on, he snapped, "Firing!"

The main gun roared and to their front the Panzer came to a sudden stop. For a moment it looked as though it was unscathed but black smoke started to pour up from it into the sky. The hatches opened and three crewmen tumbled out onto the ground. Klimov opened fire with the machine gun and the three tankers from the Panzer died before they'd covered a few yards each.

"Steer left, steer left."

Marya swung on the levers and the tank steered left. A loud boom to their right told her that they'd just been missed by an enemy shell.

Looking through his cupola ports, Berezin could see that already the Panzers had regained their composure. Soviet T-34 tanks were being knocked out left and right.

Some burned while others were disabled and abandoned.

"This is not good," he muttered to himself. Suddenly his eyes widened. "Panzerfaust, two o'clock."

Marya swung the tank to the right. She stomped on the gas and the motor roared. The violent movement threw the German soldier's aim off and the anti-tank weapon missed. Klimov fired his machine gun and the soldier fell, shot through the legs.

The tank never wavered as the steel monster lumbered forward. If he screamed in his last moments Marya didn't hear because the roar of the motor drowned it out as the T-34 went over him, the tracks grinding him into the dirt.

"Tank, three o'clock," Berezin growled.

Marya turned once more to present the front of the tank to the enemy Panzer. The armor was thickest there and offered more protection.

Both tanks fired at the same time. The Panzer missed while the T-34's shell ricocheted off the thick armor of the enemy tank.

"Marya, give it everything. Get behind him where the armor isn't so thick."

She didn't need to answer. Once again, she gave the tank everything as she tried to circle the Panzer. The one thing that the T-34s had on the enemy tanks was speed. But this enemy commander was wise to the tactic and the Panzer started backing away, all while traversing its turret to fire.

"Bastard," Berezin hissed. "Marya, faster!"

"It won't go any faster."

Berezin traversed the main gun further until it was lined up in the tank. He fired and saw the shell hit the side of the tank. A hole appeared and the Panzer stopped suddenly before disappearing. The tank commander let out a sigh of relief.

Suddenly Marya's whole world erupted in one violent burst. Her head rang like a giant bell. Her vision blurred and she could taste smoke. There was something on her face and she reached up, touching it. When she removed her hand and looked at it, the fingers were covered with blood. She frowned.

Looking sideways at Klimov she could see that he too was covered in blood. Then she realized that things seemed brighter than usual.

Marya looked up and could see the sky. The turret was gone.

Her head turned further looking for Berezin, but he was gone too. All that she could see was Grafov. Or what was left of him. He was missing from the waist up.

"Lenya. Wake up." She shoved him. "Lenya!"

He groaned. "What?"

"We have to get out."

Marya started to climb out. An enemy soldier saw the movement and opened fire. Bullets ricocheted off the hull of the destroyed tank. Marya flopped back down. Lenya, fire your weapon."

"What?"

"Fire, now. Now."

Klimov grasped at the bow machine gun and squeezed the trigger. The weapon came to life and the soldier collected a packet in his chest. Marya stood up again and said, "Come on, we need to go."

Finally aware of his surroundings, Klimov followed her out of the wrecked tank. "Where are the others?"

"They're dead, come on."

They ran as fast as they could, finding shelter behind a mound of rubble. From there they moved from cover to cover, trying to avoid the enemy soldiers and tanks as they went.

They ran behind a partially destroyed hangar and stopped. Klimov said, "Where do we go from here?"

"Further into the city. Now move."

———

Kharkov, 11th March 1943

They had thrust the first attack back but now the Germans were hitting them with mortar rounds at a regular interval. Anatoly replaced the spent magazine in the PPD with a fresh one and peered out from behind his cover.

Along one of the streets which covered the approaches was a burning tank. A victim of accurate fire from the anti-tank gunners.

Another explosion rocked the rail yard. This one closer to the 45mm 20-K. It was then Anatoly realized what the mortar crews were doing. They were walking the mortars onto the anti-tank guns. Knock them out and they can get their tanks in.

"Damn it." He came to his feet and started running across the yard. He found his sister and Lagutov hiding amongst the rubble where they had a good field of fire. "I have a job for you."

"What is it?" asked Eva.

"Find those mortars and take out the crews. They're walking their bombs onto the anti-tank guns."

"We'll take care of it," Lagutov said and came to his feet.

Eva did the same and gave her brother a crazy grin. The look brought about an instant concern for his sister's mental state. He'd seen that look before in many soldiers. Right before they went mad.

Anatoly watched them go, removing all thoughts of his sister from his mind. He had three-hundred men to worry about. Not just one.

———

"THE WATER TOWER, KARIK?" Eva asked curiously.

The sergeant started to climb, ignoring her question. It was the only place high enough and close enough to try and stop the mortars before they zeroed in on the anti-tank guns.

Eva started up after him. Once at the top platform, they settled down to find the mortars. "I have them," Lagutov said. "Northwest."

Eva brought the rifle to her shoulder and put her eye to the sights. She settled them onto the loader who was about to drop a bomb down the pipe and squeezed the trigger.

She saw the bullet impact and the way he fell side-ways. Around his fallen body his comrades panicked and grabbed for their weapons. Eva worked the bolt of the Mosin-Nagant rifle and rammed another bullet home. Beside her she heard Lagutov fire his own weapon and had no doubt that another Nazi bastard had gone to hell.

Eva picked another of the mortar crew and fired. For her it was like shooting fish in a barrel. One shot, one kill. Before long the mortar crews were down taking cover.

Eva started to reload when Lagutov called out. "Look out, more tanks coming in."

Eva rammed the bolt home and saw the metal beasts rolling along the street towards the yard. One of the Panzers opened fire and a rail car lifted clear of the tracks and flipped over. The sound was almost deafening. Beside the rail car three soldiers were torn to shreds by the blast.

"There's more coming in from the right," Lagutov called out.

Eva turned her head and saw them. The tanks had worked around to flank the position of the battalion. Now they made their own paths as they came in. "We have to tell Anatoly before they get in behind us."

"Go," Lagutov called out. "I'll be right behind you."

He fired at a soldier and then reloaded. Eva, meanwhile, stated to clamber down the ladder. Once at the bottom she dropped to her knee and started to fire at oncoming troops while she waited for Lagutov.

Two Panzer grenadiers dropped in their tracks from well-placed rounds. Eva looked up. "Karik! Karik, hurry up."

She shot two more soldiers and when the sergeant didn't appear she looked up again. Eva watched on in horror as the man she'd grown close to over the past months came crashing to earth at her feet. She yelped and jumped back, her eyes wide with shock. Then she saw the bullet wound in the side of his head, his eyes wide. The big sergeant was dead.

A screech of anguish erupted from Eva's lips as the sight seemed to push her over the edge. She rose to her feet and started walking forward without any thought of her own safety. As she went, Eva fired, worked the bolt, and fired again.

The rifle went dry, and she reloaded. How she was never hit by bullet or by shrapnel was anyone's guess. Once she had the sniper rifle ready to go, she started to fire again.

Right up until she was hit from the side by Sobol who crashed her to the damp earth. In response, Eva started to fight furiously.

"Stop it, you silly girl," he snarled. "You will get us killed."

But Eva would not stop. She shouted, "He's dead! He's dead!"

The captain was left with no choice. He bunched his fist and clipped her on the jaw. Eva went limp and he picked both her and the rifle up and carried her to cover. He tapped the large soldier fighting there on the shoulder. "Bear, keep an eye on her."

"Yes, sir."

Keeping low, Sobol ran to find Anatoly.

"Major, there are tanks coming in on the right flank. We need to pull back before they get in behind us."

Anatoly nodded. "Fine. Give the order. Have you seen Eva?"

"She is all right. She's with Bear."

"What about Lagutov?"

"He is dead."

"I must see Eva."

"You must get us out of this damned rail yard before we all die here, sir," Sobol snapped.

"Fine, give the order to pull back."

And just like that, the punishment battalion gave up the rail yard and pulled back further into the city.

———

ANATOLY TOOK his battalion further back into the suburbs of the devastated where he felt it would be harder for the enemy tanks to maneuver. Once there he set up another defensive line and had his men dig in.

Eva was a solemn figure off by herself as he organized the companies into positions. When he had time, he checked on her and found her to be withdrawn. For a moment he thought he should evacuate her, but to where? At least while she was with him, he could keep an eye on her.

For the next hour or so, reports came in with stragglers about German breakthroughs. They were slowly working their way into the city even against the stubborn resistance.

"Sir?"

Anatoly turned to see Sobol standing there with another two people. Tankers by the look of them. For a moment he didn't recognize who it was, then the gap filled. "Sir, these two wandered into our perimeter."

"Marya?"

"Anatoly?"

"Good grief, it has become a family affair."

"Nicolai, this is my sister," Anatoly exclaimed.

"Yes sir, maybe she can talk to your other sister."

Marya looked excited. "Katya is here?"

"No, Eva."

"Where is she?"

"Come with me, I'll show you. Nicolai, make sure the men have enough ammunition."

"Yes, sir."

When they found Eva, it was like the younger sister had suddenly been fixed and put back together. They sat and talked about the war and each other. None of them had heard anything about Katya or their mother. Anatoly was surprised to hear that his sister was a tank driver, just like she was to hear that Eva was a sniper and Anatoly the commander of a punishment battalion.

"I hate to interrupt, sir," Sobol said as he walked up behind them. "But the enemy is starting to move along the street. The meeting was brief, but it gave Anatoly hope of life after the war. But for now, the war would continue, and men and women would die. All for the Motherland.

CHAPTER TWENTY

Leningrad, April 1943

THE SIEGE WENT ON. EVEN IF THE BLOCKADE WAS BROKEN, and food was getting through, the siege was still in place without an end in sight. Shells still rained down upon the city. Bombers were relentless, and still the Soviet Army persisted at trying to break free.

Meanwhile, Anya worked at her new job. A lot of the time it was without uniform as she mingled amongst the homeless of Leningrad as she tried to establish the whereabouts of the Vixens, especially, Galina Sharapova.

Even though they were still getting around the city, there was no solid word about where they called home.

Until now.

"I think I know where they are?" Anya told Morova. "But it won't be easy getting to them."

"Where?" Morova asked.

"In the tunnels."

"What tunnels?"

"Are you not from Leningrad, Comrade Morova?" Anya asked.

"No."

"In the turbulent years from nineteen-seventeen to nineteen-thirty-five, a series of tunnels and chambers were built under Petrograd—you know, before it was Leningrad."

Morova nodded.

"Well, when Kirov was assassinated, it gave Stalin the reason to start his famous purge. Around forty thousand died in Leningrad alone. Some hid in the tunnels but they were found. After that they were sealed. I think that is where Galina is now."

"Why weren't they opened for bomb shelters?" Morova asked.

Anya shrugged. "Maybe you should ask those in command."

"So where will we find them—these tunnels?"

"In the east of the city. We will need a map to find out where the best place to attempt entry is."

"I'll see what I can do," Morova replied. "Tomorrow I'll gather a company and we'll see if we can flush them out of the tunnels."

Anya nodded. "Until tomorrow."

———

THE EAST of the city had been hit hard. Buildings had been brought down and it was a place where most civilians never went. The women of the Security Battalion marched through the rubble all armed with various weapons. After looking at the map Anya and Morova decided that the entrance at the zoo would be the most likely.

The zoo had been evacuated just before the siege had been locked, with tigers, panthers, and even a rhino been taken away. And judging by some of the damage, it was just as well.

Morova turned to her sergeant. "Set up a perimeter. I will take a platoon with me. Keep an eye out."

"Yes, Comrade Morova."

They entered the zoo and Anya guided them to where the old tunnel was sealed up. It was in what had once been a panther's enclosure, however, with the war it was just an empty pen—with a gaping hole in the back wall.

Morova sent four scouts on ahead with flashlights and it wasn't long before the sound of gunfire echoed through the caverns. The company pushed forward. Anya held back Morova. "Let the girls handle this," she said.

Within fifteen minutes, the gunfire had ceased and the den of Vixens had been cleared out. Except for Galina who could not be found. What they did find, however, was a large store of food, weapons, ammunition, and valuables which had been stolen over time.

"What did they hope to do with all this stuff?" Anya wondered out aloud.

"After the war this would have been worth a lot of money," Morova replied. "Do you know who Galina Sharapova actually is?"

Anya shrugged. "I assumed she was just a normal person."

"When I was first handed this assignment, I investigated who I was going up against. She used to be

Leningrad high society. Her family was one of the richest and most influential Communist supporters in the city."

"And when the war came, she lost it all."

Morova nodded. "She had to adapt."

"I'd say she did that rather well." Anya looked puzzled for a moment.

"What is it?" Morova asked.

"I know she had help, like a small army, but for something this size I'm beginning to think there was someone else involved. Someone outside the Vixens."

The captain nodded. "We've suspected that there is. Her activities have gone on for some time now and we're sure that an officer or a Commissar could be involved. It is a shame she wasn't here. But this is a good start."

Anya wasn't so sure. Somewhere out there was an angry woman who would want revenge, now more than ever, and she was sure that her name would be at the top of the list.

———

Kursk Salient, 5th July 1943

"My name is Marya Kozlova. I am your new commander." She waited to see if there would be a reaction to her words. When there wasn't she continued. "I can assure you that I have been in battle before and can do my duty. When I give an order, I expect it to be obeyed without question. Is that understood?"

The three men nodded as the sound of distant guns reached out across the landscape. Marya continued.

"We will be going into battle within the hour. But before we do, I want to know who you are."

The first man stepped forward. He was short and stocky with dark hair. "Dusa Gulin. I am the driver."

Marya nodded.

"Grigor Ivashin," the blond-haired man informed her. "Bow gunner."

The last one to step forward was a red-haired young man who looked barely old enough to fight. "Ivan Veselov. I am your loader."

"Are you quick, Ivan?"

"I can load them just as fast as you can fire them, comrade."

She liked his confidence. "We will see."

Marya looked at the T-34 behind them. "What do I need to know about the tank?"

"She's a bitch, Comrade," Gulin replied. "She has a life of her own at times."

A smile split Marya's lips. "Sometimes us ladies need a little bit of love, Gulin. Maybe you should try that."

"I wish it was just that, Comrade."

Marya looked at her watch. "We still have time. Show me what is wrong, and I'll see if I can fix it."

"Yes, Comrade."

For the next thirty minutes the three tankers watched on as their new commander worked her charms on the battered tank. And once she was finished, Marya had the metal monster purring like a kitten.

"There, you see, Gulin, a little love goes a long way."

He stared at her and smiled. "Yes, it does."

"Easy, Tiger. Now, make sure everything is in order before we go to war."

————————

North of Ponyri, 5th July 1943

Marya wasn't the only one to have a new command as the opening rounds of Operation Citadel commenced. To the north where the Germans were breaking through the lines with their armored spearhead, Karl Egger found himself in command of a new Tiger tank. A beast of a thing which mounted an 8.8 cm KwK 36 main gun which coupled with the thickness of the armor made the tank very formidable.

As they moved forward towards the battle which raged ahead of them, Egger noted the amount of destruction surrounding his battalion. Many of the hulks still smoldered. Soldiers were scattered across the battlefield, and it was hard to avoid them as they advanced.

After a one-hundred-and-eighty-mile retreat since the loss of Stalingrad, now was the time to stop and fight back. For if they kept going the way they were, then the Ivans would never be stopped from taking Berlin.

For the task at hand two Army Groups had been brought in. Some 780,000 men. Also, thousands of field pieces and 2,500 tanks. However, unknown to the German high command, the Russians had seen the build up, and had brought in a colossal force of around 2,000,000 troops and 5,000 tanks. Not to mention the thousands of artillery pieces. Now they were going head-to-head in bloody combat.

The German armor advanced across the field. To their right there were trees, to their left a patch of ground which dipped into a long gully. Egger didn't like it. The trees could be hiding anything just as the gully on the left. He was about to give an order for the gully to be explored for potential dangers when a large formation of T-34s and other lighter tanks appeared in front of the German tank battalion.

"Enemy tanks, range two-thousand meters."

"Sir, there's hundreds of them."

"Fire when ready," Egger commanded.

The Tiger roared and the 88mm shell flew straight and true. A T-34 exploded on impact incinerating the crew inside.

Soon battle was joined and tanks on both sides were taking hits. The only problem was that the Tigers had thicker frontal armor and the shells from the T-34s were bouncing off. Meanwhile the horizon seemed to be a wall of flame and black smoke as the attacking T-34s were hit hard. But now that the Tiger tanks were concentrating on the threat to their front, Egger's worst fear was about to come true.

———

"DRIVER ADVANCE," Marya ordered, and the T-34 moved forward out of the trees.

To the right and left of the tank many more had emerged from the tree line. However, to complete the ambush, from the gully on the opposite flank, many more tanks appeared.

Marya traversed the 76mm main gun so it settled onto the side of the nearest Tiger. The gun roared and the Tiger was hit. At the closer range the shell had no trouble penetrating the armor. The German tank lurched to a stop and started to smoke.

"Keep moving forward," Marya ordered.

Veselov reloaded with armor piercing before Marya traversed the main gun, looking for another target. When she found it she was almost too late, for the Tiger had traversed its own main gun and was about to fire.

The shell from the 76 hit the tank in the tracks, disabling it. Marya hissed vehemently through gritted teeth at her poor shot. "Reload! Now, before the bastard kills us."

"Ready!"

"Firing."

Veselov was right, he could load as fast as she needed them.

The second shot at the Tiger finished it off and set it burning.

Suddenly a loud clang rocked the tank as a German round glanced off the hull. Marya looked through the port in the cupola as she searched for the new threat. Then she saw it, another Tiger with a large Balkenkreuz on its side.

It fired a second shot which flew wide and vanished into the trees behind Marya's tank. The main gun on the T-34 adjusted and Marya fired. She now had three kills to her name and the battle had barely begun.

———

EGGER SCREAMED INTO HIS RADIO. He was furious at driving into a Russian trap. Even more so that the Ivans had what seemingly appeared to have had warning. "Heads will roll for this."

His Tiger rocked under another shell strike from a T-34. It might have been the fourth or fifth time, he wasn't sure but if this kept up, one of the rounds would surely disable the tank and he'd be in a world of trouble.

Already many Tigers had been lost and if he didn't do something, many more would be. "Push through," he ordered over the radio. "Push through or die here."

The tanks pushed onward, blowing the T-34s aside. The Russian tankers were game, but in a head-on engagement against the Tigers they were no match.

Eventually they broke through the armored wall that the Soviets put in front of them leaving behind them a field of burning wrecks from both sides.

Ponyri, 6th July 1943

The Germans renewed their attack on Ponyri early that morning with artillery and Stuka dive bombers. The village was of vital importance to the overall attack as well as the hill to the east of the village which would give them a tactical advantage over the battlefield. On the hill the 360th Punishment Battalion waited for the bombardment to stop so the real fighting could begin. Meanwhile the Germans continued to assault the small town which stubbornly held against the onslaught of armor.

The ground around the defensive positions on the hill trembled with the impact of the shelling. Anatoly kept his head below ground as the bombardment seemed to be endless. It had started just after dawn and had continued for two hours.

Another shell landed close and covered Anatoly with clods of dirt. "Christ," he hissed vehemently.

The Germans were pushing hard as if they knew that everything counted on this one battle. Down in the town the enemy forces supported by armored elements had managed to untangle themselves from strategically placed minefields. As yet, the attacking divisions which were assaulting the hill were still trying to extricate themselves from the minefields placed around the elevated position. But it wouldn't be long, and battle would be joined and the closeup dying could begin.

However, the defenders had a surprise of their own waiting as the German divisions were about to find out.

The guns fell silent and from his position on the hill, Anatoly could now see the advancing formations below. When they reached the barbed wire obstacles, machine guns opened fire with a savage ferocity, cutting down many young men in the prime of their lives.

Next the artillery spoke. Over a thousand guns which hammered the approaches and decimated the German ranks.

The same was now happening in the village, except instead of artillery, anti-tank guns pounded the German armor. Flames shot skyward as they were hit hard. Black smoke drifted thickly up marking the death of another crew.

Houses and buildings were set up as strong points

which meant they had to be cleared one at a time in a time-consuming advance.

Of the few that managed to break Ponyri it was like using a hammer to destroy a massive brick wall. And, even though they made further gains, they were not prepared for the Soviet counterattacks and were quickly overwhelmed.

Below the hill, tanks moved in to support the infantry. The roaring monsters thrust forward only to drive into a waiting ambush of anti-tank guns set up perfectly where the attack came in.

Before long, the German tanks were all flaming hulks on the battlefield. The infantry had suffered innumerous casualties and were forced to withdraw. Then the artillery started again followed by the dive bombers as they began to soften the line once more ready for another round.

———

North of Ponyri, 6th July 1943

As far as the eye could see the landscape below was dotted with smoldering wrecks. For a moment, Katya thought the fields were on fire until she realized what they were. The battle below must have been intense.

"Keep an eye out for enemy planes," she said calmly over the radio. There were six planes in her flight, and this was the third mission for the day.

"I think I'd rather be up here than down there," Elena said.

"It looks nasty," Katya agreed.

She turned to port as her flight started the next leg

of their patrol. Already, in the two previous ones, they'd engaged in vicious dogfights with Me-109s. However, a couple of other patrols had been mauled by Focke-Wulf Fw 190s with more than a handful of planes not returning to base.

For the next five minutes, Katya and her flight flew straight and level looking for threats. It wasn't until they turned onto the next leg when Elena's voice came over the radio. "Bandits, three o'clock."

Katya swiveled her head until she found the enemy planes. "Go get them, ladies."

The Yak responded to her touch as she turned it towards the inbound fighters. Her stare fixed on the lead plane, and once it was in range she depressed the firing trigger and felt the plane vibrate. Tracers shot forward and Katya was certain that some of them hit, but the enemy plane was unwavering.

When it was close enough, she saw that they were 190s. Their day was about to get interesting indeed.

The German pilots held their fire until the last moment before joining the battle. Multiple rounds punched into the Yaks before they blew past.

"I'm going down," Katya heard over the radio and turned her head to see one of the Yaks dropping downward with smoke trailing from it. The canopy went back, and the pilot was able to get clear.

Katya put the Yak on its port wing as she brought it around in a tight turn. The 190s seemed to have disappeared momentarily but then she saw them. They'd pulled up and were starting to come back around.

Pushing the throttle hard forward, Katya started the machine climbing to get a shot at the underbelly of one of the swift machines. The gap closed between them, and she managed to get off a good burst. Most of it missed but as luck would have it, some struck home. Debris flew from the airplane and then came the smoke before the 190 began to lose altitude.

"Yes!" Katya couldn't hide her excitement at bringing the 190 down. She lay the Yak into a tight turn and looked for another target. Over the radio she heard another of her pilots call out that she was hit along with a couple more saying they got good hits on enemy fighters.

A flash from her right and bullet holes appeared in the canopy of Katya's plane. She felt the hammer blow to her chest which knocked the air from her lungs, making her eyes bulge and it impossible to breath.

Katya reached up and tore the oxygen mask from her face, gasping to draw air.

She looked down and saw the blood and suddenly realized that she'd been hit. Shock started to give way to pain, and her head slumped backward against the rest.

Everything started to slow, and the pain turned to numbness. Katya felt tired and her head started to loll to the side.

She closed her eyes for a moment and then they opened again. Through the front of the shattered canopy, she could see the ground below and made a conscious decision to pull up. Katya tried to reach out, but her arm wouldn't move. She frowned and tried again. Then a heavy fatigue began to overwhelm her, and her eyelids seemed like lead weights. She decided that she'd fix it in a minute after she had a sleep. And just before her eyes closed, she thought she heard someone calling her name.

"KATYA, PULL UP!"

Elana watched on helplessly as the Yak plunged earthward. She desperately tried to raise her friend and commander on the radio, but to no avail. The Yak hit the hard ground nose first and exploded on impact. Elena felt the tears burn in her eyes. She shook her head and felt the anger surge through her body. Then she pulled her plane up and went looking for a German to kill.

CHAPTER TWENTY-ONE

Ponyri, 10th July 1943

THE SOUND OF STALIN'S ORGANS SOUNDED WONDERFUL AS they were fired en masse. The ground where they landed lifted violently taking with them soldiers and tanks. Another salvo came in and more men died as a result. From his position Anatoly watched on at the hell the Germans were enduring. He remembered some of the artillery bombardments he'd sustained and thanked God that he and his men weren't beneath the explosive storm.

"Sir, you're wanted at headquarters."

Anatoly turned and saw a young private standing there expectantly. "What about?"

"I'm not sure, sir."

"Lead the way."

He followed the private to the rear where he found the dugout with the current general in command inside. It was hard to keep track of because they constantly changed. The last one was killed under a dive-bombing attack.

General Efim Lukov looked tired, the burden of command taking its toll on the large man. He stared at Anatoly and said, "A major German attack is expected on Ponyri tomorrow. I want you to take your battalion into the town and reinforce the troops there. They have to be held."

"Sir, I have one-hundred men left. I—"

"I know, Major. But I'm still sending you. From what I've heard, your battalion is one of the best in the line."

"That's because they're always given the shittiest section of line to defend, sir. We're given jobs that no one else wants and they fight with pride because they've been accused of being cowards when they are not."

"Just like you?"

"Yes, Comrade."

"Well, I'm giving you another shit job, Major."

"And I'll follow orders, sir, and we'll march into that town and die like good soldiers." There was more than a hint of insubordination in his voice.

Lukov's stare hardened. "Understand this, Kozlov, if you don't hold—if Ponyri doesn't hold, then whole armies will be cutoff and slaughtered, setting us back months."

"Like I said, sir, we'll do our duty and die for Comrade Stalin."

Then something strange happened. Lukov saluted him. "Good luck, Major."

Anatoly stiffened. "Thank you, sir."

He left the dugout and found Sobol. "We're moving out into Ponyri. Reinforcing the soldiers there."

The captain shook his head. "Good grief, Anatoly.

There are other regiments in better condition than us to pick from."

"It appears our reputation precedes us, Comrade. We'll move after dark. Make sure that everyone has all the ammunition that they need. More if you can get it."

"I'll see that they do."

"Thank you, Nicolai. Let me know if you need anything else."

———

AN HOUR LATER, Sobol came and found his commanding officer. "Sir, I'm having a problem getting the fragmentation grenades we need."

"What seems to be the problem, Nicolai?"

"The officer in charge won't give me any. Says they're for real frontline units, not for cowards and deserters."

"Did he now? Let's go see him, shall we?"

They found the major in charge of supplies where some trucks were being unloaded by his men. Anatoly walked up to him and said, "I want six crates of fragmentation grenades."

The major looked at him as if he were stupid. "Who the hell are you?"

"Major Anatoly Kozlov, commander of the Three-Sixtieth Punishment Battalion."

The man looked at him knowingly. "Really? Well, as I told your man there, you criminals aren't getting shit. Now, get the hell out of here."

Anatoly pulled the Tokarev handgun from its holster and pointed it at the officer. "No, Comrade. Not before I get the grenades."

"You're done. They'll shoot you this time for pulling a gun on a respected officer."

"Get in line, asshole. By this time tomorrow I'll have a couple thousand Germans trying to do the same thing."

The man's expression changed. "You're going into the village?"

"That's right."

"All right, you can have your grenades."

Anatoly put the weapon away. "How gracious of you."

———

Ponyri, 11th July 1943

Sobol finished wrapping a bandage around Anatoly's left arm and patted him on the shoulder. "You'll live."

A sharp crack from beside them and Eva slumped back down beside them. "That Nazi bastard won't."

"How many is that?" Sobol asked.

"One-hundred and twenty-nine."

"Do you ever miss?"

"Only if I want to die."

All around them was total devastation. In their part of the line the punishment battalion had held off every attack. Bodies had piled up on both sides and now that Anatoly could take stock, he found that he had twenty men left. The battalion was done as an effective fighting force.

Anatoly said to Sobol, "Send a runner to the general. Tell him we need reinforcements. If he doesn't send them, the village will fall."

"Yes, sir."

Sobol disappeared into the ruins. Anatoly looked at the scene before him. He saw a wounded German soldier move and then heard the crack of Eva's rifle. He turned to stare at her. She looked back and shrugged. "What?"

He shook his head, really starting to worry about her. He'd seen the war take its toll on men—and women for that fact. But what it was doing to her was different.

"Mortars!"

The shout reached him moments before the first one exploded close to their defensive line. More followed and soon the chaos that had reigned for the past few days started all over again.

However, the mortars didn't last long for the barrage was the prelude to the next attack. Anatoly just hoped that they could hold one more time.

Northeast of Ponyri, 11th July 1943

Silence surrounded the tank that had been dug in so that the only part visible from the front was the barrel which protruded from the branches that had been laid across it as camouflage. Marya waited in her turret with the hatch closed, looking through the ports in the cupola. Radio messages had been going back and forth informing the tank commanders of the progression of the German tank column. They were trying to flank the Russian line but once again the Soviets had seen the attack coming.

Now they waited for them with every tank they could gather to stop the thrust.

"I wish they would hurry up," Veselov said.

"Have patience, they will be here."

No sooner had the words left her mouth when the radio came to life. "Start engines."

"Start, engine, Dusa," Marya snapped curtly.

Moments later, the German column came into view. Tanks as well as troops. The Germans were throwing everything at the flanking maneuver before they became bogged down for too long. This was it; if they failed, everything failed.

KARL EGGER WAS ONCE MORE the tip of the attack. He was tasked to lead the flanking attack to help the glorious Reich begin its eastward thrust once more to drive the Ivans back to where they had come from. To do that, the column of Tiger tanks had been given the last reserves of fuel which had been allocated.

"Tiger Leader to all tanks, keep an eye out for the Ivans. We're close."

The beasts rumbled on, further into the Russian trap. It wasn't until the tank behind Egger was hit that he realized that he'd made another mistake.

"Get off the road and into the field," he barked into the radio. "Move, now."

Tanks moved left and right as more were hit. Calls came back asking if anyone could see where the tanks were. But then they appeared. Reversing out of their positions and showing themselves.

Egger's face paled. He was staring at a T-34 no more

than one-hundred and fifty yards away. They'd driven into a perfect killing zone.

The T-34 fired its first shot, and the shell struck the Tiger a glancing blow. Determined to not let it get a second go, Egger snapped orders, his voice panicked. The turret traversed and then the gunner fired. The T-34 erupted in orange flame and lifted from the ground.

"Driver, keep moving," the tank commander snarled.

The Tiger rumbled forward towards the line of Soviet tanks. All around the chaos of battle started to descend upon the two combatants. Suddenly there was a crunch and the tank lurched wildly.

"What is happening?" Egger demanded.

"We ran into another tank, Herr Untersturmfuhrer," Blumenberg informed him.

"You dumbass idiot, get us out of here before some Red bastard kills us."

"Jawohl."

Gears grated and the Tiger jerked as the driver started to move it back. Then it did the same again as Blumenberg started it forward once more.

The main gun roared, and another tank disappeared in flames. Visibility on the battlefield became harder as smoke from burning hulks drifted across it. Egger's tank stopped once more.

"What are you doing, Heinz? Get us moving."

"We have men in front of us, sir."

"Ours or theirs?"

"Ours."

"Drive over them."

"But sir, we –"

"Do it, damn you or I'll shoot you myself."

Once more the tank moved, crushing out life as it went.

Eggers ignored everything around him as he looked through the ports in the cupola. Then, "Tank, two o'clock."

The turret traversed making a whining sound as it went. The T-34 fired, and the Tiger rocked under the impact of the shell. Then came the grating sound and the turret stopped moving.

"What's happening?" Egger shouted.

"The turret is jammed," Heinrich called back.

"What? Fix it. Get it moving."

"I can't; the last hit must have screwed it."

Egger looked through the cupola at the T-34. His face paled as he suddenly realized that they were sitting ducks. He opened his mouth to bark an order when the tank fired.

———

"THAT GOT THE BASTARD," Marya growled.

The turret on the Tiger lifted from the internal blast where the shell from her tank had hit it. For a moment she thought they were in trouble but when her first shell had hit it where the turret met the main body the turret had jammed enabling her to get in the killing shot.

Looking through the cupola, Marya sought out another target, but the battle was suddenly done. Those German tanks that could were retreating, their troops with them. The ones which couldn't burned alongside the Soviet tanks. Marya said over her intercom, "Well done, men. The Germans have had enough and are retreating."

A cheer went around the tank which had now stopped. Marya opened the hatch to let in fresh air and stood up. Her gaze drifted over the battlefield. It was hard to comprehend what she was seeing. Destroyed tanks, dead men, some missing their bottom half, others the top. Her eyes stopped on a nearby corpse., its head completely gone. Black smoke stained the sky.

Gulin appeared from the driver's hatch. "Wow. So many tanks."

"Anyone would think we fought here for days," Marya said to him.

"Unbelievable."

She nodded. "Yes, it is."

———

Ponyri, 11th July 1943

Anatoly slumped down next to his second in command and closed his eyes. Overhead the smoke which drifted across the sun turned the landscape an eerie orange color. "How many?" he said without opening his eyes.

"Ten," replied Sobol. "We have ten men—sorry, nine men and one half-crazed woman left out of the whole battalion."

"What about wounded?" Anatoly asked. "How many wounded do we have?"

"Maybe ten, if that."

Suddenly Eva appeared in a cacophony of noise. In front of her she herded a wounded German officer. The man staggered and fell. Eva walked up to him and drove the toe of her boot into his ribs. "Get up, you bastard swine," she snarled. "Get up!"

Anatoly moaned. "What is she doing?"

"Eva," Sobol called out. "What are you doing?"

"I have a new friend. His name is Klaus."

"What do you intend to do with him?"

"I am going to have some fun and then kill him."

Anatoly sat up and stared at his sister and then at the German. Eva kicked him again and he cried out in pain. "Eva, stop it," her brother snapped.

"Why? He's nothing but a stinking German. Like dogshit you tread in, and it sticks to your boots."

"Get up, Klaus," Anatoly ordered. The German officer slowly climbed to his feet and stood favoring his wounded leg. "Your lines are that way, Klaus. Get out of here."

"Wait," demanded Eva. "What are you doing?"

"Just because we have to live and fight like animals doesn't mean we have to be them, Eva. Let him go."

For a moment she thought about arguing with her brother but instead she nodded and said, "Fine, go, pig."

The officer was confused. "Go," said Anatoly motioning to him. "Go, go."

The German started hobbling away, gradually getting faster and faster as he went.

CRACK!

Anatoly's head whipped around, his eyes fixed on his sister. "What the hell do you think you're doing?"

"More than you did," she replied defiantly as she lowered her rifle.

"You may be my sister, Eva, but I'm still your commanding officer, and if I give you an order, I expect you to follow it. Now get out of my sight."

Eva stormed off and Anatoly stared at Sobol. The captain said, "You're going to have to keep an eye on her."

The punishment battalion commander turned his gaze onto the dead German officer. "Yes, I think you're right."

———

Moscow, 11th July 1943

It was late when Zhukov arrived at the premier's quarters. Stalin was still awake and looking over the latest figures for the day. He looked up when there was a knock on the door. "Enter."

Zhukov opened the door and crossed the threshold. Closing the door behind him he stood in front of Stalin and smiled. "We stopped them, sir. We were better prepared than they were and held firm."

Stalin slammed the flat of his palm down onto the desk. "Wonderful, Georgy. Wonderful news indeed. Now we must crush them. We can't stop now. Put whatever is required into the line and drive them back. Do not stop until you reach Berlin."

CHAPTER TWENTY-TWO

Berlin, Germany 1945

THE THUNDER OF GUNS IN THE DISTANCE SEEMED TO BE closer that evening. Major Gerhard Meunch stopped on the steps of the battered building and looked towards the horizon. The darkness showed the flashes of the exploding shells. The Ivans were at it again pressing into the Berlin suburbs. It brought back memories of Stalingrad.

Stalingrad. The smell still lingered with him. It took months for him to get over the slaughter. Since he'd left, he'd been teaching officers battle tactics and then he was transferred to headquarters.

Now, with the Soviet army moving into the city, he'd been called on again to command another battalion. If that's what you could call it. It was roughly a quarter strength of what it should have been. Men, soldiers not yet fully recovered from battle inflicted wounds, dragged from their hospital beds had helped boost the numbers already consisting of boys and old men.

Meunch, along with Glass, had got them together and made sure that they were ready.

Meunch turned away from the flashing skyline and went inside. He walked along a hallway and stopped at a door with two Wehrmacht guards standing outside of it. "Major Meunch to see the general."

The senior of the two men grunted and opened the door. Inside General Werner Richter sat behind his desk. In front of him was his Luger handgun. He looked up at his visitor with tired eyes and asked, "Who are you?"

"Meunch, Second Battalion, Nine-Hundred and Twenty-First Battalion. You sent for me."

"Yes, I did," he replied absently. "I have orders for you. Waste of damned time if you ask me. Time and lives. Don't they know that the Soviet Army is just out there? Just out there, can you hear them?"

"Jawohl."

"Tomorrow they'll be further into the city and doing exactly to us what we did to them. Only worse."

"How could it be worse, sir?" Meunch asked.

Richter ignored the question. "How many men do you have, Major?"

"Not enough. Roughly a quarter of what it should be."

"It'll have to do," he sighed. "You're to take your battalion and set up a defense in the Berlin Hotel. Take whatever ammunition you can get because you'll need it. But don't expect too much. There was a company of soldiers yesterday who were throwing rocks at the oncoming enemy."

Meunch nodded. He suddenly thought about taking his men and heading west before the city was surrounded. The English and Americans would be a better option then the rampaging Soviets. Maybe. "Jawohl, General."

"Good luck, to you, Major. Consider this your last order."

Meunch saluted him before he turned and walked out. The door was closed behind him and as he walked along the hallway the sound of a single gunshot rang out.

———

ANATOLY HAD FORGOTTEN how many times the battalion was reinforced since Ponyri. Three? Four? The faces had come and gone but there were the few who remained. Nicolai Sobol being one. "We're being ordered forward to take these two blocks in this suburb, Nicolai," the battalion commander told his second in command.

The order had come from their new overall commander, Colonel Stepan Andreev, the man in charge of the 451st Regiment to which they were currently attached.

Sobol stared at the map. There was at least a company of Germans to get through just to break into the suburb and then they had to secure their objective. "What about reinforcements, sir?"

"There are none. We go with what we have."

"Anatoly's Bastards at the pointy end again."

"It's what you get when you're good at what you do."

"Why don't those fat assholes come up here and do it themselves?"

"That would make them us," Anatoly responded.

"Wouldn't—" A shell came in and exploded. Sobol

waited for the noise to go away, then, "Wouldn't that be something?"

"Have you seen Eva?"

"She's here somewhere. I think I saw her going into one of the rooms that still had a roof over it."

"Which one?"

"What?"

"Which room?"

"Back there."

Anatoly found her a few minutes later

"Come on, let's go. We're going to kill Germans."

BULLETS RICOCHETED off the mound of rubble they were sheltering behind. Sobol looked at Anatoly and grinned. "Stubborn bastards."

"Take a couple of men and flank that MG42," Nicolai. "We'll try to keep them busy from here."

"Yes, sir."

Sobol took two men out of the line and started to work his way around to the right. The remainder, along with Anatoly, fired at the machine gun nest.

They had made progress into the rubble, clearing strongpoints as they went. Their objective now within reach, was blocked by one last machine gun nest.

Anatoly changed the magazine out of his weapon and replaced it with a fresh one. He rattled off half of it before dropping back down into cover. Suddenly a grenade exploded and the MG42 fell silent. It was followed up by the sound of automatic weapons and shouts as Sobol and the others finished off the survivors.

"Move forward," Anatoly shouted waving everyone on. "Into the building."

Beyond the now destroyed strongpoint was a two-floor apartment building in which the battalion commander had decided to set up. He looked for Sobol and said, "Get everyone into defensive positions just in case the Germans counterattack. Send a runner to the colonel and tell him we've taken our objective."

"As usual," Sobol said.

"Leave that bit out of the message."

"Yes, sir."

Anatoly looked around for his sister. He saw her and said, "Get up to the second floor and find a good position where you can cover the main approach." Eva pulled a face at him and then skipped off like some schoolgirl going out for lunch.

Next Anatoly grabbed the tunic of a corporal who was hurrying past him. "Get a couple of men and take all the weapons and ammunition from the dead Germans. If the MG42 is operational set it up in one of the second-floor windows. Understood?"

"Yes, Comrade."

Anatoly went inside the building. There were holes in walls and part of the second-floor roof was gone. He moved to a window where he could look out and saw further along the street the impressive outline of the Berlin Hotel. If the Nazis were to come, that would be the way. And they would be ready.

————

WHILE ANATOLY WAS ORGANIZING his Bastards, Meunch was organizing the defense of the Berlin Hotel. "Major?" Felix Glass said, interrupting his thoughts.

Meunch turned to see him standing there with another Feldwebel. One he'd never seen before. "What is it, Felix?"

"Sir, this is Feldwebel Wolfgang Schmitt. He's wandered in here with twenty or so veterans and wanted to know if we could use him."

"Schmitt, is it?"

The tired looking NCO nodded. "Jawohl, Major. We are all that's left of the Three-Fifty-Sixth Regiment."

Meunch nodded. "We can always use men like you, Feldwebel. Eastern front?"

"Jawohl. You?"

"Stalingrad. Both Felix and I."

"Tough business."

"Very. Take your men and set up to the east of our position. I think the Ivans are gathering there for an attack."

"Major," Glass interrupted. "Some of the men are reporting that the enemy has moved into a building along the street to the north as well."

"Let's worry about the east first. It'll be easier to defend against a frontal attack if they come from the north."

"I'll see to it."

"Walk with me for a moment, Felix."

The man looked confused. He followed his commander through the partially destroyed hotel. "Felix, I'm thinking of getting out before the Russians can encircle the city."

"I'm not sure I understand what you mean, sir," the Feldwebel said cautiously.

"I'm talking about getting out to the west and surrendering to the Americans or British."

He waited for his friend to react.

"If you do, sir, I'll come with you."

Meunch patted him on the shoulder. "There are two people in this world that I count as close to me. My wife, who is out of all this shit, thank God, and you, Felix. We've been in it for a long time."

"Wouldn't be anywhere else but by your side, sir. Just say the word."

"I'm glad to hear you say that to me, Felix. Really glad."

An hour later, the Russians on the east flank made their move. They started with a mortar barrage and then followed it up with an all-out assault. The hardest part was keeping control of his men. The old hands from the eastern front stood firm, even to their own detriment. The younger ones under his command were greener and unused to the Russian way of doing things. Some turned and ran while others just stood up and waited for the inevitable. However, of those who fought stoically, it was Glass who provided the glue which held them together.

When it was over, the defenders were battered and bloodied but they still controlled the hotel.

But for how long?

That night the men under Meunch ate the last of their rations and distributed the last of their ammunition. The following morning the heavens opened and a bombardment rained down.

Then the enemy came from the north. The Shtrafbat. The political prisoners, deserters, murderers, and all those considered scum of the Soviet Army. The ones who neither cared whether they lived or died. But by God they could fight.

———

PAIN!

As he slowly came awake, Anatoly wasn't sure which hurt him more. His back or his chest. He groaned and tried to roll over. A voice said, "Do not move."

Anatoly's eyes flew wide at the sound of it. His vision swam into focus, and he was staring at the same German officer who was about to shoot him when the floor gave way. "Go on, shoot, Nazi bastard."

Meunch grunted. "I am just a German. I'm not a Nazi. I am like you. I follow orders and fight for my country."

"And murder innocent people."

"No."

"What shall we do with him, Major?" a new voice said.

"I'm not sure, Felix."

"Then there's the other one," Glass reminded him. "She needs a medic."

Anatoly looked at Glass. "Did you say she?"

The feldwebel looked at Meunch who said, "Yes. A young woman who is missing an arm. Had it blown off. I had Felix tend her wound but if she's not seen to by a medic she will die."

"I must see her," Anatoly blurted out. "Now."

"Why?"

"Her name is Eva. She is my sister."

Meunch stared at his anxious face for a moment before saying, "Follow me. Felix, shoot him if he tries anything."

The major led Anatoly into the next room where he found his sister laying on a clear patch of floorboards. She looked pale, probably from the loss of blood where her left arm was gone above the elbow. Various other shrapnel wounds dotted her body and there was blood and dirt on her forehead. Anatoly gasped and sank to his knees beside her. "Eva? Eva, can you hear me?"

Her eyes fluttered open. When she saw his face, a faint smile passed across her lips. "A—Anatoly. My arm. Find my arm."

"It's all right, Eva. Just hang in there. We'll get you to a doctor. A medic even."

He looked up at Meunch. The major said, "We have nothing. I can't even treat my own wounded."

"What am I to do?"

"Keep the tourniquet on her arm. Can you pick her up?"

Anatoly frowned then leaned down and scooped his sister up. A low moan escaped her lips. Anatoly looked at Meunch. "Now what?"

"Find her a doctor. Do that and she might live. Go."

"Why?" Anatoly asked confused.

"The war is done. Germany has lost. The killing is senseless. I don't want to do it anymore."

"You are letting us go?"

"If your sister is to survive it is the only way. Get her better, go home."

"What is your name?"

"Major Gerhard Meunch."

"I am Major Anatoly Kozlov. I will not forget you, Meunch. Good luck."

"You, too."

Meunch watched Anatoly leave the hotel carrying his sister in his arms. He looked down at his chest where his Iron Cross was pinned, awarded after Stalingrad. He reached up and tore it from his chest, throwing it into the rubble. Turning to Glass, he said, "Come on, Felix, let's get out of here. I've always wondered if the Americans and British were fed better than us. Shall we find out?"

"I'm right behind you, Major."

———

ON THE 30TH OF APRIL, 1945, Adolf Hitler committed suicide in his bunker along with his new wife, Eva Braun. Then a week later, on the 7th of May, at Reims, General Alfred Jodl signed the unconditional surrender of all German forces. The war in Europe was officially over.

CHAPTER TWENTY-THREE

Leningrad, November 1945

IT WAS COLD. THE DEEP SNOW ON THE GROUND FORETOLD of another bitter winter on the way. Leningrad was already starting to rebuild as the evidence all around explained. Anatoly pulled his coat around him tighter to block out the chilled wind. He turned to Eva and looked at her. She was starting to get some color back into her face. It had been a hard road to recovery, but she'd made it; had the scars to prove it.

"Everything is so different," Eva said to her brother.

He nodded. "It feels different."

"Where will we meet Marya?" she asked.

"She said she'd be here."

Eva looked down at her feet. "Damn shoelace has come undone again."

Anatoly looked at her. "We're not soldiers anymore, Eva."

She nodded. "Sorry."

He bent down and tied the lace for his sister then

stood erect again. She smiled at him. "Thank you. At least I didn't lose my right arm, otherwise you'd have had to wipe my ass for me."

He chuckled and said, "It is good to see you smile."

"I wonder if mother and Katya will be with her?"

"I don't know."

A truck drove past with a load of debris in the back of it. As he looked around Anatoly knew that there would be no shortage of work around that he could do. Eva must have read his mind because she said, "I wonder if there's any work for a one-armed sniper?"

"I'm sure you'll find something to do."

"Anatoly! Eva!" They turned to see Marya waving at them from across the street.

Eva said, "It's her. She looks different."

"I'm sure we all look different," Anatoly said.

Marya hurried over to them. "It's so good to see you."

The three of them hugged and only then did Marya notice that Eva was missing her left arm. "Oh, Eva."

Her little sister smiled positively. "I still have one good one. Others lost a lot more."

"Yes, they did."

"Where is Mama and Katya?" Eva asked. "I thought they might be here."

Marya glanced at her brother and kit was enough to tell him what he needed to know. "What happened, Marya?"

"What do you mean?" asked Eva. "Did something happen?"

"Katya and Mama are both gone," Marya said.

"What? No."

"Katya was killed in her plane in 1943—"

"No, no, no," Eva moaned. Gone was the war-hardened exterior which she'd often showed. She looked more like the little girl Anatoly remembered. He put an arm around her, holding in his own pain for the next lot of news he knew would be just as devastating.

"Keep going, Marya," he urged her.

"Mama's gone too."

"What happened?" Anatoly asked.

"Come with me and I'll tell you all that I know."

———

Leningrad, February 1944

The siege had finally been lifted the previous month. After 872 days the German forces had finally been driven back leaving behind them a tortured landscape of destruction.

Anya, now a permanent part of the Women's Security Battalion, was with her captain and a company of women who were tasked with documenting the destruction of the Gatchina Palace.

From what she could see, the outside surrounds had been damaged from bombing and artillery shells. Morova had said that the palace had been evacuated of most of its valuables when the Germans had invaded Russia.

However, before the Nazis had left, they had set fire to the historical building destroying a good portion of its interior. Now, as Anya stood in the snow looking at the windowless, building, scorch marks where flames had licked the exterior leaving it blackened.

"Svoloch'," Anya hissed.

"I agree," said Morova.

"I came here once, with my children. It was a beautiful place."

"It will be again," Morova told her. "Your children. Do you know where they are?"

Anya shook her head. "I have no idea. I don't even know if they're still alive. Do you have someone?"

Morova shook her head. "No one. Let's look around."

The security battalion commander talked to one of her sergeants and had her set up a perimeter while the rest walked towards the devastated building. Suddenly, just before they were to enter, three trucks pulled up loaded with soldiers. The armed men clambered out and started to surround the group.

Then a few moments later two officers climbed out. A man and a woman. The first was a commissar, the second, the female, was a captain, one that Anya knew by sight. Galina Sharapova.

"What are you doing here?" the commissar demanded.

If Morova recognized Sharapova she didn't let on. "We have been tasked to secure the palace."

"And who are you?" the man demanded.

"Captain Sabina Morova, officer in charge of the Leningrad Women's security Battalion. Who are you?"

"Commissar Alexey Runov."

"What can we do for you, Commisar?"

"You can take your people and leave, Captain," he instructed.

"I beg your pardon?"

"You heard. We will be taking over from here."

Anya glanced at Sharapova and saw the smug look on her face. Her blood boiled. The woman saw her looking and said confidently, "Do I need to get my men to remove you?"

Morova glared at her. "I would be quiet if I were you, Captain Sharapova."

The wanted woman never batted an eyelid. "I think you have me confused with someone else."

"I do not think so, Galina Sharapova, leader of Vixens. Wanted for the murder of innocents and for stealing from the glorious Red Army."

"Enough, Captain," the commissar snapped. "You have been given your orders. Leave now."

Morova's face hardened. "My general will hear of this, Runov. Especially the part about you harboring a wanted fugitive. Come on, Anya."

They turned and started walking away, the other soldiers following them. However, something didn't feel right to Anya who turned to look back over her shoulder. Her eyes widened as she saw that the newly arrived soldiers had changed their stance and had their weapons pointed at them.

Anya opened her mouth to shout a warning, but her words were drowned out by the sound of automatic weapons. The last thing she ever knew was the pain of multiple rounds which slammed into her just before she died.

Leningrad, November 1945

"So this woman, Sharapova and the commissar are the ones who murdered Mama?" Anatoly asked. "Are we sure?"

Marya nodded. "Yes."

The flames in the fireplace crackled. The house where Marya resided in was small, but it was all she needed. The orange glow filled the room making shadows dance across Anatoly's face. "Where can I find them?"

"Where can *we* find them, you mean," Eva corrected, tears in her eyes.

"I'll show you tomorrow," Marya replied. "What do you plan to do?"

"What's right," Anatoly replied. It looked as though their war wasn't done with after all.

———

IF THE DAY before had been cold, today it was bitingly so. Thoughts of Stalingrad filtered into Anatoly's thoughts as he and Eva studied the large house before them on the outskirts of Leningrad. The overgrown gardens were covered in a sea of white while smoke lifted into the leaden sky above from two of the four chimneys. "This brings back memories," Eva said to her brother.

"Yes, I can still smell it."

"We're only missing one thing," she replied.

"All in good time," Anatoly told her.

They had been watching for most of the day, like the day before, and the day before that. Trying to get the movements of the occupants nailed down. Now they were reasonably sure that they had. Every morning, not long after nine, both Sharapova and Runov would leave in a car.

"I've seen enough, Anatoly," Eva said. "It's time to end this."

"I agree. Come on, let's go."

They left their hide and walked back home. Once

there, Anatoly excused himself while Eva told Marya about their day.

Once again, Anatoly went out into the cold. This time, however, there was another purpose. He walked three blocks before he turned into a narrow alley where two men waited for him. "Do you have them?" he asked.

"Do you have the money?" a big-bearded man asked.

Anatoly shook his head. "No."

"Go away."

"I need them," Anatoly persisted.

"And I need the money."

"Shit—"

The man stepped in closer and produced a Tokarev handgun. He pointed it at Anatoly and said, "Go away or I will shoot you here."

Anatoly's hands moved with blinding speed. His left hand clamped on the man's wrist while his right grabbed the gun and twisted savagely. The man yelped in surprise and pain but before he could react, Anatoly had the Tokarev in his own hand.

The bearded man's eyes widened. "Wait—"

The single report rang out and the man staggered back, the wound in his chest already bleeding below his coat. He sank to his knees and fell onto his side. Anatoly looked over at the dead man's companion. "It's your move, Comrade."

The man swallowed hard but never moved.

"Good idea. Now, where are they?"

"Over here," the man replied pointing back over his shoulder with his thumb.

Anatoly followed him until they reached the two bundles wrapped in old blankets. "There."

"How much?"

"What?"

"How much are they?"

The man told him.

"Meet me back here in two weeks and I will give you the money."

"But—"

Anatoly said, "If he had listened to what I wanted to say, he would still be alive. I was going to make him the same offer. Do we have a deal?"

The man nodded vigorously. "Yes."

"Fine, two weeks."

———

ANATOLY PUT the two bundles on the table and stood back. "What do you have there?" Marya asked.

Eva stepped closer to the table and reached out. She stroked one of the bundles and started to unwrap it. When she was done, she was looking at a Mosin-Nagant sniper rifle, complete with scope. "You got one."

"This one isn't for you, Eva," Anatoly said. "Try the other one."

Eva gave him a puzzled glance before starting to do the same to the second bundle. When she was done, she looked up and smiled at her brother. "A Tokarev SVT Forty. Semi-automatic. I love it, brother."

"I figured if you didn't have to work the bolt, then it would be easier for you."

"I will only need one shot. You on the other hand— when will we go?"

"Tomorrow."

Marya looked at her brother. "I am coming with

you."

"It would be better if you stayed here," Anatoly said. "This won't be like driving a tank, little sister."

"She was my mother too, Anatoly. I have a right to go. I wish I did have a tank; it would give me pleasure to drive slowly over the bitch."

Eva said, "Let her come, Anatoly. She deserves to be there."

"All right. We can all be there."

"Thank you, Anatoly."

———

THERE WAS a light snow falling the following morning when the sun rose. The stark white landscape looked peaceful in the dull morning light. Four hundred yards from the house, concealed by white snowsuits, Anatoly, Eva, and Marya waited for the occupants to appear.

The rifles, like themselves, were wrapped in white so they couldn't be seen. Overall, they blended into their surrounds rather well.

They waited patiently and soon all of them were covered in a light dusting of snow. For over two hours they lay there unmoving. Marya said, "I need to pee."

"Go in your pants," Eva said.

"Are you joking?"

"Or not. I don't care."

"We've got movement," Anatoly said.

His two sisters focused their gazes to the front, Eva through her scope. She found the movement her brother was talking about. Their targets were coming out of the house. Early.

Anatoly said, "It has to be now. Eva, take the woman.

I'll take the commissar."

Eva adjusted her sights so they were focused squarely on Sharapova. For a moment she was unsure whether she would pull the trigger. Her mind flashed back, first to Karik, then the killing fields of Stalingrad, then to Berlin where the last thing she remembered was the flash of light. Lastly, she remembered her mother, how she did all she could to keep her safe, even if it hadn't worked.

Anatoly said softly, "Anytime you're ready, Eva."

She let out a slow breath and said, "Now."

———

"WHAT DO WE DO NEXT?" Marya asked her brother across the table.

"We survive, rebuild our lives. Just like Mama would have wanted for us."

Eva nodded. "I am going to apply to the army as an instructor. I might only have one arm, but I can offer them something. I know someone I can turn to who might be able to help me."

"Vasily?" Anatoly asked.

"Yes. What about you, Marya?"

"Not a lot of jobs for a tank commander, I'm afraid," she pointed out. "However, I'm a good mechanic, so, I might be able to find something there."

"I'm sure you will," Eva said smiling. "Anatoly?"

He looked at them both waiting patiently for his answer. They'd come a long way since the day he'd left on the train; been through a lot. He thought about the two men he'd met the day before and then gave a nod. "I think I might try my hand at being a salesman."

FOOTNOTES

Chapter 5

1. Eventually, when the battle for Kiev was over, the Red Airforce would have lost 1,561 aircraft.

TAKE A LOOK AT: THE IRON HORSE
BY JAMES REASONER

The race is on to span the continent with steel rails—and someone is willing to do anything to stop it, even if it means spilling rivers of innocent blood!

Matthew Faraday is president of the Faraday Security Service, a detective agency specializing in work for the ever-expanding railroad empires. Hired to find out who is stirring up the Sioux and sabotaging the Kansas Pacific line as it builds westward, Faraday sends tough young agent Daniel Britten to the railhead, where he finds himself embroiled with surveyors, track layers, buffalo hunters, and a pair of beautiful young women. But there's a killer stalking the railhead as well, and not only the fate of the railroad but also Britten's very life depends on him uncovering the truth.

An epic Western adventure full of historical sweep and gun-blazing action.

AVAILABLE NOW

ABOUT THE AUTHORS

Robert Vaughan is one of America's best loved writers of fiction with a career that has spanned nearly sixty years. He has published over 500 books, under his own name and various pseudonyms. We, at Wolfpack, are pleased to present many of his classic books as well as the introduction of a new series, The Western Adventures of Cade McCall. This series is provided exclusively for Wolfpack.

Mr. Vaughan has had a storied career, primarily writing in the Western genre. In addition, he has written war stories, action and adventure, crime stories and the critically acclaimed, The American Chronicles, a decade by decade account of the twentieth century.

He is a retired Army Warrant Officer, having had three tours of duty in Vietnam. His books, Brandywine's War and the sequel, Brandywine's War: Back in Country, draw upon his personal experiences, bringing an iconoclastic look at that war. The Valkyrie Mandate, The Quick and the Dead, and The Other Side of Memory provide a more sober window on the Vietnam experience.

———

A relative newcomer to the world of writing, **Brent Towns** self-published his first book, a western, in 2015.

Last Stand in Sanctuary took him two years to write. His first hardcover book, a Black Horse Western, was published the following year.

Since then, he has written a further 26 western stories, including some in collaboration with British western author, Ben Bridges.

Also, he has written the novelization to the upcoming 2019 movie from One-Eyed Horse Productions, titled, Bill Tilghman and the Outlaws. Not bad for an Australian author, he thinks.

Brent Towns has also scripted three Commando Comics with another two to come.

He says, "The obvious next step for me was to venture into the world of men's action/adventure/thriller stories. Thus, Team Reaper was born."

A country town in Queensland, Australia, is where Brent lives with his wife and son.

In the past, he worked as a seaweed factory worker, a knife-hand in an abattoir, mowed lawns and tidied gardens, worked in caravan parks, and worked in the hire industry. And now, as well as writing books, Brent is a home tutor for his son doing distance education.

Brent's love of reading used to take over his life, now it's writing that does that; often sitting up until the small hours, bashing away at his tortured keyboard where he loses himself in the world of fiction.